IF ANYTHING SHOULD HAPPEN

*A Selection of Recent Titles by
Bonnie Hearn Hill*

GEMINI NIGHT
GHOST ISLAND
MISTRESS
LAST WORDS
IF ANYTHING SHOULD HAPPEN *

* available from Severn House

IF ANYTHING SHOULD HAPPEN

Bonnie Hearn Hill

Severn House Large Print
London & New York

This first large print edition published 2016
in Great Britain and the USA by
SEVERN HOUSE PUBLISHERS LTD of
19 Cedar Road, Sutton, Surrey, England, SM2 5DA.
First world regular print edition published 2015 by
Severn House Publishers Ltd.

British Library Cataloguing in Publication Data
A CIP catalogue record for this title is available from the British Library.

ISBN-13: 9780727894359

Severn House Publishers support the Forest Stewardship Council™
[FSC™], the leading international forest certification organisation. All
our titles that are printed on FSC certified paper carry the FSC logo.

MIX
Paper from
responsible sources
FSC
www.fsc.org   FSC® C013056

Typeset by Palimpsest Book Production Ltd.,
Falkirk, Stirlingshire, Scotland.
Printed and bound in Great Britain by
T J International, Padstow, Cornwall.

For Jen Badasci and Christopher Allan Poe, who have taught me the meaning of family

Acknowledgements

My thanks to my agent Laura Dail, for believing in this book and providing valuable feedback. It wouldn't have happened without you. Thanks to my brilliant Saturday critique group, Jen Badasci, Ann and John Brantingham, Hazel Dixon-Cooper, and Chris Poe. And to my husband Larry Hill and my talented support sisters and brothers, Brandi Bagley, Stella Barberis, Meredith Booey, Lisanne Harrington, Rochelle Kaye, Michaelsun Knapp, Michael Ko, Kara Lucas, Stacy Lucas, Brenda Najimian Magarity, John Milburn, Bob and Carol O'Hanneson, Sylvia True, Unni Turrettini, and Anne Whitehurst.

Prologue

'If anything should happen to me,' my mom said, 'I want you to know that I wrote you a letter.'

If anything should happen to me. It was just like her to resort to euphemism for anything unpleasant. Funny thing, though. Right then, in the middle of the long, crowded hall of the Seattle airport, I couldn't say the D-word either. Not that there was any reason for us to be discussing my mother's mortality. A borderline health nut, she ran to the doctor as frequently as she did to Joyce, her dermatologist, and Doug, her *colorist*, as she called him.

With auburn highlights, weekly Pilates classes at one of the health clubs she owned, and a diet that included a kale breakfast juice so green that I had to look away when she drank it, my mom looked vibrant and, yes, young enough to be my older sister. Now, that was a scary thought.

She stopped. I leaned against the handle of the bag I'd been dragging along behind me and came to a halt as well.

'Fifty is hardly terminal,' I said. 'Pardon the pun.'

'That's not funny.' Her lips tightened the way they did only when she was thinking of Mick, my dad. She picked at the fabric of her black jacket, as if lint could possibly have the poor judgment to settle there. 'Fifty-one, and I'm serious, Kit. Families do need to discuss these

1

things. There's a letter for you in the safe, right on top of my other papers.' She reached out and stroked my hair the way you'd touch a dusty car that belonged to someone you cared about.

At that moment, I didn't want to know how I looked to this near-perfect woman, with my braid a little too messy, my tank top a little too tangerine-orange, and my jeans a little too tight.

'You're telling me this at an airport?' I asked. 'Ten minutes before I'm supposed to take off?'

Although her expression was as perfect as carved stone, I saw desperation in her hands. She patted her hair with stiff fingers. 'It's the only chance we have to talk.'

'We've had a whole weekend to talk.' I glanced down at my watch. A gift from her, it looked more like a bracelet, and I feared those stones gleaming like multifaceted stars around the band might be 'the real deal', as my best friend Tamera suggested. If I ever wore it to work, Farley would laugh me off the air. 'Mom, if we stand here much longer, I'm going to miss my plane.'

'Go, then.'

'I'll see you as soon as I can. Mother's Day, for sure.' We began walking again, moving closer to security, where I would go on, and she would go back. I felt a heaviness pulling me, and knew it wasn't just my luggage. 'You could come to Sacramento.'

'And sit in that little house of yours? They never let you off the air long enough to have a life.'

'I have a life,' I corrected her. 'It's called a blog. The radio show just feeds it. That's all.'

'You don't have to tell me about radio.' She

glanced past me, as if focusing on the past or maybe the future. 'Just remember, you can be on top today, thinking the way you sound on the air is enough to see you through the rest of your life. And then, time passes, and in a moment, it's all gone.'

'I'm not my father.' I lowered my voice so we didn't become the airport's free entertainment. 'Farley and I talk about unsolved mysteries. We aren't playing records or anything.'

'But you are on-air talent, regardless of what you call it, and regardless of the attention that crime blog of yours gets.' She touched my arm with icy fingers. 'I know you're much more down-to-earth than your father, but you're a little bit of a dreamer too.'

'I always thought I got that quality from you.'

She started to speak. Then she bit her lip and tried again. 'I just don't want to see you get hurt the way Mick did when his ratings dropped.'

'I won't get hurt,' I said. 'I have a cause.'

'Unsolved crimes.' She made a face.

'What's wrong with that?'

'Nothing, I guess. As long as that young man's family continues to fund you.'

That stung. 'One day, I hope I can help the Brantinghams find out who killed Alex,' I told her.

'It will never happen, regardless of the number of blogs you write. Whoever killed their son is long gone and not listening to talk radio.'

'Well, it's my dream,' I repeated, as I had to her many times before. 'In the meantime, I'd like to see anyone whose lives have been destroyed by crime get the answers they deserve.'

3

'You're not listening to me.' She sighed and followed me to the security line.

'I'm trying, Mom, but I need to go now.'

She continued holding on to my arm. 'I'd like to just stand here if you don't mind.'

I took off my shoes and tossed them in a gray plastic tub. Then I removed her hand, squeezed her into a hug, and said a parting, 'I love you.'

'I love you, too.' Her tight lips, the same shade as the fuchsia camisole under her jacket, curved up in a way that was both self-righteous and endearing. 'Remember what I said.'

'I always remember what you say.' The line through security picked up speed. I threw my backpack and my phone into another bin. She stepped away, and I waved.

On the plane, I turned up the music loud enough to let me forget how much I hated to fly. I cranked it up each time I remembered that there was nothing between me and the ground.

My goofy mom. The thought sneaked in there somewhere between Portland and Beyoncé. My crazy, goofy mom, with her melodramatic mention of a mysterious letter at the same time my career was taking off and I was actually doing some good in the world. How much of a coincidence could that be? She had to be scared for me. That was all. Afraid her nerdy little girl would end up like my dad, spirit broken and trying to live in the past, regardless of how much I earned. I cranked up the volume, leaned back, and closed my eyes. No way to tell. With my mom, there was never a way to tell.

The next day she was dead.

One

My dad called from Vegas at the end of my shift at KWEL Radio on Monday morning. Our show had been about as uneventful as my flight home. For reasons I couldn't figure out, Farley and I were both off our game, and the half hour limped to an inconclusive end. Before we finished, an investigator called in to say that a tip we'd received from an ex-con about Alex Brantingham was false. Knowing that Alex's parents and sister, the current mayor of our city, were listening only worsened our situation, and everything we said to each other after that sounded like Pollyanna on speed.

For a moment, I was jerked back to an early memory: a pre-school teacher telling my mom there was something wrong with me because I rarely spoke. The teacher mentioned medication. Not long after, about the same time my parents separated, I began attending private school. Only later did I realize my mom financed that education we couldn't afford with the first gym she bought with her divorce settlement.

Now, though, as Farley and I left the studio, I knew we hadn't delivered the show we could have. Not that I was worried about losing the Brantingham sponsorship. Alex's parents had committed for the long haul. I was just sorry the tip fell through, and I was embarrassed that we hadn't done a better job on the air.

'Happens to everyone,' Farley said, and I nodded.

'Not too often with us, at least.'

'Breakfast?' he asked and gave me that surfer-boy grin.

'Next time.' I needed to work on my blog, and Farley never needed a reason.

I said hi to Tamera as she passed me in the narrow hall. All hair, jewelry, and sass, she was on her way to the control room to debate with her conservative partner Jimmy J Vincent, probably over immigration reform. That's what they'd been at all week. Jimmy J, as he was known on the air, sailed through the door right behind her. Short, with spiked salt-and-pepper hair, he could be annoying if challenged, but the station was big on multiple viewpoints, and Jimmy J fit the profile.

Tamera flashed me a grin that lit up her dark eyes. 'Meet you for lunch?' she asked.

Before I could answer, Jimmy J stopped in front of me. 'Hey, why don't I join you two?'

'Another time,' Tamera told him before I could come up with an excuse. 'I haven't seen Kit since she got back, and we need to catch up.'

'Cool.' He gave me his version of a seductive smile. 'Another time it is.'

So I *hadn't* imagined that he'd been subtly hitting on me since Richard and I separated.

I nodded and made eye contact with an amused-looking Tamera. 'See you there.'

Our Monday lunches at the sandwich shop down the street from my place had pulled me through those last four months without Richard.

Tamera hurried to catch up with Jimmy J, and

I continued thinking about the bad lead Farley and I had chased. Someone had to know who had murdered Alex Brantingham.

I'd barely gotten to the door when my phone rang.

'Kit?' My dad, Mighty Mick Doyle, as he was known to his shrinking legions of Top Forty fans, spoke in the deep, raspy voice they used to call *ballsy* in the industry. Never mind that too many cigarettes had kept it that way.

My mom had feared more than anything that I would end up like him. Not that he was such a poor role model. His voice still collected residuals from syndicated oldies stations, and in real life he operated a recording studio and advertising agency from the motorhome he shared with his wife Rachel, the widow of one of his clients.

'Hi, Mick. How're you doing?' That's the way I'd been raised. First name only, at least after he and my mom broke up.

'Where are you?'

Where did he think I was? A year ago, he wouldn't have known my schedule, but from the day Richard and I separated, he'd checked in at least once a week.

'I'm almost to my car,' I said. 'My shift just ended. I'm heading home to do some work on the blog.'

'I know. That's why I waited.'

I stepped into the parking lot. In spite of the purity of the day and the rush of fragrance that meant the rose bushes clustered around the edges of the station were aligned with spring, I felt a chill. 'Waited for what?'

'Kit, I hate to tell you this way.'

I leaned against my car. 'What's happened?'

'Elaine. I mean, your mom,' he said. 'She had some kind of attack this morning, and they couldn't save her.'

'What do you mean they couldn't save her? What kind of attack? Where is she?'

'She's dead, Kit.'

Dead.

'She can't be. No, she can't be.' My mom couldn't be dead. She couldn't. Not my mom.

'I'm sorry.' His husky voice broke, and I knew he was crying, something I'd never seen him do.

As quickly as the surroundings had blurred, they clicked into focus. Trees, asphalt, white lines, tight green bushes. My mom was dead. Just yesterday she had hugged me and said she loved me. She was too young to be dead, too healthy.

'How?' I choked out.

'They don't know yet. They're doing an autopsy.'

'Why would they do an autopsy? What happened to her?'

'She'd been jogging in a park. I think that when you— When it happens in a public place, they have to—'

I unlocked my car, like a creature emerging from ice, moving in short, exaggerated gestures. Once I was safely in the front seat, I asked, 'Are you sure?'

'I am.' Mick's voice was soft. 'They found her a couple of hours ago. I waited until after your shift.'

I started to swear at him. Then I reminded

myself that he couldn't help it. He wouldn't dream of calling me while I was on air. My father was a radio machine who believed *the shift*, as he called it, had priority over real life, real people. And, oh my God, my mom was dead. I'd never see her again. I'd cut her off at the airport, been abrupt, maybe rude. That would be my final memory of her.

'I need to see you.' I almost added *Daddy*.

'Say the word, and I'll be in Sacramento tomorrow.' An unspoken *but* trailed at the end of his voice.

'I'd love that.' I wiped tears from my cheek. 'What about services?'

'She wanted to be buried in Seattle. I'm working with a big automotive client on a series of commercials and I can't leave the day gig for long, but I'm going to fly up there as soon as they release her.'

So, in spite of his offer, my father couldn't come to Sacramento, couldn't leave his job voicing commercials long enough to see me until the funeral.

'Then I guess I'll meet you there, whenever it is,' I said.

'Sure, honey. We'll be able to spend some time together, just the two of us.' I'd studied his voice like a road map all my life, but just then I couldn't read the meaning behind his tone.

'Do you know anything about a letter?' I asked.

A sudden click was followed by the unmistakable sound of a cigarette being lit and someone blowing out smoke. He told me he quit a year ago. 'What letter?' he asked.

'She wrote me one,' I said. 'If anything happened to her, she wanted me to have it.'

'Shit.'

I sank deeper into the seat, and then forced myself to stiffen my back and sit tall. That's the way my mom would handle this, and it was the way I had to handle it now.

'Is there a problem?' I asked.

'I don't know anything about any letter,' he said, in a voice so thin with dishonesty that I almost felt embarrassed for him.

'She said it was in her wall safe,' I told him.

'She had a wall safe?'

The curiosity filling his voice sounded too tense to be idle. I knew right then that I had to get to that safe before he did.

'Maybe I didn't understand,' I said. 'Maybe it was a post office box.'

'Yeah,' he said, in the voice of a stranger. 'Yeah, maybe.'

Something was wrong. From the moment I'd mentioned the letter, his tone had changed. Farley always kidded me about my so-called photographic memory. Just then I used it and saw my father's expression and heard his voice every time he tried to lie. He was lousy at it then and now. My mom was dead. I couldn't change that, and I couldn't even take the time to grieve. What I did have to do was get on the first available plane and fly back to Seattle. She wanted me to have that letter, and nothing was going to stand in my way, not even my own tears blurring my drive to the airport. Not even my own father.

Two

My mom's death was like her life, orderly and, yes, secretive. On my way to the airport, her attorney called me. His name was Matthew Breckenridge, and according to him, I was the executor of Elaine Carter-Doyle's estate, as he called it. Her ashes and burial were paid for, he told me, and her obituary written. He spoke in a soft funeral-home voice as tears ran down my face, and I wondered why this stranger knew so much more about the details of my mother's death than I did.

I reminded myself that she had been the strongest woman I'd ever known. Few strived as hard as she had to be perfect, first as a fitness instructor at one of the Gold's Gyms, later as the owner of that gym. The only reason I had majored in communication studies with a minor in computer science at Sac State was to show her that I could be successful with a 'real education', as she called it. She'd only had a short community-college experience, which had been interrupted by my birth. After I left for my internship and she opened her fourth gym in her home town of Seattle, I had hoped we could reach some unspoken peace between us. I would never be as perfect as she. Yet my mother needed to acknowledge that I – at least part of me – was my father's daughter, and I could come across well on the air.

So, yes, I wanted her approval, even now that

I knew she was dead. Maybe I'd find it in her condo, off Seattle's Vine and Third. Now I had to get there before Mick did, and something about our conversation, something that hadn't been said, convinced me he would be going there too.

On the plane, I wondered if I was just being paranoid. Had Mick known about the letter? And now he knew that *I* did, would he really try to find it before I could? I'd sensed something wrong with his voice on the phone, though, and I wasn't about to take any chances.

I landed in Seattle that night, my eyes burning with grief and lack of sleep. I ached from shoulders to skull and couldn't turn my head without pain. Only when the cab driver asked me if I had luggage did I realize I'd left without as much as a toothbrush.

When we arrived at Mom's place, I looked out the window through the glass doors of the condo and saw what looked like a shouting match. A uniformed female security guard was arguing with a short, wiry man who seemed to be holding his own.

I sank back into the seat of the cab and then made myself open the door. I'd recognize the beat-up yellow suede jacket anywhere. Mick didn't just wear it; he resided in it. I got out of the cab and walked up to him.

'I'm her husband,' he shouted to the guard, a short but muscular young woman.

'Ex-husband,' I corrected him.

He turned, as sharply as if I'd fired a gun. 'Kit?' It was too dark for me to see more than a hint of guilt in his features.

12

'I thought you were staying in Vegas until the memorial service,' I said.

'Changed my mind.' He glanced back at the guard. 'Considering.'

'I have a key,' I said.

'Then let's get inside.'

I didn't move, and neither did the guard. 'Would Mom really want you in there?'

'I've been in there plenty.'

'When?'

He paused. Mighty Mick wasn't much of a liar. That was another trait I must have inherited from him. I watched his face and waited.

'Last year. Christmas.'

'I was here last year at Christmas,' I said.

'You came Christmas Eve.' He backed away from the security guard, toward the entrance, as he spoke. 'I came the day before. Elaine let me stay.'

'She did?'

'In the guest room.' His voice dropped. 'Come on, Kit. Let's talk about it inside.'

We climbed the winding black iron staircase. Outside the door to her condo, I couldn't believe that my mom wouldn't be waiting on the other side of it, that she never would be again.

'I'm not sure I can do this,' I said.

'I sure as hell can't.' He frowned at the door, then back at me. 'Why don't we stay at a hotel? We can come back tomorrow and get whatever you need.'

It was a good idea, I knew, but there was something I had to do first, and I couldn't do it with that hound dog gaze on me. 'I don't know any hotels here. Could you call around?'

'If that's what you want. Sure, I can do that.'

He knew I was trying to get rid of him, and he didn't like it.

I moved away from the door, and he followed my lead. 'Do you know where the roof deck is?'

'Sure,' he said. 'We've been up there. I mean, Elaine and me. We were up there a few times.'

'Would you mind making your calls up there?' I asked. 'I'll meet you in a few minutes.'

He hesitated and looked back at the door. 'Do you really have to go in there right now?'

'Please,' I said.

He stared at me hard and finally nodded. 'OK, then. But hurry.'

The moment he was gone, I let myself in. The first sensation was the rainwater scent that I now realized was my mom's. She lined her drawers with it and sprayed it in the air. I'd always thought of it as a light fragrance, but now it was almost a presence. Her presence.

I knew where the safe was, inside the closet of the master bedroom, and I knew the combination. I opened the door, and before I flicked on the light, a garment wafted across my face, so airy it could have been a ghost. I grabbed for it, and it turned into insubstantial silk. Her bathrobe. As I stood there among the clothes she'd never wear again, I had to repeat to myself that this was what she wanted me to do, what she'd asked me to do. *If anything should happen to me . . .*

I reached into the safe and pulled out a smooth, hard envelope with my name printed on it. She'd made it easy for me. I turned off the closet light, stepped out into the bedroom, and removed the single handwritten sheet of white paper.

14

Dear Kit,
Know that I have loved you, even before
you were born. For years, I imagined how
you would look, how you would feel in
my arms. And when there was a chance
that you weren't going to be my daughter,
I moved heaven and earth to make it
happen.

It was too soon for this, but I knew I had to keep
reading.

Your first word was, 'Mama,' your second
and third words, too. I scooped you up
and ran into the house, telling Mick that
our daughter could talk. He was different
then, back when he was still at the top of
his radio career. He cried. We both cried.
You giggled and said it again. 'Mama.'
I'd never felt so much joy and never felt
like such a fraud.
*   This is what you need to know, Kit. I*
am not your biological mother.

Not my mother? I tried to look away from the
thin-as-veins blue ink scrawling out a truth I
couldn't imagine or accept. But there it was. First
I felt confusion. Then anger. Then the need to
keep reading, keep learning.

I'm sorry I couldn't just say it to you. I
am not your biological mother. The
woman who gave birth to you is Kendra
Trafton.

15

I read the name again. *Kendra Trafton*. Yet I felt no connection.

> *She is single and lives outside of Tucson, in Buckeye, Arizona. I always planned on telling you, but then Mick and I split up, and there was always a reason I couldn't. Now, it may be too late.*
>
> *I want you to know that the happiest moments of my life have been because of you. You were a miracle beyond what I could have ever imagined, and you forced me to be a much better person than I would have been without you. Maybe that's what any mother would say about her daughter. But in this case, I owe you something. I owe you a biological mother. I'm sorry it took me so long.*

She left no signature. No initials. Nothing. That piece of paper in my hand felt unfinished, as if she had planned to add more to it before death had stopped her.

I read it again, unable to make the words real. Still, I felt the truth in them and knew what I was reading was more real than the life I had led until now. I left the room, locked up the condo, and then took the elevator to the roof deck.

'It's about time,' Mick said. 'I made our reservations.'

I stood trembling at the railing.

Mick stepped next to me, as if attempting to see what I saw, trying to understand. 'Kit, what is it?'

16

'Leave me alone.'

'Don't make me the bad guy, Kit. We need to talk.'

'You want to talk? Why now? We've never discussed anything except format, air sound, and radio.'

'Judging from your success, we must have had some good conversations.'

'Why didn't you tell me you aren't my real father?'

He stiffened, as if I'd shot him. 'Who the hell defines *real* these days?'

'Kendra Trafton,' I said. 'Is that real enough for you?'

'How do you know about Kendra?' The color drained from his face and left him looking older and drawn. I didn't like watching it, but I was the one who'd been lied to.

'Mom's letter.' I looked down and realized I was clutching it in both hands. 'It's all here. I know I'm not your daughter, and I know Mom wasn't my mother.'

'She was more mother to you than anyone could have been.' He backed away from me, as if wounded. 'Elaine wanted you more than anything. You'll never know what she went through to get you.'

I walked closer to him, away from the railing, trying to read him, to understand. 'You came here to destroy the letter, didn't you?'

'That's crazy. I didn't even know about it.'

'I told you about it on the phone. Nothing can make you leave your work. What I told you about the letter did.'

17

'You're right.'

I hadn't expected that. Nor had I expected the dropped voice or the mournful eyes.

'I hoped I could get here before you found it.'

'Why would you do that?' Tears threatened again. All I could think was that everything in my life had been a lie.

'I only wanted to see what was in it.' He patted my shoulder, as if I were a pet dog. 'I wouldn't have destroyed it. I wanted to read what was in it before you did.'

'Why? What did you think it would say?'

He looked away. 'I don't know. I just wanted to protect you.'

'Protect me from what?' I demanded. 'The truth?'

'Hold on,' he said. 'Get one thing straight right now. I never wanted to keep the truth from you, not ever. And I paid a price for it, too.' Something in his voice terrified me, but I couldn't turn away from him.

'What price?' I asked.

'My marriage, Kit.'

And then I knew. I could see it glistening in his eyes. 'You got divorced because of me?'

'Not exactly.' Still, he nodded. 'I never stopped loving her, but it wasn't enough. She didn't want to tell you, and I knew you had to know. She wanted this perfect little life for you, a make-believe life.'

My lip began to tremble. 'But you kept quiet about it too.'

'Quiet as I could. She kept saying she'd tell you when the time was right.'

18

'When was that going to be?' I demanded. 'I'm twenty-six years old.'

'Twenty-five.'

'Twenty-six in December, Mick. You knew she wasn't going to tell me, not ever.'

'That's what we fought about.' He stared out at the night, and I felt almost a sense of relief coming from him. Not from me, though. 'Kit, honey, she didn't just want that perfect life for you. She wanted it for herself.'

'And that included not telling a child she was adopted?'

'Elaine needed perfection.' He squeezed my shoulder, as if to say he knew how little he offered me. 'She wanted it more than was good for any of us.'

'But why?'

'I'm not sure,' he said. 'It goes back a long way. I knew that when I married her, but I also thought we'd be good for each other. I loved her so much. I still can't believe she's gone.'

So my parents, the people I'd been raised to believe were my parents, hadn't hated each other all of these years. They'd loved each other and broken up because of me, because they couldn't agree on whether or not they should tell me I was adopted.

'Oh, Kit, I'm sorry.' Mick put out his arms.

Still holding the letter, I stumbled into them and buried my sobs against his shoulder.

Three

Rat-a-tat roar.

Rat-a-tat roar.

Part drum, part gun, its music followed her everywhere. Rena Pace was used to it by now. In a way, they had a pact, the nail gun and her. As long as she could hear it, she knew her husband, Dale, was working, not sneaking around trying to spy on her, or, just as bad, chatting up Bryn in their store.

She walked out back, and the heat sucked the breath out of her. Dale was standing on top of the tin shed, his face blistering with color, like meat frying.

'What do you want?'

'Nothing, honey. I just wanted to tell you I need to drive into Tucson. I'm supposed to help Kendra out at her shop this afternoon.'

He made a face and waved her away.

She couldn't hear what he said, but she could guess. 'She's paying me, Dale.'

'Who's going to cook dinner?' he yelled down.

'I'll be back way before then,' she said, but he had already reached for his tools again.

Rat-a-tat roar.

Rat-a-tat roar.

Back inside the store, she picked up a couple of bottles of strawberry soda from the cooler. Even with the gas prices climbing, people kept filling their tanks, the way the hooked still bought their cigarettes.

Bryn Coulter turned from where she'd been counting out change for a gas customer and stopped when she saw Rena come in. She was what Rena's dad would have called fluff, with hair so thick and shiny that calling it blond was like calling the moon yellow.

'I'm going over to Tucson.' Rena pressed the cool bottle against the back of her neck.

'Helping that Injun with her witchcraft again?' She drawled it out with just enough disrespect and a slow up-and-down look to make Rena feel old and stupid.

Bryn's jeans were frayed at the top and barely cleared her pubic area. What would happen if she reached up for something, and they slipped? That was probably the question meant to burn in the minds of every man who looked at her, Dale especially.

Rena slammed both bottles on the counter. 'I don't allow any race talk in here. Now, give me a bag for these.'

Bryn took her time reaching behind the counter. 'Question is, I guess, what does *Dale* allow in here?' She blinked those secretive gray cat eyes and rocked back and forth on her platform sandals.

'My husband respects my wishes in here as he does at home.' She pressed her palms on to the scarred counter and went face-to-face with her. 'When you get older, you'll understand.'

Bryn slid a brown bag over the counter and didn't look away. 'I'm old enough, don't you think?'

'Wonder what your daddy would say about

21

that.' Rena snatched the bag, put the bottles inside, and headed for the door.

'You leave my daddy out of this,' Bryn shouted from behind her. All of a sudden, she didn't sound as sure of herself.

'I'll leave him out of it, 'til he needs to be brought in.' Rena reached the door, wondering if she was being mean because Dale had been mean to her. It didn't matter right then, though, with her blood still boiling so hard that it burned as harsh as one of Dale's slaps. 'Just so you know,' she said, looking back, half-in, half-out of the open door. 'This is my place. I hire and I fire, so don't you ever again call Kendra Trafton an Injun or a witch.' The door swung shut behind her before she could hear what Bryn said back.

She was still cursing Bryn and her jeans when she parked on Fourth Street and entered The Smudge Shop, part of a tiny collective of healers.

Two women stood chatting over the candle collection in the west part of the store. Five older women and three men – tourists, for sure – carried on sniffing the scented soaps for sale. The whole store smelled like vanilla and freshly mown hay.

At the glass counter, Kendra was bent over a series of short, brittle-looking sticks. A chamois-colored shirt draped over her black tank top hid her height and her large build. Her ponytail was dusky gray except for the widow's peak in front, which was still a vibrant black. A witchy contrast. No wonder Bryn was afraid of her. And Rena knew that was all the bad-mouthing amounted to in the end: just fear.

Kendra looked up as she drew closer. So many

22

years. How had Kendra spent them? How had *she* spent them? Dale and his nail gun? The store? It had been different before her folks died, different when Daniel had still been at home. They'd shared some pretty good times back before Dale got mean.

'What's wrong?' Kendra had that way about her. Rena didn't have to say anything. Kendra just knew.

'Heat's just getting to me, I guess.' She placed the bottles on the open newspaper beside the counter. 'I brought us something to drink. And this time I remembered the opener. No twist-off caps on these babies.'

Kendra reached for the bottle, but kept her gaze on Rena's face. Her eyes glinted with that look Rena would take for amusement if she didn't know better. 'What'd he do this time? Tell you I'm a lesbian because I haven't had a man since Eddie and I split up?'

'Not this time. In fact, he didn't say a word. It was more his attitude.'

'Because he doesn't want you coming over here. Forget the fact that we were all friends in high school. Forget the fact that I've been back here almost a year, and that I am your best friend in this town.'

'It's not just you.' She took the bottle opener from her purse.

'He doesn't want you to have anyone at all, Rena. That's how it starts. They try to isolate you.'

'Why?' Rena's eyes burned, both with tears and the sweet, hot smell of the store.

'So they can control you.' Kendra sighed. 'Classic

23

abuse syndrome. You think he just has bad moods, but it's a whole lot more than that, Rena.'

'I don't know.' This kind of talk made her fidgety. What happened at home stayed at home. That's how she was raised.

'Well, I do know,' Kendra said. 'He's going to say I'm a witch, or anything else to keep you under his thumb.'

'You think?' That made her smile. 'Kendra, if you're a witch, you're the sweetest one I know.'

'Come on, Rena. I'm just a woman who has learned how to take care of herself. That's all. My own daddy doesn't like some of the things I do, but even he says the vehicle of spirit is not important. All that matters is the source, and mine is good. I wish I could say that for Dale's.'

Rena picked up one of the bundles on the counter just to have something to do with her hands. 'Is this what we're making today?'

'White sage wands.'

Kendra never pushed her more than she could handle. Rena could feel her back off.

As Rena fingered the leaves and smelled the scent of white sage, she remembered the way it could overpower the ugliest thoughts – her own or someone else's. 'I haven't burned one of those for a long time. Not away from here, I mean.'

'I didn't think so.' Kendra tugged at her ponytail and nodded at the pile of straw. 'Used for purification, strength, wisdom, and cleansing,' she said in a school teacher voice. And with a grin, 'I think I'd better send one home with you.'

'You know what Dale would do if he caught me smudging?'

'So, don't let him catch you.' She lifted a bundle to the light.

'He doesn't even want me burning candles. Says it's against his religion.'

'And when was the last time that man saw the inside of a church?'

'You have a point. He only remembers that his daddy was a preacher when he's trying to win an argument or keep me from doing something I want to. Still, I don't dare let him catch me smudging.'

Kendra glanced out on the patio, where the stone Buddha sat, rain or shine. 'It all has to do with intent, you know. What you think about and wish for when you burn it.'

Rena looked from Buddha to the candle customers. 'My only intent is to help you sell them.' She went around the counter to her usual work-table, a scarlet-painted bench with a matching folding chair.

'I've got some sweet grass, too,' Kendra said. 'Thought we could make some braids, if you have time.'

Rena leaned down. 'Oh, that's what I smelled when I came in.'

'Sweet grass.' Kendra chuckled. 'Especially good for people who are starting fresh or want to release old patterns.'

Maybe it was the scent of the grasses and sage. Maybe it was just the healing spirit of Kendra. Whatever it was, it soothed Rena and mellowed her out faster than a cup of herbal tea. She'd take some of the sweet grasses home with her and stuff them into her smocked pillow.

25

'Release old patterns?' she asked with a chuckle. 'You don't say.'

Her serenity lasted until she had to turn off the highway toward home. What if she kept going, she wondered, just kept driving into the desert and let the crusty, dusty land swallow her up? Where would she be when she stopped, and would it be any better?

She went around the store, straight to the back, to let Dale see that she'd hurried to return. The tin roof glinted in the light, but there was no one up there. Well, she couldn't expect him to stay up there all day. Lord, she hoped he wasn't in the store with Bryn. She started to turn around and go back, but before she could, she felt someone grab her by the hair and jerk her around. She screamed and tried to pull away.

'Shut up.' Dale's face shoved into hers, his mouth so close to her nose that his features blurred.

'Let me go.' Her scalp felt raw, and her neck ached from being held at such an angle. She sniffed for liquor, but smelled only sweat.

'You're not going anywhere, Rena Pace. Not until we have a little talk.' He yanked on her hair to make his point, and she let out a yelp. No one would see them out here. He could do anything. Why hadn't she gone into the store first?

'What's wrong?' she begged. 'What's happened?'

'You running your mouth, that's what.' His watery blue eyes came into focus. 'You told Bryn this is your store, that you could fire her anytime. What do you mean talking about our personal business like that?'

'I didn't mean anything. Let me go, Dale.'

26

Through her pain, she felt a glimmer of anger. Bryn had tattled on her. Bryn was the reason for Dale's rage.

He tightened his grip again. 'Quit your whining. I don't know what's wrong with you any more, Rena. You're losing it again is what you're doing.'

She was losing it, too, tears gushing down her face, her stomach so twisted up that it made her dizzy. 'I'm sorry.'

'You're going to be more than sorry if you don't learn to keep your trap shut. Where the hell do you get off threatening to talk to Leighton Coulter about Bryn?'

Finally, he released her. She wrapped her hands around her throat, trying to quiet her trembling and hold back the sobs.

'Leighton is Bryn's father. And he's a friend.'

'A wimp lawyer who thinks he's way smarter than he is.' He punched his fist into the air like a boxer, and she jumped back. 'Don't piss me off any more than you already have. Don't make me think about you and Leighton Coulter. I swear, if I ever catch you talking to him—' His voice trailed off, and he lowered his hands. 'And just because your daddy left you this miserable store doesn't mean it's not mine. Understand?'

She nodded and looked down, hating the words that had deserted her, hating her fear as much as she hated him.

'OK, then, baby. Just do whatever it takes. Keep away from Kendra Trafton and that sick stuff she's into. Get yourself some hormones. Start acting like a wife again instead of a crazy woman. All right?'

27

'All right,' she whispered. 'I will.'

He reached out, and she winced.

'Calm down,' he said with a grin that terrified her even more. 'I was just going to wipe off that little mascara spot there on your cheek.' He reached out again and touched her with his fingertip. 'I don't know about you, but I'm wrung out. I'm going to go inside and get me a beer, maybe stretch out on the bed while I drink it. You want to come along?'

'Maybe later,' she said.

'Fine, then. But don't stand out here all day. The heat will kill you.' He turned and walked back to the store, his blue shirt clinging to his back, his boots digging into the dust.

The tears left along with him. Rena felt empty, almost separate from her body. *Please, don't let him be right. Don't let me be losing my mind again.*

Four

My life had been slashed down the middle, and I could think in only two compartments. Life before the letter; life after the letter. The weirdest thoughts flickered through my head at the least likely times. The checkout line in a supermarket, for instance.

'Credit or debit?' the clerk asked, and all I could think was, was I illegitimate? Was Kendra Trafton married when she gave birth to me?

'Credit or debit, ma'am?' the clerk asked in

what my mom used to call a gratey voice. My mom. Why hadn't she told me? Why?

'Debit,' I said, with a gratey voice of my own.

On the way out of the store, I remembered what my mom had written. Kendra Trafton was a single woman. Had she always been? My Internet search for her had shown only a real estate company in Washington and a man. Maybe she had married since my birth. Still, there should be some kind of record. If it existed, Farley and I would find it.

Richard called sometime between my flight to Seattle and my return.

'I heard about Elaine. Let me know if I can do anything.'

What had my soon-to-be ex-husband heard about my mom? That she died? That she wasn't my mom? And who told him? If I were a betting person, I'd put my money on Mick. They'd always been close, and Mick had made no secret of the fact that he thought we would get back together.

I didn't return Richard's call; I would not have to deal with him unless and until I chose to. Part of me dreaded seeing even my friends at work, especially Farley and Tamera. Their pity would only underscore how much I had lost, and when I told them the rest . . . I would tell them the rest, wouldn't I?

When I got to the station that Wednesday, I realized how glad I was to pull into that familiar lot, park my car, and walk across the lot toward the side door. In a few minutes, I would have to put aside my feelings and become part of a team. I welcomed the familiarity of business over the uncertainty that had overtaken my life. At least here I would have no time to focus on anything but the job.

The state-of-the-art station, with its glassed-in announce booth, natural woods, and white walls covered by constantly changing paintings, was the brightest spot in a neighborhood that refused to give into the decay around it. Several rows of loft apartments had attracted young people and other dreamers to the area. A church had purchased a long-closed Art Deco-style theater next door, painted its high, brick side-wall white, and printed it with the giant sheet music for 'Amazing Grace'. Looking at it, I felt comforted, not so much because of the lyrics as by the fact that it had probably taken someone hours to print them on the side of that two-story building.

I stood there for a moment and stared up at it. Then, I heard the door open, and Farley stepped outside. His expression was solemn, and his forehead glistened. It's tough to sweat in Sacramento in early spring when the air is all floral and as soft as a commercial for online dating and hope is as natural as breathing. But he was. I hesitated, and then made eye contact and finally put out my arms. He crossed the lot to me, and we hugged without a word.

'I'm so sorry, Kit,' he finally said as we made our way through the station's side door. 'I did my best to carry the show yesterday. Let me know if you need anything.'

'Thanks.' I kept my voice low and even. 'I can't really talk about it yet.'

'I understand.'

'I'm behind on my blog.'

'It's all right. Leave early today. I can cover.'

Even in the chill of the morning, Farley wore a T-shirt. It was the same solemn green as his eyes. We got seated, and he clutched a crudely crafted little KWEL mug between his fingers, his thumb over his own likeness, my image untouched. I hoped I didn't actually come close to looking that young or having wads of unruly dishwater-blond hair like the woman on this very tacky piece of pottery.

'We need to change the topic,' I said. 'Wing it the way we used to and just see what we can get.'

'Change the topic?' He gave me that wild-man stare. 'What's wrong with the coed murders? I know my sources are a little flaky, but the listeners dig conspiracy stories. Jimmy J keeps trying to sneak in stuff like that.'

'Tamera will keep him in line,' I said. 'I thought we agreed the college-student murders were random crimes. There's not enough to substantiate the connection.'

'There wasn't enough to substantiate the Gomez case either.'

'But DNA was involved. Once we raised the question, they could prove he was innocent. This is drunk-cop speculation.' It sounded meaner than I meant it. I washed down my words with scalding coffee. This was going to be more difficult than I'd thought.

'So was the Gomez case.' He tried to maintain eye contact, but I looked away. 'You didn't seem to mind the strokes we got for helping an inno-cent man get out of prison.'

31

'That was a good show. Of course it was, Farley. One of our best.' I couldn't say much else. I was choking on tears.

'Kit.' He reached across the narrow console and grabbed my hand. Distant as I was, I felt the jolt of connection. 'My contract's up for renewal. You know that. And while everyone reads your blog, no one cares about mine. Two of the college girls were found in the same park.'

'Years apart.'

'But still, I think we can keep building the show on that.'

'It's not real,' I said. 'I want to do the show on something that is.'

'You're not thinking,' he said. 'What's going on?'

'My mom.' That was all I could get out.

'I know. Want me to do this by myself again today?'

I shook my head. 'She wasn't really my mom, Farley. I mean, she was, but she wasn't. Not really.'

'What are you trying to say?' Finally, I had his attention. I had to convince him to agree to the only show I could do with him right now.

'She and Mick adopted me and never said a word. I have a mother out there, my biological mother.' I looked from him to the mic. 'We can wing it. We've done it before. Some of those shows were our best. You know they were.'

'Too soon,' he said. 'It's just too soon. It'll tear you to pieces.'

'I have to do it.' I swallowed more coffee. 'Someone might know something. We've been able to help other people. Maybe we can again.'

'Maybe.' He patted my back in an awkwardly affectionate way that felt more genuine than I would have expected. 'But why didn't you call me if you wanted to do this? Why talk it over with me two minutes before we have to go on?'

'I only just decided,' I said and hoped he could feel how determined I was. Then I pulled my professional voice out of wherever it had been hiding. 'I'm ready, and I can do it. I promise you I can.'

He nodded, and his eyes confirmed what I already felt. 'Let's go for it, then. You're going to have to do the lead-in, and then I'll play catch-up.'

My partner. At that moment, I would have done anything, paid anything to demonstrate my gratitude, but the mic was on, and I had to talk. 'Thanks for joining me, Kit Doyle, along with Gnarly Farley,' I said. 'We've looked at lots of unresolved cases on this show and helped a lot of people. Today, I'm the one asking for your help.' My voice was shaky, and I stopped to take a breath.

Farley leaned into the mic. 'What's happened to Kit is what we believe happens more than most people know. She's just discovered that she's adopted. Twenty-something years of believing one thing, and then, bang, she realizes she has a biological mother, maybe an entire family out there she's never met. Right, Kit?'

'And I don't have a clue.' I'd managed to compose myself while he spoke. 'All I have is the name of my mother.'

He shook his head and put up a hand. 'Are you sure you want to give her name on the air?'

My skin tingled. Maybe I shouldn't have risked

33

this, but it was too late now. 'It's the only way,' I said. 'My biological mother's name is Kendra Trafton. She lives or lived in Buckeye, Arizona. If anyone knows anything, please call us.'

'We want to hear from you.' Farley took over, his voice rich and resonant. 'Give us a call or email us at our website if you can help Kit connect to her biological family. And we'd like to hear from any of you who've had to struggle to find your own biological parents. Start calling, folks. We want to hear from you.'

The first call came through almost before he finished speaking. I spent the rest of the hour immersed in other people's pain. I hadn't realized there were so many whose situations mirrored my own – children who didn't discover until they were adults that their biological families were not the ones in which they had been raised.

'My aunt was really my mother,' one woman said. 'Her name was Edith.'

'My lab offers DNA testing,' said another. 'We've helped many people reconnect with their loved ones.'

I frowned at Farley as if to say: *Who let her in here?* Farley shrugged and kept taking questions.

Just before we finished, a familiar voice came over the line. 'Frank Vera is innocent.'

Now, Farley got to frown at me. I shrugged and didn't bother answering. We both knew Bert the Troll vanished as fast as he appeared.

'Thanks to all of you for calling,' I said. 'Well, almost all of you. Let's talk again tomorrow.'

Farley and I exchanged glances, and I could have hugged him. The show had worked. I knew

34

we'd still be getting calls for the rest of the week. But I didn't have much personal hope. No one we'd talked to on the air or off knew anything about Kendra Trafton of Buckeye, Arizona.

Tamera was waiting for me after my shift. Her yellow shirt and white cargo pants made her one of the brightest spots in the colorful, art-filled lobby. She put out her arms, and I realized she was crying. I hugged her, and we stayed like that for a moment, my cheek pressing into her shoulder.

'I heard it on the way over,' she said. 'What a show. God, you're brave.'

'Not brave. Desperate. And I have no idea if we'll get any leads.'

'But this is the first day. Anything can happen.' She wiped her eyes. 'I know what you're going through.'

'At least you found your siblings,' I said.

She nodded, her amber-brown eyes shiny. 'Only, it was too late to find my father while he was still alive. You can't wait on this, Kit.'

'But I don't know where to start.'

'Your blog. Blast her name all over the Internet. Go to Arizona. Knock on doors.'

'I have a job,' I said. 'I can't just drop everything.'

'That's what I said.' She wiped her eyes. 'I kept thinking I'd never find him, and finally, once I was away from my mom and living on my own, I realized he was a part of me, regardless of what she thought of him. At least you have a town.'

'But that's all I have.'

'I did everything, even tried to trace military

35

records. I'll never know him, and he'll never know I tried.'

'Oh, Tamera, I'm sorry.'

'Well, shoot.' She tried to laugh, but the sadness didn't leave her eyes. 'Knowing my mama's taste in men, he was probably as big a jerk as the rest of them.'

I put my arm around her. 'I just want to know. I want to look at her and know that she's my mother, no matter what she's like, no matter why she gave me up.'

'Then don't do what I did,' she said. 'Don't waste any time, Kit.'

We walked together out the back door. The morning felt clean as fresh laundry, and I wanted to bury my face in the scent of it. I loved these hours, loved having my official work day over when most people's had barely begun.

When Richard and I were falling in love, there weren't enough hours in the night to contain us. I'd drive home from his apartment at five, maybe six, drinking in the new day like a drug. In those hours, wearing the same clothes from the night before, I came as close as I ever had to unabashed happiness.

Dawn could still conjure those feelings for me, fleeting as they were. And now, with the show behind me, and most of the day ahead, I felt something akin to hope.

Tamera stood beside me, staring off, as I was, into the clear sky. 'You better go in,' I said. 'You're on in a few minutes.'

She nodded but didn't move. 'What are you going to do?'

36

'I'm going to find her.'

'Good.' She gave my arm a tight squeeze, and the shadows lifted from her eyes. 'I'm going to help you, Kit.'

Five

After Dale left on Thursday morning, Rena counted one thousand one, one thousand two, all the way to one thousand ten. Then, she smudged the house.

Intent, she thought, just as Kendra had said. She lit the sage bundle with Dale's old Zippo lighter and held it over a bowl to catch the ashes. Then, she walked through the living room, the bathroom, the TV room Dale called a den, and, finally, their own bedroom, even passing the smudge stick over the rocking chair where she kept the lavender smocked pillow she'd made back in high school.

Burn away, burn away. Those were the only words in her mind as the stinging smoke followed her from room to room. That must be her intent, then.

Dale had said he was going to check out a construction job in Phoenix, so she could finally relax. She'd barely been able to breathe since he'd grabbed her.

Start acting like a wife again instead of a crazy woman.

The words hammered into her skull like nails

driving into tin. *Rat-a-tat roar.* But she was all right now. She wasn't crazy.

Maybe he'd get this job. Maybe he'd be gone for a couple of days, maybe a week. She looked around the hazy room. At least he'd be gone long enough for the smell of smoldering sage to sink into the house so that he wouldn't notice that she'd done the one thing he'd warned her against – listened to Kendra Trafton.

Her scalp still ached. Her neck too. All of a sudden, the room felt too warm. Not so smart to try to smoke out evil spirits on the hottest day in weeks. Besides, Dale had said she had to work the store today. She'd better get back there.

She started toward the front of the house. Something small – the wrong kind of noise, but nothing she could name right off – stopped her. She began to tremble. *Don't let it happen again. Please don't let it happen.* A floorboard cracked out in the living room. No, she wasn't making up the noises. They were real.

Dale. The thought skittered across her mind. He'd lied, set her up, hadn't gone to Phoenix at all. Now, he was here, sneaking back to catch her. And he would, too, if she didn't get rid of the sage bundle and the smell – most of all, the smell.

She shoved the bundle into the bowl Kendra had given her Monday and stuck it under the sink. Then she grabbed a green dish-towel off the counter and started waving it around the room. When he came sneaking in, she could tell him she'd burned something on the stove – soup, maybe, or chili. Yes, chili, and she'd had to pour it down the drain. Oh, Lord, why had she done this? She rubbed her scalp and waited for the worst.

Nothing happened. Her neck continued to ache. The smell of sage continued to fill the kitchen, but Dale didn't come busting in to grab her hair and yell at her again.

She heard the little whoosh sound of the front door closing, and not on its own. It didn't make any sense unless . . . No, not *unless* anything. She wasn't imagining one moment of this.

Sweat broke out on her palms, and she rubbed them against her shorts. Maybe Kendra was right about Dale and all that abuse-cycle stuff. Maybe he was just trying to make her think she was going crazy. She'd catch him trying to sneak out, though. Maybe that's what the sage had done, just forced him out of here like the evil, lying thing he was. Still, she'd catch him, and even though she wouldn't say a word, he'd know she was smarter than he thought.

She ran through the house and threw open the front door. But it wasn't Dale heading down the stairs.

He turned toward her. The same face, only sadder, and with lines pulled so deep at the corners of his eyes that it must hurt him to smile. His body was the same, with the tight muscles pulling back the shoulders, the long legs in black boots.

'Leighton,' she said. He wasn't supposed to be here. He was supposed to be out of her life. Gawking at him, trying to compare his body and his face with her memories, she realized that he was probably doing the same with her.

'Sorry if I scared you.' Still on the stairs, he turned and kept his gaze on hers, not on her grungy, dirty shorts, not on her gray T-shirt that felt suddenly too tight.

'You didn't scare me.' Her voice came out as a croak. 'I didn't realize anyone had come inside the house.'

'I knocked first.' He took the last step down and pulled off his baseball cap. His damp hair waved around his ears. The gray mixed in made it more of a brindle color than the curly reddish blond she remembered. 'I shouldn't have come in, but there was no one in the store, and the front door was unlocked. I thought maybe Bryn was in there with you.'

'She's off today.' She followed him into the yard, more dirt than anything else. So that was why he'd come by, after all these years, to check on his daughter. But of course. That's what a parent should do. More than Bryn could expect from Debby Lynn. That was for sure.

'Off?'

'That's why there's no one in the store. I'm supposed to be working it.'

They stood close now. She could smell the sweat and the worry on him.

'She told me she had to work,' Leighton said. 'You haven't seen her?'

'Dale told me he gave her the day off.'

'And where's Dale?'

With a sickening thud, she realized something wasn't right. 'He's supposed to be checking out a construction job over in Phoenix.'

Leighton didn't change expression. Only his

40

fingers flexed in and out. 'You haven't seen Bryn, and you don't know where Dale is either?'

'You don't think she's with him?' she asked.

'Do you?'

She stared into his eyes. 'Leighton?' That was all she could say. His name.

He touched her cheek, and she cringed.

'No. Don't pull away from me. You know I'd never hurt you.'

'I do know that.' But, when he reached out, she shrunk back again. 'I'm sorry. But you're not supposed to be here. You promised.'

'I want to know what's going on,' he said. 'With Dale and Bryn.'

'I told her if she didn't behave here on the job, I was going to talk to you about it.'

'What do you mean, behave?'

'She's at that age,' she said, speaking rapidly, so she couldn't change her mind and try to sugar-coat it. 'You know, when everything's brand new, and you just want to try it out. No, that's not it. I'm not saying it right.'

'You mean when a young woman wants to see if she can attract a man?' he asked.

'Exactly.' She exhaled, drained from even this short contact with him. 'That's what Bryn's doing. Trying to find out if she can get a man to notice her. Every girl goes through it.'

'You didn't.'

'Yes, I did.' She allowed herself a smile. 'Dale's a grown man, Leighton. He's not going to let anybody make a fool out of him, most of all not some young girl who . . . Not Bryn, OK?'

'You sure of that?'

41

'Yes, I think I am.' She was. There were problems in their marriage, sure, and parts of their past were more nightmare than real life. Still, Dale wouldn't cross certain lines.

'I need to find out for myself. Bryn's had enough to deal with, and I blame myself for all of it.' He moved beside her, and an unmistakable sound, out behind a cactus taller than she was, sent chills down her neck.

'Rattler,' Leighton said.

'They're everywhere. I'll never get used to them.'

'You hate this place as much as I love it.' He studied her neck, the place Dale had grabbed her. She felt like a bug under some scientist's microscope.

'Got no right to hate it,' she said. 'I've never been anywhere else that's better.'

'There are places.' The sun caught him just right, and the curls around his neck glistened. 'I've seen those places, and they would blow your mind.'

'Nothing, except maybe winning the lottery, is going to blow my mind,' she said.

'And what would you do with the lottery?'

'Just run.'

'You could do that right now.'

'Don't start, Leighton.'

'I'm not starting anything.' His knuckle brushed her cheek. 'You think he's with her right now? Tell me the truth.'

She shook her head and met his eyes again. 'Why would he do something that crazy?'

'Because of us.'

'He knows that was all in the past. Besides, I've never told him much.' Never told him that

42

she loved Leighton. She'd never said it in those words.

The knuckle again. More than a brush this time. 'He knows, Rena.'

'No.'

'I can tell by the way he acts around me.'

'That's just his way. The war messed him up. He's a good person. A good father,' she corrected. 'He knows Bryn's the same age as his own son. And he knows what you'd do to him if he laid a hand on her.'

'You're right there.' His pale eyes went dark. 'I'd do the same thing if he ever laid a hand on you. You understand that?'

'I'm his wife.' Such a weak answer that she had to turn away, too ashamed to watch the reaction on his face. 'You'd better go.'

'Is that what you want?'

'What I want?' She looked out as far as she could at the dry, dead land that held her life and always would. 'What I want is just to get through the day without any trouble.'

'You've got my office number,' he said in a voice that appeared to fade.

'Yes. Yes, I do.'

'You can call it anytime. There are laws, you know.'

'And you're a lawyer,' she said. 'I know that, too.'

'Then, why—?'

'I've got to get back inside,' she said. 'I left something burning.'

'I smelled it from the porch. What is it, anyway?'

She couldn't help grinning to herself. What would he think if she told him? 'Something I got over in Tucson.'

'From Kendra's herb shop? Have you seen her much since she got back?'

'It's been almost a year now. I work in her shop sometimes.'

He gnawed on his bottom lip the way he had back in high school, as if to say he was figuring out all of her secrets. All of them. 'So what was that burning smell? You're not smoking any of that wacky tobacky, are you?'

She looked for meanness in his face and couldn't find any. Nothing in either his voice or his eyes. 'Not hardly. Kendra sells herbs that can heal and help you. She knows how to use them too. I can't tell you what a comfort she's been to me.'

'I'm glad for that.' He reached out for her bare arms, and for that moment, she let his fingers press lightly against her flesh.

A horn honked like a shotgun blast between them. They broke apart, and Rena whirled around to see Dale's truck screech into the side yard. It kicked up enough dust to surround them like an angry cloud. Bryn sat beside him in the passenger seat.

Leighton sucked in his breath in a harsh gasp. As the dust still danced around the truck, Dale sat glaring through the windshield at Rena, his face red and twisted with anger.

Six

Tamera convinced me of what I had already started believing. I could not waste any time. After that talk with her, I spent most of my free time studying missing people on online sites. An eighteen-year-old whose deserted van was found in Arizona. A mother whose son was convinced she had tried to flee an abusive relationship. A fifteen-year-old described by her sister as *wearing long sleeves; otherwise covered with scars and cuts*. A young man who was *a nice guy but off his meds*.

I saw their faces, their guarded smiles. I glimpsed their secrets and the highs and lows of their lives. In the past, I had studied only crime blogs similar to mine. Now, I observed the world of the missing. Most of the seekers on the family sites were women, and most, like Tamera, asked for help finding their fathers. Others tried to connect with children. Almost all of those seeking biological mothers had grown up knowing they were adopted. As far as I could tell, no one in Buckeye had reported a missing daughter.

Kendra hadn't exactly tried to find me. At one time, that might be reason enough for me to put off this search. But not after I saw the regret that haunted Tamera. I would blog and speak for as many hours as it took to find any answer, even one I didn't want to hear.

Late that week, Carla Brantingham called and

asked for a meeting downtown at the Crocker Art Museum, and I could already guess what the soft-spoken, heavy-handed mayor of our city would want. The Brantinghams had funded my show to publicize unsolved crimes, to shine the light on victims like Alex, Carla's murdered brother. She probably wasn't all that thrilled that I was using the show as a forum for my own search. As I drove toward O Street, I tried to memorize a response – anything from: 'It won't happen again,' to: 'Take your funding and shove it.' As if I could ever best Carla in the mildest debate.

I still hadn't gotten used to the remodeled museum's contemporary structure, which resembled a rocket about to take off. Carla looked as if she might do the same. Her teased blond hair blew around her narrow face, which was always prettier at first glance. That thought made me guilty. This woman's family funded my life, or at least a big part of it. She'd never been anything but nice to me, and I knew she had loved Alex. But I was sure she wouldn't have picked my blog to spread the word about unsolved crimes if he and I hadn't interned together for that short time.

She hurried toward me in a tailored suit so fitted and blue that I almost had to blink, not only because of the color, but also to be sure I was in the right decade.

'How are you?' I hated that question and the defensive way it made me feel.

I took her extended hands. 'How are you, Carla?' She paused. Then with a brief squeeze, she released me. 'Quite well, actually. Thanks for meeting me here. I wasn't sure how long this event would go on. Our timing is perfect.'

Hers, she meant, but I was OK with that.

'What can I do for you?' That's how our meetings always started.

We began walking though the spring morning toward a destination only she knew. 'May I be candid?' she asked.

'Of course.' *It won't happen again. Take your funding and shove it.*

'It's about the radio show.' A breeze caught us, and we ran across a narrow street. 'Our mission statement and all.'

'To honor Alex,' I said from memory. 'To expose unsolved crimes and—'

'Exactly.' She stopped on the sidewalk, and I realized her eyes matched her suit. Had to be contacts. 'Here's my concern.'

'The current topics?' I asked. 'Farley and I do try to keep to the unsolved theme.'

'And you're doing a fine job.' She flashed me a rich-girl smile. 'But Kit, you simply cannot give that freak any more air time.'

'What freak?'

She shook her perfect head. 'You have no idea what I'm talking about, do you?'

This woman, the mayor of our city, was far from stupid, and I didn't enjoy being treated as if I were.

'Carla, with all due respect, we get more than one so-called freak calling in. So if you can't be more specific, I'm afraid I can't help you.'

I wanted to turn and head the other direction.

47

She must have sensed that because she reached out and touched my arm.

'It's that horrible man, the one who calls in a whisper.'

Then I knew. 'The one who says Frank Vera is innocent.'

She cringed. 'Yes. That one.'

'We call him Bert the Troll,' I said. 'Every station has at least one, and blogs have many more. People like him make outrageous statements just to get attention.'

Her lips curved, and I didn't know if it was because she had read Tolkien or because she hadn't.

'And every time this Bert creature, as you call him, invades your show and says my brother's murderer is innocent, my parents' hearts break a little more.'

I stood on that Sacramento street corner and wanted to sigh with relief. The mayor didn't want to stop my search for my mother. She wanted only to stop the station troll.

'We don't like him any more than you do,' I said.

'You aren't just using him for drama?'

Relief flooded through me. 'Are you kidding? He mumbles the same thing every time and hangs up before we can respond.' I took a breath. 'Is that all you want? To get rid of Bert the Troll?'

She gave me a professional nod, and I read relief in her expression. I felt it in myself too.

'Can you do that for me, Kit?'

'I'll do my best,' I said. 'I'll be sure they screen callers better. Promise.'

'That means the world to me and even more to my parents.' She leaned toward me, and for a moment, I feared she might kiss my cheek. Instead, she reached out and shook my hand. 'And, Kit,' she said. 'Family really is everything. No one understands that better than I do.'

Seven

Dale had barely spoken to her since he and Bryn had pulled up in the pickup together, but Rena could tell by the way he almost crept through the house that he blamed her for Leighton being there. The only reason he hadn't said anything was that he had some explaining to do himself. Bryn had claimed they'd just run into each other in Phoenix, and he'd given her a ride home. The deadly look in Leighton's eyes made Rena pray it was true. No way had Dale been able to get to Phoenix and back that fast, though. He and Bryn must have been together from the start. Leighton had ordered Bryn into his car and left without speaking another word. Yet she was back at work the next morning, and Rena told herself everything would be all right now. Only, it wasn't.

For the last two days, Dale had taken to going into the convenience store for a beer, hiding it behind the counter as he sat on a stool and talked to Bryn. Whispering was more like it. And smirking, like two kids telling dirty jokes. They were still at it when Rena left to meet Kendra, and she hoped they wouldn't be when Daniel drove in from college for the weekend.

Truth was, Dale was the guilty party. Not her, and certainly not Leighton. She'd wrestled with what she had seen and suspected, and she knew she'd have to do her best to find out the truth. Bryn was Leighton's daughter, not to mention way too under-age for what might be going on. She owed it to Leighton and even Debby Lynn. She owed it to herself. As she pulled up in front of Kendra's store, her legs went weak, and she knew she couldn't get out of the car.

Let go, and let God. That's what her mama had always said.

Rena lifted her hands from the wheel. 'I'm letting go,' she said, just in case God or Mama was watching. 'I'm doing it.'

If only she could talk to Kendra alone about what was going on, but her job was helping Kendra, not heaping more problems on her. Besides, Kendra had enough to deal with anyway, especially with those people in town who remembered the reason she had left there all those years ago in the first place. Bad mother, they said. Possibly in cahoots with the devil. Maybe even giving up the little girl as a sacrifice.

So, no. She needed to do what she could to help out Kendra at the shop.

The moment she walked inside, she felt her anxiety lighten. The smell in there and the soft lights could do that to her.

Wearing a sleeveless dress with one of those blue batik patterns, Kendra stood next to a curly-haired brunette younger than both of them. The woman hugged Kendra, and then hurried toward the door so fast that she almost ran into Rena.

50

'Sorry,' she said. 'I'm just so relieved. Kendra's wonderful, isn't she?'

'Yes, ma'am, she is.'

The woman left the shop, and Rena wondered how that kind of joy, that kind of freedom would feel.

'You're early.' Kendra joined her, radiating whatever it was that made the simple act of standing beside her feel safe.

'Wasn't sure about the traffic,' Rena said.

'It was a weird morning.' Kendra leaned down and whispered, 'Debby Lynn actually showed up.'

'Why?' Hearing Debby Lynn's name jerked Rena back to a place she didn't want to be.

'Said she was still Leighton's wife, in spite of the divorce, and she wanted to know what was going on with Bryn.'

Rena didn't know whether to feel grateful or scared. 'Maybe she's finally turning into a decent mother.'

'I doubt it.' Kendra pointed to the patio behind the store where the Buddha statue had sat. Only its outlined shape remained on the dusty tiles.

'How?' Rena asked.

'I have no idea.' Kendra studied that spot where the Buddha had been. 'She said she wanted to look around the back garden, and I was stupid enough to let her do it. Lifting lip gloss and nail polish is one thing, but how did she walk out of here with an eighty-pound statue?'

As they studied each other, Rena gave into the smile tugging at her face. 'You always said everyone has an art.'

Kendra smiled too and shook her head. Then

she grew serious. 'She may try to cause trouble.'

'Maybe that's a good thing. Do you think she actually might care about Bryn now?'

'Who knows? She might just be trying to get Leighton back, and good luck to her on that one.'

They began walking toward Kendra's table in the back of the shop, and Rena willed her courage to build with every step.

'Bryn's too young to know her own mind,' she said.

'What are you talking about?'

She stopped and faced Kendra. Smoke from the candles stung her eyes. 'I'm worried about her. Bryn, I mean. Her and Dale.'

'Then you ought to be talking to Leighton, not to me.' Kendra's expression stayed the same, but her posture stiffened. She could do that – just shut out everyone but her own thoughts, her own will. 'Rena, that girl is a baby, regardless of her age. If you think something's going on, you owe it to Leighton to tell him.'

'He was there when she and Dale drove in after Dale said he was going to Phoenix.'

'Leighton caught them together?'

'We both did, but we were together too. They had a good story, but I didn't believe it. Kendra, you've got to help me.'

'And how do you think I can do that?' Her voice went low. Her expression still didn't change.

'Isn't there something you can do? Some kind of smudge or spell or something?'

'I'm not a witch, Rena.'

52

'I know that, but you're trained in healing, and you're the smartest person I know.'

'Not that smart.'

Kendra walked away from her, toward her table, and then past it, her back to Rena. Before her, the patio and its adobe pots looked naked without the Buddha Debby Lynn had somehow shoplifted. Without Kendra saying it, Rena knew she was thinking of her daughter again, maybe even remembering the nasty things people said about what kind of woman could let her baby get stolen.

Kendra couldn't help her now. Maybe no one could. Rena tried to remember what her mama would say, but all she could think about, all she could see, was that empty blank circle on the back patio. Debby Lynn always took what she wanted even if someone else wanted it more.

'Kendra?'

'I've told you all I can.'

'And you're right,' Rena told her. 'I know you are. I need to talk to Leighton.' But she didn't want to. More than that, she didn't even know where to start. 'Guess I'd better get to work,' she said.

That seemed to revive Kendra. She turned around and reached like a blind woman for the closest bunch of herbs on her table.

'More braids?' Rena asked.

'Yes, more braids,' Kendra said. 'For now, at least.'

Eight

To my horror, Bert the Troll managed to jump on the line the Monday after I'd met with Carla Brantingham.

'Frank Vera is innocent.' That same flat, muffled voice, and then nothing.

I gasped and gestured to Farley. We broke for a commercial, and I said, 'We've got to stop that guy.'

'Good luck with that. At least he's quick about it.'

'Doesn't matter,' I said. 'Carla made herself all too clear. It upsets the family.'

'Understand.' He remained silent for a moment, no doubt to remind me that what Carla's family wanted affected me more than it did him.

I felt exposed, surrounded by glass on three sides.

Finally, he said, 'I do understand. We won't feed the trolls. How are you doing otherwise?'

'OK,' I lied.

Regardless of how late he worked the night before or how early he had come in the next day, he always looked rested and straight from the shower. He reminded me of my dad that way. No matter how old the T-shirt or how decrepit the jeans, he always smelled like fresh laundry.

'Kit, I've been thinking. What do you say we do a special show for Mother's Day?'

'What kind of show?'

'Line up the best stories we can find. Play it up big on the website and your blog. Put your own experience out there again. Get media coverage.'

First, I felt joy. Another chance to find my mother. Then that nasty fear took over again.

'What's wrong?' he asked.

'I don't think the Brantinghams will go for it.'

'If they had a problem with your situation, Carla would have told you when you met with her.'

'I don't know,' I said.

'That's the best way to find your mother, Kit. Publicize the hell out of it.'

The best way to get ratings, too. I knew he was thinking that, and I didn't blame him for it.

'These people who call in are largely anonymous,' I said.

'But you don't want to be. You want to be found.'

'What I don't . . .' I couldn't finish the statement. What I didn't want, what I could not deal with, was hearing, along with our radio audience, that my mother had no desire to find me.

'Ten seconds,' said John, the engineer, through my headphones.

'I'll take this one,' I whispered.

'If you're sure.' Farley took a slug of coffee, and I could tell he was craving a cigarette.

'I told you, I'm fine.'

The phone blinked, the commercial faded, and I was as ready as I could be under the circumstances.

'Yes, hello. I'm trying to find some information about my mother?' The caller said it as a question, in a high-pitched voice trying to sound strictly businesslike.

'Do you know her name?' I asked.

'She's my mother. Of course I know her name.'

When it came to callers, rude usually meant scared. I glanced over at Farley, who pretended not to watch me.

'What details can you give our listeners?' I asked. 'Maybe someone out there has information that will help you.'

'I doubt that,' she said. 'I'm only doing this because I don't know where else to turn.' Twangy music played behind her, and I wondered if she were calling from a bar.

'Let's start with her name then.'

'Edith Marie.' She sighed, and I realized that her voice sounded familiar. 'They told me she was my aunt. And then, when I was in high school, my aunt disappeared. I got a copy of my birth certificate last week, saw the name on it, and I realized my aunt was really my mother. Only one problem. I have no idea where she is.'

'Someone in your family knows the truth,' I said.

'That's a no-brainer. Probably all of them. Those people aren't about to tell me where she is.'

'You need to find only one person who will talk to you.'

'If it was that easy, do you think I'd be calling you?'

Farley glanced at me and moved close to his

mic. 'If you had a chance to find your mother, wouldn't you do anything?' Making his point, I knew, and shook my head at him.

'I'm calling you,' she replied, 'against my better judgment. I'm starting to see what a bad idea that was.'

'It's not easy, but you can't give up.' I could have been talking to myself. 'Start with your family members.'

'You got a hearing problem, lady?' Her voice shot up, even more strident than before. 'I told you they lied to me my whole life.'

'But now you know,' I said. 'It's different. Someone will tell you something, a little piece of the truth. That will lead you to the next something.'

'So you don't know anything about any Edith Marie?'

'Not that I recall,' I said. 'Let's ask our listeners.'

But she had already hung up.

Farley glanced over at me. A lock of hair covered most of his left brow. For the first time, I noticed a glimpse of scalp beneath it.

'I did my best,' I said.

'Let's hope she finds what she's looking for.' His fingers brushed my arm. 'I hope both of you do.'

'So do I, Farley.'

I started to stand, but he shook his head. 'You don't want to be like her, Kit. Let's do the Mother's Day show and get the information out there.'

A Mother's Day special and the magic ingredient of social media might give us the power we had lacked before. Once more I thought of Tamera and what price she would pay to have the opportunity I did. No guarantees, but even the slightest chance was something.

'I'll need some time to think about it,' I said.

That was the best I could do for now. I would go home, work on my blog, and try to decide how much more public I wanted to make my life.

Mick sent me a text right after the show asking me to meet him at Virgin Sturgeon. A hang-out for news people, the restaurant, located just two miles from where I had met Mayor Carla Brantingham, floated on the Sacramento River along the Garden Highway.

In the wintertime, the river's ambience consisted of hide-the-bodies bramble. In the summer, the place fit Farley's definition of Mosquitoville. But for a moment in spring, it looked and smelled as if someone were shaking baskets of blossoms on to the water. I stepped out of my car and looked at what could be a Japanese woodcut, give or take an old speedboat or two.

Mick's copper-colored state-of-the-art motorhome was parked outside the restaurant's long gangway, which in its past life had served as a jetway for Pan American Airlines at San Francisco International.

To her credit and mine, I liked Mick's wife. Rachel was almost the reverse of Carla, a slender blond who didn't work her looks. Maybe she didn't have to, or maybe she really was as comfortable in her own skin as she appeared. She must have seen me park because by the time I got out of my car she had started across the parking lot toward me.

Her pale hair and fern-green tunic blended her in with the scenery. I had hated my parents' divorce and the steady assortment of women who followed it so much that at first I'd thought Rachel was just one more in a line of younger but fading-fast blonds. She'd soon set me straight, letting me know she had made enough poor choices to know what she wanted – and miracle of miracles, she wanted Mick.

'I made some fresh tea.' She put out her arms and hugged me as if she meant it. 'Right now, I'm going to the restaurant to pick up some sandwiches for us.'

'Meaning Mick wants to talk to me alone?'

'Something like that.' She grinned and gave the shrug that said she wasn't about to snitch on her husband. 'I'm sorry about Elaine, Kit.'

'Me too.'

'And I had no idea about the rest of it. If you need to talk, you know I'm here for you.'

'Thanks,' I said, 'but it's too soon. And I don't have time to eat, so you don't need to order anything for me.'

'If you're sure.'

She hugged me again and headed toward the gangway that led to the restaurant. I had no choice but to walk back to Mick's domain.

The vehicle equivalent of his phones and gadgets, it was a technophile's dream. A complete recording studio, located before the master bedroom and bath, dominated most of the living area with gleaming precision. Although Mick's personal life may have been sloppy at times, he maintained his possessions with loving care that bordered on obsession.

'Hey, Kit.'

He'd dressed up in a clean T-shirt and jeans. When we hugged, I realized how glad I was to see him.

'I can't stay long,' I said. 'I have to work on the new blog.'

'What's it about?' He laid his glasses on the console and settled on his chair in front of the recording equipment. I sat across from him at the table.

'One of the missing girls I read about online. She's a cutter. Her friend said she'd be wearing long sleeves. I can't forget that girl.'

'What do you want to happen as a result of your blog?'

I could have fallen into one of our easy conversations, but I needed to get out before I demanded to know how he could have lied to me all these years.

'I want her to matter. I mean, no one cared about her, that's all. I want to understand her story and maybe help her friend find her.'

'Sounds like your kind of story.' He leaned forward in his chair. 'Rachel and I are on our way to Washington. Thought we'd take our time, go along the coast. Elaine planned the service down to the last flower. We just have to pick a day. What about a Wednesday? We got married on a Wednesday, got you on a Wednesday, too, by the way. You want me to call Richard?'

'That's fine,' I said.

'And Richard?'

'He's not part of our family now.'

'Elaine loved him, and he loved her.'

Although there was no accusation in his tone, I felt it nonetheless. I had no right to say who was or wasn't part of 'our' family. I didn't even have a family – not one I knew. Not one who could or would answer my questions. I glanced down at my wedding ring; the department-store diamonds had once looked like stars to me. I wore it on my right hand now.

'Tell him if you want,' I said. 'I'm not up to calling him, though.'

'I understand, Kit.'

So this was why he'd insisted we meet – so he could try to convince me to ask Richard to the memorial service. Yet, I felt anxiety in the air between us, as if one or both of us had more to say.

'Well, then.' I glanced down at the cherrywood floor and realized I had absorbed more of his habits than I'd admitted to myself, difficulty with making eye contact being the most obvious. 'I'm considering doing a Mother's Day show with Farley.' I forced myself to look directly at him.

'The less you do of that, the better,' he said.

'Why? Farley thinks it's a great idea.'

'Because Farley wants ratings.'

'So do I,' I said. 'You should understand that better than anyone. But even more than that, I want to find my mother.'

'We have resources.' Mick stood, grabbed a folder off the counter, and joined me on the other side of the dining table. 'Private investigators, for instance. We don't have to spread our private business all over the place.'

'I've been denied the truth my entire life.' As much as I wanted to open the folder, I didn't. 'At this point, maybe I should stop caring what people think.'

'It's not so much what people think.' He pushed the folder closer to me. 'It's what they say. You've been in radio long enough to know what I'm talking about, and you don't need it.'

I also knew I couldn't bear the thought of Kendra Trafton rejecting me on the air. I wasn't sure I could deal with that in private either, though.

'But if it helps us find Kendra,' I said.

'I told you. We have other ways.' He rose from the table and to the coffee area, closer to the back of the motorhome. 'Damn, I forgot to tell you. Rachel made tea. Something she picked up on one of our trips.'

'I need to go now.' I rose from the table.

'Kit, please.' Mick shot from the stove top to me in record time. Without his glasses hiding his eyes, I could see the fear in them. But fear of what? 'You know how radio can be.'

'I do,' I said and tried to move a step back from him.

He touched my arm. 'I want you to find that Trafton woman, Kit. I gave up my marriage because I knew you deserved the truth. But not like this. Not on the air.'

I sighed and realized it was the second time in one day I would have to say the same words

– first to Farley, this time to him. 'I'll need some time to think about it.'

'Sure, Kit. I understand.' He picked up the folder and walked me to the door. 'Take a look at this when you have a chance. As I said, we have options.'

I took the folder from him. 'Have you heard anything about the autopsy report?' I asked.

'Nothing suspicious.' Mick looked down at his hand and seemed to will it to remain steady. 'They think it was natural causes.'

'They think?'

'It was her heart. No one knows why these things happen, and Elaine had her share of medical problems.'

'That's not true,' I said. 'She was obsessive about her health. I want to see the autopsy report. Is it in here?'

'Of course not. Just a summary. I wouldn't want you to have to go through the whole thing.'

'I want to see it,' I told him. 'All of it.'

'OK. If it makes you feel better, go ahead. I'll get a copy of it for you.'

'You don't have one?'

'No. Why would I? But if you want to read it – if that's what you need – we'll make it happen.' At the door, he kissed my forehead the way he always did. 'Love you, Kit.'

'Love you too, Mick.'

'Re-think this Mother's Day thing, will you? There are easier ways to find Kendra Trafton.'

Nine

Barely noon, and already the day tasted like dust as she and Kendra shopped for groceries for that night's supper. Rena had pulled her hair up, but she could feel strands that had escaped the clip sticking to her neck like thin, wet ribbons. She rubbed at the tickle they left and hoped she didn't look as bad as she felt.

Kendra pushed the cart, taking charge of the trip, which was fine with Rena.

'You look tired,' Kendra said. 'What's going on?'

'I'm all right.'

'Dale still making life miserable for you?'

'Not so much that,' she said. 'He and Bryn are still at it, though. The girl won't leave him alone. They've always got their heads together.'

'I told you to talk to Leighton.'

'There's nothing I could add to what he already knows.' Rena reached for a can of green chilies and put it in the cart beside the cheese. 'I can't believe Dale would be stupid enough to do more than flirt, considering her age and what Leighton would do to him.'

'Never overestimate that one.' Kendra pointed at the shopping cart. 'And put those canned jalapeños back on the shelf. I got some great Anaheim chilies to stuff for my Daniel.'

'He'll be so glad to see you,' Rena said. 'I wish

64

he could stay longer, but he had a lot to do over his spring break.'

Kendra stared at the canned goods, as if she wanted to look anywhere but at Rena. They both knew why Daniel didn't like to come home from school, but sometimes Rena needed to pretend.

'You must miss him,' Kendra said finally.

'The only way I can stand it is to tell myself how much better off he is going to college and getting out of Buckeye.' Rena tried not to cry, but Kendra's features blurred. 'Sometimes, though, the missing him just takes me over, and I can't think about much else. You know how it is with your own child.'

Kendra nodded. 'I do.'

'I'm so sorry.' Rena covered her lips with her hand, but it was too late to stop the words. 'I wasn't thinking.'

'It's all right.' But Kendra's face wasn't all right, far from it. Rena knew she had to be thinking about her daughter.

'We've got a long list here. We'd better get hopping. Next stop, Rotel tomatoes. Can't have decent chalupas without Rotel tomatoes, can we?'

Kendra didn't move. 'All these years I told myself running from the past only made things worse. But now that I'm back here, I'm not so sure.'

'My mama would have called what you did "pulling a geographic",' she said. 'Taking off so soon after and hoping that would fix it. At least now maybe you can heal a little.'

'They call it closure.' Kendra stared down at the cart. 'Such a cold word.'

Here Rena had been thinking about herself,

65

worrying that Dale was right about her mental state, and all the time Kendra was the one who needed support. 'The world's changed so much since then,' she said. 'With computers and DNA and all, there are so many ways to find lost people.'

'If they are alive.' She sighed and seemed to force a smile. 'Enough of that. I do all right most days, but then something will come out of the blue like that and just flatten me.'

She'd been that something out of the blue. 'I shouldn't have opened my mouth, Kendra.'

'No.' Kendra took her arm and squeezed hard. 'You and I. We shouldn't have to measure our words. We were best friends when we were girls, and we have to accept each other for who we are now.'

'I do accept you,' Rena said. 'I just feel bad I caused you to hurt.'

'I'm all right now.' Kendra smiled and reached for the cart. 'Let's have fun, and you remember what I said, OK? You and I can say anything to each other.'

'It's a deal.' Rena made herself smile too. She had made a promise to Kendra, and now she needed to keep it.

Ten

The responses to my blog and the phone calls to the station continued. With each conversation, I hoped for a reunion of my own, for someone who wanted to find me as much as these people had wanted to find their families. But did Kendra want that? She'd put me up for adoption. She probably had reasons, maybe good ones at the time. I tried to imagine myself in her place and wondered if she would welcome my intrusion into her life.

Tamera convinced me to hire the online detective agency she had used. They took credit cards and touted their successes at reuniting families. The photos of hugging, joy-filled relatives on their website were enough to convince me that hiring help was worth a shot. The blanks on the screen asked for names and dates, some of which I knew and some I didn't. I filled them out. When I came to the name and relationship of the missing person, I hesitated, then typed in the name that was still so new to me that entering it on this site made me feel like a fraud, as if I were putting in the number of someone else's credit card. Name: Kendra Trafton. Relationship: Mother.

I thought of little else apart from that. Getting through the memorial service, Richard or no Richard. And, until then, getting through each broadcast. Showing anyone who doubted me that I could handle this.

After today's show, Farley pushed back his chair with an expression that was impossible to read. He seemed to have mastered the art of hiding his thoughts from me.

'How are you doing?' he asked.

'I'm fine.' I got up and stretched. The shifts seemed longer and longer these days.

'That last caller got to you, didn't he?'

'They all do. I never thought about how many people had to deal with this.'

'A lot.' He spoke as if on the air. 'Imagine what it's like for them being cut off from half their families. Imagine the not knowing.'

'I don't have to imagine, Farley.'

A flush crept into his tan. 'I didn't mean to sound like an ass,' he said.

'You didn't. I'm too irritable these days. Sorry.'

'So am I.' He toyed with his notes, and then met my gaze. 'It's just that since all this has happened, you're different.'

We had been linked once, connected. In the confines of the studio, we fused into one unit, our identities blended so perfectly for that time on the air that I wondered how we'd be as a couple off the air. We'd never got around to finding out. Now, we were two individuals, separated by what should be just another topic for us. Another commercial and we'd be back on for a final phone call.

'What do you mean? You think I've changed?'

'Of course you've changed, and I have to remember it. One minute you're my partner, just the same as always. I need to tell myself that when we talk about this subject, you're somebody else.'

'Are you saying I'm not being professional?' I felt like walking out the door and letting him handle the last caller. But, well, that might not have been so professional. Instead, I sat back down.

'I'm saying you're hurting.' I could feel as much as see his concern. His long hair glinted in the light from the windows, making him look as young and golden as one of those singers from my father's past.

'I can still do my job,' I said, not sure which

68

one of us I was trying to convince. 'I can relate to these people because I know how they feel.'

'And because of you, I can too.' The engineer signaled, and Farley took the last caller. 'Hi, it's Farley and Kit on Perp Talk.'

'Frank Vera is innocent.'

Before I thought about it, I shouted into the mic, 'Why don't you call back when we're off the air and tell me why you're such a coward.'

No answer.

'Bert alert,' Farley said. 'He's trolling, but you don't have to. Visit our website and share your tips and stories.' He switched to a recorded newscast. 'Not the best segment ending we've ever done. Let's hope no one was listening.'

I sighed and rested my forehead in my hands. Farley squeezed my shoulder.

Just then the phone rang again. I glanced at Farley. He shrugged. I grabbed it and waited.

'I'm not a coward,' the man said in a clear voice.

I signaled with my thumb to Farley and mouthed *Bert*. 'Then why won't you tell us the truth for once?'

'Price tag's too high.'

Farley nodded. We had him. And we were off the air, which was all Carla Brantingham had asked for. She didn't say we couldn't talk to the guy. Besides, if he really did know something, and we could offer her solid evidence about her brother's death, she wouldn't care how we got the information.

'What if we keep your name out of it?' I asked.

'You won't.'

'Then why do you keep calling?'

'Because Frank Vera didn't kill Alex Brantingham. You need to write about it, talk about it on that show of yours.'

'I can't do that if you don't tell me what you know,' I said. 'Could we meet somewhere?'

Farley shook his head vehemently, and I put my hand up, signaling him to stop.

'There's a diner off J Street. I'm five minutes from there.'

'I'm on my way,' I told him. 'What's the name of it?'

'Not sure, but it's the only crêpe place on the block. I'll know you when I see you.' He hung up again, but this time I didn't care.

'Hold on just a minute,' Farley said.

'I can't wait,' I told him and headed toward the door.

He followed me. 'We need to go together, Kit. You have no idea who this guy is.'

'I appreciate the offer.' My heart beat so fast that my chest ached. 'But, Farley, it is daylight, very public, and if the two of us show up together, we might scare the guy away for good.'

'Or we might get a better story out of him. Good cop, bad cop.'

As hopeful as his expression was, I still shook my head. 'For now, at least, I need to do this alone.'

'You see what I mean?' he said.

'About what?' I asked, and we headed through the door and into the studio.

'You've changed.'

I stopped for long enough to sigh. 'This guy has been hanging up on us for months. I have a chance to talk to him. That is all this is about. I'll check in with you as soon as I can.'

I left him there like that and hurried through the side door to the parking lot.

Regardless of what he said, Farley was thinking about himself and about whatever relationship we did or didn't have. For some reason, he could no longer see how important this interview was for us, and more than that, for Alex's family. No, I thought as I pulled out of the parking lot. I wasn't the one who had changed. Farley was.

The tiny restaurant had that energetic caffeine-and-sugar vibe that defined such places more than any business being done there. In the early after-noon, it was packed, mostly with coffee drinkers, who from the looks of them were on their breaks or just trying to get lost with their newspapers and laptops. Any of them could be our caller. To the counter on my left, a man in a polo shirt sat with a large fruit crêpe that had more whipped cream than strawberries. At a table beside me, a guy in a tank top and flip-flops held an espresso and checked me out. I glanced back, and he smiled an unspoken invitation.

No, thank you. Mr Flip-Flops was not my guy.

'Ms Doyle? Kit?'

I jumped at the sound of my name and realized I was more nervous than I had admitted to Farley or myself. Next to me stood a young guy – early twenties, maybe – with studious-looking glasses and black, longish hair shoved behind his ears.

'Thanks for meeting me,' I said.

'I'm taking a big chance.'

71

I put out my hand. 'It's good to meet you, Mr . . .?'

'I could make up a name,' he said, without taking my hand, 'but that would just confuse the issue.'

'At least you're honest.' I glanced around the packed room. 'Could I get you some coffee?'

'No,' he said. 'We need to get out of here.'

'You won't even tell me your name,' I said. 'No way can I go anywhere with you.'

'That's the only way it can be. My parents. They could get in big trouble.'

I guessed he was telling the truth. He was too jittery to be lying. 'It's a nice day,' I said. 'Why don't we just walk around a little?'

He nodded, and we went outside.

The only way I could speak to him was to pretend we were on the air, not face-to-face. 'Why do you think Frank Vera's innocent?' I asked.

'Because . . .' He bit his lip and signed. 'Frank's had his problems, all right. But he didn't do it. You got to the bottom of that other murder. Investigate this one, and you'll find out I'm telling you the truth.'

'If Frank didn't do it, who did?' I hit him with the question the way I would if he were only a voice on the radio. He seemed almost to recoil from it.

'All I care about is clearing Frank's name. If he goes to prison for this, I'll never forgive myself.'

'You're friends?' I asked.

'No, man.' He shook his head. 'I hate his guts.'

'Then why do you care if he goes to prison?'

'Alex wouldn't want it that way.' He fumbled

in his pocket and shoved on some dark glasses.

'You knew Alex Brantingham?' I asked it too fast, too forcefully, and he stepped back as if I'd lunged for him.

'I can't do this. I'm sorry.'

'Wait,' I said. But he was already walking, and then running, down the street.

Eleven

Rena followed Kendra down the narrow aisles. They should be able to say anything to each other. She should be able to say anything to Kendra, and Kendra to her. Yet she didn't want Kendra to think she was crazy, and more and more lately, especially after something set Dale off, she felt that way.

'Hey, girls,' a male voice hooted. Then, a whistle from behind them.

Rena turned around and felt Kendra do the same. Two young men about Daniel's age stood there, shamefaced. Rena felt her cheeks heat up with embarrassment for them and herself, too, for not being what they'd figured them for.

'Sorry, ma'am,' one of them said, his face so red that he looked as if he'd been scalded. 'We thought—'

Kendra chuckled and glanced down at her long, tan legs. 'No problem, guys. We'll take it as a compliment.'

'Oh, I know who you are,' the other one said.

'My girlfriend buys herbs at your store, Ms Kendra. We didn't intend any disrespect.'

'No disrespect taken,' she said. 'Have a good day.'

The kids took off down the closest aisle.

'We must look younger from behind,' Rena said to her. 'Dale told me these jeans were too tight. Guess I should have listened.'

Kendra laughed and pulled her ponytail tighter. 'You look young coming and going, girlfriend.'

'Don't lie to me. I can see it in the mirror. Not the age, so much. I just look tired all the time.'

'Probably because you *are* tired all the time. You need to take a vacation, get away from Dale for a few days.'

'I wish.' Rena stood before the meat case. She didn't want to talk about Dale right then. She just wanted to find a decent pork butt for Daniel's chalupas. She picked up a plastic-sealed package, stared at it, and tried to figure out ounces from pounds.

'Wishing won't make it so,' Kendra said, 'but you can. Why don't you come stay at my place after Daniel goes back to school? I could use the help.'

'And leave Dale and Bryn alone together? No way.'

'They're going to do what they're going to do, with or without you. Besides, Leighton's going to keep his eye on Bryn. Rena, you can't blame yourself for things that are out of your control.'

'I'm not blaming myself, but I'm no fool, either.' She put the package of pork back into the cooler. No way to concentrate on how many pounds she needed with Kendra harping at her like this. 'That Bryn is a crafty little thing. It's hard to believe she's Leighton's daughter. Must be the Debby Lynn influence.'

Kendra gave her the look that others would say was witchy – the look that saw straight through you. 'Why in the world did you let his daughter come to work for you, anyway?'

'Leighton asked me to,' she said. 'It was right after Daddy died last winter. I wasn't thinking straight, and I hadn't talked to Leighton in a long time.' Make that a long, long time. She still couldn't believe they'd spoken again, couldn't believe she'd actually been able to see him.

'And?' Kendra asked.

'And that was that. He just called out of the blue. Said Bryn was having some trouble in the city college and would it be all right if she worked for us for a while to find out the value of an education. I said yes before I thought about it. Of course, I didn't know her. Now that I do, I don't like having her around. I just liked the idea of it, I guess, her being Leighton's daughter and all.'

Kendra picked up a bundle of red chilies. She didn't seem satisfied, turned back, and lowered her voice. 'So, how'd that braid work out? Did you use it?'

'Oh, yes. I can't say it brought me the best luck, though.'

'It's not about luck. It's about cleansing.'

'Right,' she said. 'And the house does smell fresher, just like it does after a rainfall.' She wanted to ask Kendra what had been bothering her, but she didn't know how. Maybe once they were out of the store, she could get Kendra alone and demand that she tell her the truth. There wouldn't be another chance today, once they got back to the house and started cooking.

The checkout line snaked down the aisle, with too much traffic and too few checkers. Displays of chocolates reminded her that it was almost Mother's Day. The holiday never seemed for her. Looking at the foil-wrapped boxes, she thought of her own mother and missed her.

The two young men – boys, really – stood in front of them, no cart. The one in cut-offs carried a twelve-pack of Rolling Rock. Neither turned around.

'Bet that blond guy has a fake ID,' Rena whispered.

'He's got a nice butt.' Kendra stared openly. 'Not like those sorry pancake asses on most the guys our age.'

'Hush,' Rena said. 'They'll hear you.'

'Next time, I might just get me one of those,' Kendra continued in the same tone. 'Lots of women are going for younger guys, you know.'

'I already raised one son,' Rena said, and then bit her lip again.

'Nobody said anything about raising.' Kendra shoved her sunglasses into her hair. 'That's way too long term for what I have in mind.'

'Kendra, stop it.'

'Come on.' She nudged Rena. 'Tell me you don't fantasize about something young and fine now and again.' Then, shaking her head, 'You really don't, do you? Can't you even let yourself have a silly little fantasy?'

'Wouldn't be a fantasy to me. It'd be more like a nightmare.'

'What's wrong with you, anyway?' Kendra gave her that look once more.

Rena didn't answer. They walked out into the blast of heat, the sunlight, and Kendra opened her trunk.

Rena planted herself in front of it. 'Do I look any different to you?'

'Different, how?' Kendra squinted at her.

Rena's arm froze and prickled, as if a cricket had landed on it. She didn't know how to put her feelings into words without sounding like a total nutcase. 'Dale's been saying some stuff. I don't believe it, but I need to hear it from you. You're the only person I can trust to tell me the truth.'

'What's he been saying now?' she asked.

She said it the only way she could, standing there in the honesty of that hot, dusty sun. 'That it's happening again. That I'm losing it.'

'Oh, Rena.' Kendra put down her bags and gave her a hug. 'The only thing crazy about you is the fact that you stay with that man.'

'It's only lately that it's gotten bad.'

'That it's gotten worse, you mean. It's been bad as long as I've known you two, and that's most of my life. Why can't you just leave him, Rena? I'll help. You won't be alone.'

The possibility seemed almost real as they stood out there in the sunlight, the way a lot of plans seemed possible when Kendra spoke them.

'Where would I go?' she asked in a voice that shamed her with its hopelessness.

'Rena, you don't have to go anywhere. Your daddy left the gas and convenience store to you. You could stay with me until you figure out what to do with it. And I'm sure you could find someone to give you legal advice, if you know what I mean.'

Rena's face burned, as if she'd been slapped. 'You really think all this trouble we're having is because of Dale? Tell me the truth, Kendra. Do you think he's the problem, and not me?'

'Of course he's the problem. He just says it's you making him mean. He was mean before you, and he'll be mean after you.'

'You think so?' The words were freeing, yet the dark memories tugged at her, pulling her back.

'Just leave the abusive creep, Rena. It's time.'

They got in the car. 'I don't know,' Rena said. 'I just don't know.'

Kendra eyes gleamed. She looked like a little kid, with her dark glasses tucked into her hair like a headband. 'You don't believe you're strong, but you're like the sphinx. A woman's head and the body of a lioness.'

'Where do you come up with this stuff?' Rena shook her head. 'I never saw any sphinx that looked like a woman.'

'The Egyptian one did,' she insisted. 'And that's you. Want to stop for some coffee?'

'Daniel might be home by now. I'd better not.' On the dry fields on either side of them, one cactus after another flashed by, the landscape of her life. 'Sometimes, I forget things,' she said.

Kendra turned with a frown that made her eyes seem harsher than they were. 'What kind of things?'

'Nothing important. Just sometimes I do. And

when I was smudging the house the other day, I had the strangest feeling.'

'What kind of feeling?'

'Like I wanted to do more than just smudge, more than just smoke out whatever was in there.'

'What do you think was in there?' Kendra asked, her voice almost too careful.

'I don't know.' She turned in the seat so she could see Kendra's face better. 'When you smudge, it's about intent, as you said. Is it normal to think *burn away*? Is it normal to just want to burn away every trace of evil in your life?'

'I don't know, Rena. I'm not on close terms with normal.'

'But you don't think I'm weird because I was thinking those thoughts?'

'Of course not.' Kendra pulled down her glasses, and Rena could no longer see her eyes. 'Just don't say anything about them to anyone else, all right?'

That meant Kendra thought Rena's feelings weren't the kind regular people had. If she didn't hide them, her life could crash down around her the way it had before. She would do anything to keep that from happening.

'Don't look so worried.' Kendra reached over and patted her hand.

'Just thinking about those chalupas.'

Rena tried to force herself to picture that big old platter full of meat and beans, the smell of garlic, and everyone gathered around. Instead, she thought about how much heat and pressure it took to reduce a solid roast to shreds that you could scoop up with a single tortilla chip.

As they pulled in front of the store, Rena spotted Daniel's little car in the driveway. 'He's here,' she said, and prayed that she could make this a good day for him. There'd been enough bad ones. She owed him this, and she had to be strong. *Face of a woman, body of a lion,* she thought.

A suitcase lay propped against his car. As he walked up to it, he spotted them pulling in and broke into a grin. 'Hey. Hi, Mom.' She couldn't hear the words, but watching him mouth them was enough. 'Mom!'

'He's gorgeous.' Kendra screeched to a stop. 'Oh, Rena, he's looking more and more like you.'

Kendra dashed out of the car and was the first to hug him. Second was just fine for Rena. He smelled like damp grass and some kind of after-shave straight out of the sixties – patchouli, maybe.

'You're going to be as tall as your grandpa,' Rena said, and stepped back to look him over. 'Sorry we're late, baby. We've been shopping for supper. Kendra's fixing chalupas and *chile relleños* with fresh Anaheim peppers.'

'Awesome.' Daniel hugged her again. Her son. He just got more and more handsome.

'I'm so glad you're here,' Rena said. 'I was afraid—'

Before she could finish speaking, he reached for the handle of his bag. 'So, tell me about the babe behind the counter.'

'The counter?' She hoped she was wrong, but the look in his eyes made it clear.

'In the store. You, know. Bryn. Is she hooking up with anyone?'

'Is that what you kids are calling it now?' Rena felt as if he'd struck her. 'Forget about it, and let's start supper.'

'In a minute.' For the first time, she could see his resemblance to Dale in the obstinate set of his chin, his narrow eyes, the color of hers but the shape of his father's. 'I'm telling you that girl is hot. And I think she kind of likes me too.'

'Do not talk to that girl.' Rena realized her voice was out of control, but she couldn't stop it.

'Mom, calm down.'

'No, Daniel. No, you calm down. You calm down right now. I mean it. That girl is trouble.'

The sky turned black. Somewhere beyond her vision, she heard the rattle of a snake. She was slipping. *Please don't let this happen again, not in front of Daniel.*

'Rena?' Kendra asked, with a strong grip on her arm. 'Leave this fool kid to his fantasies, and let's get in there and kick ass in the kitchen.'

It was as if Kendra had passed a magic wand over her. She felt safe again. 'Absolutely,' she said, her cheeks still burning. 'Let's get started. Son, I'll bet you haven't had food like Kendra's chalupas since you were here last winter. Let's go inside, all right?'

'Sure.' He pulled the bag behind him, its tiny black wheels clattering through the pebbles. Rena was afraid he'd mention Bryn again, but he didn't. Still, his face had changed. He no longer looked happy to see her.

'Let me take care of that, son.' Dale appeared from the side yard.

Rena gasped, and she knew they all heard it.

81

He'd dressed up, in a clean T-shirt and slacks the color of the land around them. Daniel's face filled with something that looked too much like relief.

'Hiya, Dad.' He put out his hand.

Dale pulled him into a bear hug. That had to be a first. As she walked past them, following Kendra into the house, she heard Dale's voice. 'Now you know what I've been telling you about, son. This is the kind of stuff I have to deal with every day.'

Rena turned back to the car as if she'd forgotten something, embarrassed that they might know that she'd overheard. And, yes, embarrassed that her son suspected the truth about her.

Twelve

Bert the Troll no longer called the station. Carla Brantingham congratulated me on the fact, as if I had somehow made him disappear.

Farley and I had been invited – make that coerced – to a fund-raiser for her next election. 'Not that you're expected to contribute,' Ray, her secretary, had said. 'The mayor will be honored just having you there.'

'Especially since she's the hand that feeds us,' Farley said as we drove to the event.

'At least she didn't ask us for money.'

'She's asking for more than that. Did you actually vote for her?' He swung his car into one of the few remaining spaces on the street.

'What do you do?' I asked. 'Smell these things? No one finds a parking place around here.'

He leaned close to me and fixed those pale-green eyes on me. 'I asked you a question, Kit.'

'No, I did not vote for Mayor Carla. Are you happy?'

'I didn't either. Yet if we show up here, we're endorsing her in a way.'

'We work for her,' I said. 'Besides, she's going to be re-elected with or without our votes.'

He started to get out of the car, and then paused. 'There's something else going on, isn't there? Another reason why you wanted to come tonight.'

'To keep my job?' I asked.

He shook his head. 'I don't think so. I'm not going far away from you inside there, though. I want to see what you really have in mind.'

'I'm not so sure,' I told him. 'Playing it by ear, I think.'

That was the truth. I did know I needed to talk to Carla Brantingham and maybe even catch her unguarded. The best way to do that would be in the safest environment she knew – a ballroom full of supporters her family's money had paid for.

When we entered, I could see that Carla was surrounded by several hundred thousand dollars of supporters, so Farley and I walked around the ballroom trying not to look obvious. Farley had cleaned up nicely in a black suit and khaki tie a shade darker than his eyes. I wore a deep-green dress covered with hot-pink scribble-print roses. The clingy fabric was more Tamera's style than mine, but when she tried it on, she said it looked more like me and insisted that I buy it. I had to admit Farley and I looked as well-heeled as the room of donors. True, some of the women, including Carla, had more cleavage than I, and some of the men wore more diamonds on their fingers than their dates did. But Farley and I blended in, and that was all I wanted.

Joseph and Bette, Carla's parents, entertained an entourage almost as large as Carla's. It figured, I guess, since their money had launched their daughter's career. Bette spotted us through the crowd and waved that palms-forward, fingers-up-and-down way some people do to let you know that even though they're too busy to actually say hello, you really do matter.

I waved back. Bette Brantingham was a tiny pastel woman. Her platinum hair, rose-tinted cheeks, chalk-blue knit suit and matching eyes took understatement to an art form. Even the alcohol she sipped was as clear as the stemmed glass that held it.

'Is it my imagination,' Farley asked, 'or does Carla's mom look a little tipsy?'

'Not tipsy. Just vague. And she's always that way,' I told him. 'The poor woman lost her only son. At least she's trying.'

'She does look happy to see you.'

'As happy as royalty can. Make that ag royalty. They're surrounded by rich farmers.'

'I'm not going to ask how you can tell that.' He nudged me. 'You probably ought to go over and say hello to her.'

'Can't you see she's involved up to her eyeballs?'

'With old Joseph's friends, maybe. But I saw

84

the way she looked at you. Maybe she needs a friend of her own.'

As much as I liked that decent part of him, I had no desire to dive into that murky pool of politics just across the room from us. 'You're the one who didn't even want to come,' I said. 'And now you want me to go pay homage to the sponsor.'

'The poor woman, as you call her, looks lost.'

I glanced up at him and realized he was serious.

'Besides,' he added, 'saying hello is not exactly paying homage.'

'Just for the record,' I told him, 'Bette is the mother of Carla, remember? I'm not sure how far the metaphorical apple falls from the tree there.'

'Speaking of metaphors.' He grinned, as if to remind me I'd better think twice before trying to talk over his head. 'Bette wasn't born with a silver spoon, was she?'

'Far from it,' I admitted. 'But she's been married to privilege for a very long time.'

'But, as you pointed out, she also lost her only son.'

'That's true.' I glanced over at Bette again and got what looked like a hopeful smile.

'You liked Alex, didn't you?' Farley asked.

'As much as one intern can like another in a month,' I said. 'From what I remember, he was polite and sweet.'

'She doesn't seem that bad.'

'If you're so eager to make sure she gets some attention,' I said, 'why don't you go with me, Farley?'

'Good idea.' He took my arm, and we crossed the room.

'So good to see you.' Poor Bette did look starved for company, in spite of the crowd that surrounded her. 'Kit, you are doing such an excellent job for our non-profit. And . . .'

'Farley,' he replied, and put out his hand.

She shook it eagerly. 'Good to see you,' she said, although as far as I knew, she had never before laid eyes on him. 'It's an honor to have you two young people join us.'

'Same here,' I said.

'May I get you a drink?' She asked it as if this soulless room were her home and the bartenders her houseboys.

Farley made too-obvious eye contact with me, and I shook my head as politely as possible. 'No, thanks. We just wanted to say hello.' I glanced back at Farley as if to say so much for his great ideas.

'Alex had the highest regard for Kit,' she told Farley. 'He always remarked on how smart you were, how you taught him to never give up.' Her eyes got glassy, and I knew tears weren't far behind.

'He was a good guy,' I told her. 'A good man. We should probably go now.'

'Of course.' She became the pastel lady again. 'So happy you came out tonight. We must catch up.' She held out her nearly empty glass to a passing server. 'Oh, waiter. Over here, please.'

'You might be right, Farley,' I said as we drifted away.

'About her seeming lost?' he asked.

'About her being tipsy.' I sighed and wished I hadn't had to witness Alex's mother's pain at such a close distance. Not that I was a coward about pain. I had some of my own, especially

86

lately. But I hated being exposed to a problem I had no way of solving.

'You think she is?' Farley nodded back toward her as she took one more clear class from the server's tray.

'I'm not sure. Let's discuss it later.'

We continued to move around the room. At every conversation cluster, we heard the same word packages, the same praise for this mayor, who had made it clear by what she didn't do that her goal of higher office was her only priority. That, and seeing her brother's killer incarcerated for the rest of his life.

A half-hour or so into the mindlessness of it all, Farley grinned and nudged me. 'I guess getting drunk is out of the question.'

'You do whatever you like,' I told him. 'I'm getting high on the fumes in here.'

'High?' Carla's tall, handsome secretary asked from behind us. 'Fumes?' His white tux and matching hair looked more suited for the Oscars than this paint-by-number ballroom. 'Is everything all right?'

'Just a little talk-radio humor,' I said. 'How are you, Ray?'

'Managing pretty well considering how crazy it is in here tonight. Can you believe this crowd? Carla's going to free herself up for a few minutes, though. She'd like a photo with you two.'

Farley frowned, but I linked my arm in his and flashed Ray the most obedient expression I could conjure. 'We'd be happy to.'

'This had better be good,' Farley said as we followed the white tuxedo across the room.

'Just be quiet.' I squeezed his arm. 'I'm still not quite sure how I'm going to do this.'

As we approached, Carla extracted herself from the embrace of a short elderly gentleman whose dye job was as subtle as hers. Highlights. Lowlights. I couldn't keep them straight. But the braid over Carla's left shoulder, resting on the beaded bodice of her turquoise gown, looked expensive enough to be real and almost made me forget how much shorter her hair had appeared the day we met at the museum.

'So good to see you.' She brushed her cheek against mine and shook Farley's hand.

'Thank you for inviting us,' I said.

'We'd like just one quick photo.' She emphasized the *quick*, and Farley rolled his eyes.

I knew I had to move fast if I were to move at all.

'Of course.'

'Ray, hurry it up, would you?' Her voice was as charming as always, but her expression could have been carved out of ice.

'Sure thing, Carla.' He got in position with his camera. 'Move closer to the mayor, you two, please.'

I didn't budge.

'Come closer.' Carla put out her right arm, as if I were falling and she must catch me.

'I met someone recently,' I said, 'and I really need to talk to you about it.'

She motioned to me to move closer. 'We don't have time for anything tonight but this photo.'

'The man I met insisted that Frank Vera didn't kill Alex.'

'What man?' She seemed to freeze in place. 'What are you talking about?'

'The one I told you we call Bert the Troll,' I said.

'Dark hair?' she asked in a clipped voice. 'Wavy black hair?'

'Yes, but that could describe a lot of people.'

I could feel Farley's gaze boring into me but didn't dare make eye contact with him. I had to go for this while I still had the nerve.

'Was his name Luis Vang?'

'He wouldn't give me his name and said he didn't want to bother with making up a fake one.'

'Sounds like him,' she said. 'The man you met with is no doubt Frank Vera's friend Luis. He's a teacher who doesn't belong anywhere close to young people.'

I hoped the man I met wasn't this Luis, because if he were, he would be in trouble come Monday.

'I'm not sure who the man was, and I'm not trying to involve anyone.' I stared into Carla's glassy contact lenses. She didn't even blink. 'I only wanted to share with you what this man told me. I believe he's sincere. He said he hates Frank, but knows he's innocent.'

'Get out.' Her voice dropped so low that I almost didn't hear her.

'Did you say . . .?'

'Get out of here now before you expose my parents to your lies.'

I stepped close, so that only she could hear me. 'The angrier you get, Carla, the more I tend to believe they're not lies.'

Ray frowned and tried to focus his camera,

89

clearly unsure about how to proceed. 'Still need you a little closer, you guys,' he said.

'Forget it.' Carla turned and started to walk back into the crowd, where the old man with the good dye job hovered. Then she walked back to me. 'You were my brother's friend,' she said. 'How could you try to hurt us more than we already have been?'

'Because your mother and father both told me they wanted the truth,' I said. 'What if this man, Luis Vang, knows something we don't?'

'He doesn't. And, Kit, as unsettling as it might be finding out that you are illegitimate, you should focus on that, and on finding your biological mother, as we have allowed you to. Now get out of here before I call security.' She drifted toward the older man, her posture straight, her arms outstretched.

'Could I at least get a photo of you and Farley together?' Ray asked.

Farley put his arm around me and shrugged. I clung to him, still trying to make sense of what had just happened.

'Is that a no?' Ray asked.

Without a word, Farley and I headed for the door.

Thirteen

As a rule, weird behavior didn't shock me. After fending off blog trolls and the relatively sane people with out-of-the-ordinary problems who called our radio show, I was accustomed to any kind of behavior, however bizarre. But so convinced was I that Carla Brantingham would do anything to find her brother's killer that her nastiness regarding Luis left me stunned. For the first time, I wondered if the Brantingham Crime Fund was really designated for unsolved crimes . . . or for Carla's re-election. And I resolved to find Luis Vang.

That Friday, Scott waited for me in the parking lot right across from that white brick building painted with the 'Amazing Grace' sheet music. He had dressed for the occasion in one of his gray KWEL T-shirts and black pants, gelled hair pinched to a minimum height. Talk-radio program directors don't spend their time hanging out in station parking lots. I could think of only one reason why Scott was.

I got out of my car and said, 'Carla Brantingham got to you, didn't she?'

'I don't know what you're talking about.' Yet his expression remained guarded, as if he had no idea what to say next. 'But you've been under a lot of pressure, Kit. I think you should take a week off and try to find your mother.'

'Was that Carla's idea?' I asked.

'It's my idea that you have too much going on in your life right now.' He grew more confident by the moment. 'You can do today's show, Kit, but after that, you have a paid week off. Check in with me after that, and we'll discuss how to continue from there.'

'Suppose I leave right now?' I said.

He sputtered. 'I need to check it out.'

'With Carla?'

91

'That's none of your business.'

'You're right, Scott. It's none of my business. I'm going to drive home now. Tell Farley I hope he does a great show today.'

'You have no right . . .' he began.

As he stammered to a finish, I turned around, climbed in my car, and drove away. I'd write a blog today, maybe more than one. But before I did anything, I would do my best to find Luis Vang.

He lived in East Sac. That I knew because he had told me he didn't live far from the crêpe diner. Come to think of it, so had Alex. I had picked him up for work there one day.

Less than thirty minutes after I arrived home, Farley pounded on my front door.

'What are you doing here?' I asked.

'Helping you.'

'You're supposed to be on the air.'

'So are you.' He walked inside and squeezed my shoulders. 'When Scott said you'd been suspended for the week, I told him I was taking my vacation time. Screw them.'

'Oh, Farley.' The gesture was the last thing I expected from him, and even though it touched me, I didn't want to get him fired over my battle.

'Carla is behind it,' he said. 'You know that.'

'And we need to find Luis. He's the key to everything.'

'He barely talked to you,' Farley said. 'I'm sure he didn't give you his contact information.'

'I think he might have been Alex's room-mate. And he did say he lives on the east side.'

'You know where the house is?' He looked skeptical.

'I went there once. I might be able to find it again.'

'This time you aren't going alone.'

I could no longer argue with him. 'OK,' I said. 'But you're driving.'

While Farley cruised through the east side, the neighborhoods, and the streets, I squinted house-to-house and tried to remember. As it turned out, we hadn't been able to leave until late afternoon. Scott called and demanded that Farley come in to talk to him, and I insisted that he go. I felt guilty that he was endangering his career out of loyalty to me.

'That one.' I pointed.

The yellow porch awoke something in my memory. We parked and started to the door. But it was protected by an iron gate.

'No,' I said to Farley. 'It's not this one, after all. It only looks like Alex's house.'

'OK. We'll find it.' He put his arm around me, and I remembered why we were such a good team. No egos, no put-downs. We really did want the best for each other.

Then I looked across the street and saw the simple olive-colored Tudor with the arch on one side and the driveway on the other.

'Farley, that's it.'

'I thought you said it was yellow.'

'They painted it. Farley, I know that's the house.'

'We have nothing to lose, do we?' He tried to sound cheerful, but I knew he was as worried as I was.

Together, we crossed the street.

I knocked at the door. No one answered.

I knocked again. 'Luis,' I said. 'Please let us in.'

I heard movement from inside, as if someone were pulling furniture away. I glanced up into Farley's eyes and knew that whatever happened I would be safe.

Slowly, the door opened. Before us stood the young man with the serious expression and the dark-rimmed glasses.

'Hey, Luis,' I said.

'You figured out my name?'

'Kind of remembered it, I think.'

If he were surprised by this visit, he didn't show it. Wearing khaki shorts and a matching T-shirt, he didn't seem at all out of place in Alex's home.

'How are you, Kit?'

'You live here, don't you?' I asked, even though I already sensed the truth.

For a moment, I thought I might lose him again, the way I had that day outside the crêpe place. But then he seemed to settle down into himself.

'Yes,' he said. 'I do. Please come in.'

'I was here once before,' I said.

Farley squeezed my arm, as if to say I was talking too much, and I forced myself to slow down.

'You were picking up Alex for work, I believe.' Luis ushered us in. 'Could I get you a glass of wine?'

'Red would be great,' Farley said.

'Pinot noir OK?' Luis asked, and Farley nodded. 'What about you, Kit?'

'I'm fine.'

I knew I needed to take my time with this. He had run from me before. I couldn't risk it again.

We followed Luis across the honey-colored hardwood into a small but elegant kitchen with marble countertops and glass-brick accents. From a wine cooler, he pulled out a bottle of red and poured it into a squat Italian-looking glass.

'Nothing for you?' he asked me.

'I need a clear head,' I told him. 'And I need you to tell me the truth, Luis. I'm about to get fired for talking to you, and I'd really like to avoid that if possible.'

'Of course.'

'I need to know what's really going on.'

He adjusted his glasses and studied me for a moment. Then he put out his hand and said, 'Come with me.'

'Farley too?'

'No,' Luis said. 'Just you.'

Farley looked uncertain, as if to say no way would he leave me alone. He put his wine glass on the bar. 'Are you sure, Kit?'

'We're just going upstairs,' I said.

'Why can't I go with you?'

'You can in a moment, but right now, I think Luis and I need to do this together.'

'Five minutes,' Farley said. 'Any longer, and . . .'

I shook my head, turned, and walked with Luis toward the stairs.

'Thank you for understanding.' He took my arm, as if the conversation with Farley had never happened. 'And thank you for coming. I was afraid to call again. I'm so worried about my

95

parents, so afraid to risk their safety. They could be deported.'

'What makes you think that?' I asked, and then wished I hadn't.

'You really don't know?' He paused on the stairs.

'I don't agree with Carla Brantingham's politics,' I said, 'but I didn't think she would harm innocent people.'

'Trust me, she is not my friend. And she would do anything to erase my family from her life.'

We reached the top of the stairs, and, with him behind me, I walked into the master suite. A long, white brocade chaise took up most of the room leading to a large bedroom, and from what I could tell there was a tiled bath beyond that.

'It's beautiful,' I said. 'More than that, it's peaceful.'

A powder-blue carpet led to the patio. I glanced back at Luis.

'You had to know,' he said.

Of course. Although I had never consciously thought about it, being in this house brought everything into focus.

'You and Alex?'

'This was our home.'

His hand trembled, and I felt myself doing the same. My fingers reached for his arm. 'I didn't know him that well, Luis.'

'You knew he was gay?'

'I guess so, but I didn't think about it. We worked together only a month. But I knew he had someone, and I knew he was in love. He didn't hide that.'

'Thank you for telling me.' He put his hand over mine and squeezed my fingers. 'He said he was going to introduce me to you, but at the end everything got crazy, and I wasn't sure what you were aware of.'

'Only that Alex was in a serious relationship,' I said. 'How did everything get crazy, as you put it? What happened?'

'Frank Vera didn't kill him.' He sank down on to a black sling chair. Tears filled his eyes. He lifted his glasses and wiped them away.

I sat on the love seat beside him. We stayed like that for a moment, for many moments.

'Luis,' I said as softly as I could manage. 'Who killed Alex?'

He turned to me, tears streaking his face. 'I can't . . . I don't know.'

I started feeling pulled in, the way I had when my mom Elaine had said she'd left me a letter, and then when I had read that letter and learned about Kendra.

'You must have some idea.'

He shook his head. 'I only know it wasn't Frank.'

'How do you know?'

'I'm sorry. I can't tell you that.' He stood. 'Thank you for finding me. I swear I am not a coward, and I don't want to see Frank punished for something he didn't do. But my situation is sticky. I just got a teaching job, and I am all my parents have in this country.'

'Are you sure you can't tell me anything else?'

The person who spoke first would lose. I bit my lip and stared into his eyes.

97

He met my gaze. 'They sent him away. He was supposed to get cured at some kind of camp. Never again look at another man.'

'Who sent him away?' I asked, and then realized it as soon as I said it. 'The family?'

He nodded. 'There's nothing else I know for sure.' He stood with a sigh. 'It's best you leave now. I've gotten you in enough trouble.'

I tried to think about Alex's family. The jovial father, his light dimmed by tragedy. His mother, who did nothing but smile and nod. Carla, with her surgeon husband and plans for re-election.

'His parents sent him away?' I asked. 'Or his sister?'

'All I know is she walked in on us. Carla. Two days later, Alex was in some kind of rehab for gay souls trying to find their way back to normal.'

'You've got to tell his parents,' I said. 'They are convinced Frank Vera murdered him.'

'Maybe they are, and maybe they aren't.' He glanced over at me, the hope drained from his expression and from his voice. 'I thought by calling your show, I might make you curious enough to investigate, but it might be too late for that.'

'Maybe it's not,' I said. 'What really happened?'

'Frank didn't have a gun. Alex did. When Frank found him, he picked it up, of course. He didn't know what to do.' Luis shrugged, as if trying to free himself of the memory. 'By then, the police officers had arrived.'

'But surely Frank explained.'

'He wasn't sure,' he said. 'He thought an intruder might have come in, and by the time he

98

did figure it out, it was too late. If it's up to the family, he'll be convicted for sure.'

'Why would they allow that?' I asked.

He gave me that steady gaze. 'You know why.'

'Not in this world. Do you really think Alex's family would rather see an innocent man be convicted than just admit their son was gay?'

'They're doing it.' He sighed and leaned back in his chair, as if the confession had drained the energy from him.

'I don't believe it.' I felt better just saying the words. 'I've met his parents a few times. They're decent.'

'Until it comes to their son's orientation.'

'I know you believe that.'

He stood. 'And you don't?'

'I'm not sure,' I said. 'I want to help you if I can. All those times you called the station, I wanted to hear more. I wasn't ever convinced you were a troll. But then Carla kind of let me know my job depended on keeping you off the air.'

'She's the one trying to cover this up,' he said.

'Are you sure? She adored Alex.'

'Until he let her know he wasn't who she thought the brother of a mayor should be.'

'They said Frank knew that he kept cash in the house.'

'In the closet, yes. On the floor.' He pointed behind him. 'Alex didn't have the wall safe installed in there, but he used it. I'm not sure why, but in spite of his parents' wealth, he always wanted his own money.'

'And Frank knew where it was?'

'He didn't touch it,' he said. 'Every dollar is still right there. I told the police that, but then an officer asked me how I could know the exact amount.' He tried to grin. 'That's when I got the bright idea to start calling you.'

'I'm glad you did,' I told him. 'But first, we need to figure out what Frank Vera wanted from Alex if it wasn't money.'

He got up and joined me at the window. As he looked out at that peaceful landscape, I couldn't help wondering how what he saw compared to what I did.

'I already know that,' he said. 'They had been lovers, and he wanted to get Alex back.'

'Alex and Frank Vera?'

'He's an angry bastard,' Luis said, 'but I don't think he's the one who went to Alex's family. Someone else told Carla.'

'But Frank Vera was caught holding the gun,' I said.

'Frank got there after Alex was . . .' He turned away from me. 'That's all I'm going to say. Frank arrived after the above.'

'Can you prove that?' I asked.

He nodded, his eyes dull with what must be pain.

'If you want me to help you, you've got to tell me the truth. When did Frank arrive?'

'I pulled in right behind him. We found Alex together. If I'd touched the gun first, I'd be the one going to prison right now.'

So that explained why he wanted to help Alex's former lover. Guilt, the great motivator.

'I'm sorry,' I said.

'So what do we do now?' he asked.

'Only one thing we can do. You said Alex's family sent him away. Maybe others were sent away as well. Do you know who his friends are? Can you get into his email account?'

He paused again, then stared out the windows, as he must have done the many times he had shared this room with Alex. 'I didn't think I had a right to.'

'Maybe you're the only one who can connect us to other men who went through what Alex did,' I said.

'You really think finding them will help?' he asked.

'I do. But I can't do it without you.'

Although Luis and I had spent more than ten minutes upstairs, Farley hadn't interrupted us. We found him sitting with his wine as we came down to the kitchen.

Luis seemed to be holding something back, but I wouldn't be getting any more information out of him tonight.

Luis and I hugged at the door. Farley shook Luis's hand. Then Farley and I drove back to my place together.

'What can you tell me?' he asked.

'Not much for now.'

'Luis seems like a nice guy,' he said and braked at a stop sign. 'But you have your own problems right now, Kit. Maybe he ought to go on the back-burner.'

'He can't,' I told him. 'But you have to promise me that you won't tell anyone what I'm about to share with you.'

'Of course I won't.'

'Farley!' I grabbed his arm. 'I need to tell you this so that you can help me, but you have to swear to me that you won't share it with anyone – at least until it is common knowledge, which it probably will be.'

'You can trust me, Kit. You know that.' He pulled into my driveway, took his phone out of his pocket, placed it on the dashboard, and stopped the car. 'All right. Tell me whatever you need to. I promise you I won't repeat it.'

'Luis and Alex,' I said.

He nodded, and I could see, even in the dark, that he got it. 'Of course. I should have known that just being in the house.'

'The family tried to stop it,' I said.

'I'd believe that of Carla.'

'You've heard of gay-conversion camps, right?'

He winced, as if I had shouted the words. 'Those camps are illegal.'

'But they exist. Luis told me. The family sent Alex away to a place that was supposed to cure him.'

He crossed his arms and shook his head. 'We've got to go public with this, even if it means our jobs. Maybe Luis is right, and Frank Vera didn't kill Alex. Someone knows the truth. We have to put it out there.'

'We can't,' I said. 'Not yet. And you promised me you wouldn't say anything. Carla could yank that teaching job from Luis as easily as she got me suspended. She could get his parents deported.'

'We have to do something,' he said. 'But what? Do you have any idea?'

'Maybe.' I shrugged. 'Maybe we need to appeal to the voice of reason in the family.'

Fourteen

For a moment, lying there, twisted in and around the sheets, Rena feared Dale might still be in bed behind her. Then she heard the *rat-a-tat roar* outside and knew she was safe. She turned over and squinted at the clock on the nightstand. Almost seven, and the heat had already settled into the air.

A cool shower revived her. At least she'd get to work with Kendra today. Of course, that would leave Dale and Bryn to their own devices, but she couldn't dwell on that, and she sure couldn't dwell on how Dale had tried to turn Daniel against her. No, what she had to do today was what her mama had always said – just keep her side of the street clean.

After making the bed and rearranging her pillow on the rocker, she smoothed a tank top over her jeans. She had to smile when she remembered the hoots from the boys at the grocery store. Maybe this old body wasn't as worn out as Dale liked to say.

'You're getting too skinny.'

She jerked around, her breath shallow. Dale stood leaning against the door, the nail gun hanging from his right hand.

'I'm no different than usual.'

'Trying to look like that Trafton woman, aren't you?'

'I'm not trying to look like anyone, Dale. Besides, I'm smaller than Kendra.'

'I'm not talking about her size,' he said. 'I'm talking about how tight she wears her clothes.'

'Kendra doesn't wear her clothes all that tight.' She had to bite her lip from mentioning the way Bryn wore hers. But Dale still looked angry. 'Come on,' she said. 'I'll fix you some breakfast.'

As she started into the kitchen, he grabbed her by the arm. 'If God wanted women to be skinny, don't you think he would have given skinny women boobs?'

She couldn't believe, staring up at him, that he had once made her feel safe. Sometimes, she wondered if she'd married his size as much as anything else. Now, his strength and the possibility of what he could do with it was a quiet threat, as heavy on her as the heat.

'You've got to be hungry,' she said, and looked down at his huge hand.

He didn't let go. 'I'm gonna eat later.'

'Where?'

He nodded in the direction of the store. 'Over there.'

A chill sprang from the back of her neck and spread. With Bryn. He didn't have to say it. 'Nothing over there could be that good for you.'

'What's that supposed to mean?' His fingers tightened. Her nerves felt ready to snap, like the brittle bundle of secrets she'd burned in here last week. Little good that had brought about.

'Nothing in the store but stale doughnuts,' she

104

said. 'You need eggs and bacon, some real food. Come on.'

Slowly, he released her. She wanted to bolt for the door, but she made herself stay calm.

'Guess I could use something now, considering everything I have to do today.'

'Sure, Dale.' She wiped her sweating hands on her jeans, but the perspiration seemed to pour from her. Did he notice? Had he realized how frightened she was? She used to be able to tell everything from his eyes, but they didn't change much any more. They just stayed that same shade, like a watercolor of the sky with not enough blue in it. 'I still have some of the ham left. I could fry it up,' she said, trying to get his mind off of whatever was making him smirk the way he was.

'Why don't you just do that?' He started out the door and then stopped.

Rena looked up, wondering what she'd done now. There, propped against the back of her grandma's rocking chair, was her pillow. The tiny tip of an envelope poked from the seam in its middle.

'What's that?' Dale's voice eased out soft, more frightening than when he shouted at her.

Rena moved between him and the chair. 'What's what?'

'You know what.' He cocked his head. 'Are you hiding something? You wouldn't be crazy enough to hide anything from me, would you?'

He was going to hit her, plow through her like a dirt clod in a field. Sweat ran down her face. She couldn't let this happen. 'It's nothing. Just leave me alone. Quit picking on me.'

105

'Get out of the way.' He was shouting now. He grabbed her again, the heat of his fingers stabbing pain through her.

'Dale,' a voice shouted. 'Dale?'

Bryn. Why was she here? What did she want?

He stopped, let go. Rena gasped and slammed her hand over her mouth to keep from screaming.

Bryn stood just outside the bedroom. 'What is going on in there?' she asked.

Dale looked sheepish, but even Bryn should have seen past his rotten excuse for a smile. 'Nothing but a little marital disagreement, that's all.'

She looked back at Rena, but Rena couldn't find her voice. She could only ask herself what the girl in the lace top so skimpy that you could see her nipples through it was doing coming into her bedroom.

'My dad just phoned.' Although she said it to Rena, she was looking at Dale, as if still trying to figure out what she'd interrupted.

Rena's heart skipped, and she felt as if she were strangling. Leighton had called.

'What's he doing sniffing around here?' Dale said. 'You know you're not supposed to take personal calls at work.'

'Personal calls are guys,' Bryn said. 'This is just my dad, all right? He's driving out here right now and wanted me to let you know. There's something going on with Kendra Trafton, that woman over in Tucson. He's been trying to reach her on the phone, and when he couldn't, he called here.'

To hear Bryn speak Kendra's name sent a rush of panic through Rena. Lord, let Kendra be all right. 'What's happened to her?' Rena asked, fearing the answer.

'Nothing's happened to her exactly,' Bryn said. 'My dad just heard from some detective firm out in California. There's a woman looking for Kendra.'

'Why would anyone be looking for the Trafton woman?' Dale glared at Rena, as if demanding that she answer the question for him.

'I don't know,' she whispered.

'Well, I do.' Bryn angled her hands on the low rise of her jeans, smug-faced as always, recovered from whatever had ori-ginally bothered her. 'This woman. She's claiming Kendra is her mother.'

'Her mother?' Rena asked.

Bryn ran back outside, and Rena stood alone with Dale.

'Son of a bitch,' he said. 'Leighton has no right coming here.'

'He's her father.'

'I said he has no right.' He ran his finger along her arm. 'You of all people ought to know that.' He headed for the door. 'I'll be right back.'

Running after Bryn like a fool, she thought. Good. She could whipstitch the pillow, and it wouldn't take her more than a couple of minutes.

She touched her arm where Dale had grabbed her and brushed away the bruise. No, not a bruise. He hadn't grabbed her that hard. The way the light fell just cast a shadow for a moment. Her arm was fine. She was fine. She just had to hurry and stitch up the pillow, so she could get ready to see Leighton. Yes, she'd see Leighton again, even though Dale would be watching them.

In about fifteen minutes, Dale came back,

sulking. He kept quiet as she cooked his breakfast, not even watching to see if she got the bacon
crisp enough and that she remembered to baste
his fried eggs with the drippings.

He ate in silence, too.

She'd like to think that, after all these years,
he had finally figured out she knew her way
around the kitchen. But no. He was chewing on
more than breakfast. She remembered what her
mama had said when she worried like this.
Stinkin' thinkin', she called it. Better to just turn
off her thoughts and ease their day into something
better than the way it started.

'Eggs taste all right?' she asked.

He glanced up from his plate, as if surprised
she was in the room. 'They'll do.'

Standing beside the stove, she wasn't sure if
she should say more to him or just head down
the hall. Fluff her hair up, maybe put on that
green T-shirt Kendra said brought out her eyes.

'Ham cooked the way you like it?'

'I said they'll do.' He shoved a piece of bacon
into his mouth.

'So, what do you think about all that?' she said.

He finished chewing, swallowed some coffee,
and asked, 'What do I think about all what?'

'About this woman claiming Kendra's her
mother, of course. About her coming back and
trying to find Kendra after all this time.'

'You know what I think?' Dale's eyes went
watery again. His lips trembled.

She backed into the stove and wondered what
button she'd pushed this time. 'What do you
think?'

'I think it's a goddamned lie.' He pushed himself away from the table, stood up, then picked up his plate, bacon and eggs still on it, and threw the whole mess across the room in her direction.

She slid to the side, just as what was left of his meal hit the stove. 'Dale,' she begged. 'What's wrong?'

'It's a lie about Kendra's girl,' he said. 'That bastard Leighton made it up, I'll bet you anything.'

'But why would he lie?' Leighton wouldn't make up anything. She knew that. 'He's an attorney. He can't just go around lying about a woman trying to find her mother.'

'He'll say anything to get back in this house again.' Dale sat back down and picked up the one thing he hadn't thrown at her, his coffee cup.

She ducked, and then realized he was only taking a sip. Slowly, she leaned down and began picking up the broken plate. Leighton wouldn't lie. She knew that. And if he could find Kendra's daughter, it would be worth every strand of fried yellow yolk stuck to the front of her white stove.

'Don't cut yourself,' he said. She could hear his chair drag across the floor. Dear Lord, don't let him kick her. His boots came closer, until he was standing beside her. She concentrated on the task, on placing the small, white pieces of stoneware on to the larger, jagged piece. *Burn away. Burn away.*

'I *said* don't cut yourself.'

'I'm being careful,' she told him. 'I just wish you wouldn't get so mad all the time.'

'I'm not the one who's mad,' he said in that

109

insincere voice he used when he was trying to be sweet. A thin voice; it was as watery, in its own way, as his eyes.

Still crouched on the floor, she looked up at him. Kendra was right again. He wasn't getting better, and he wasn't the big, safe guy from high school who got mad sometimes. No, he was getting worse. 'You threw your breakfast at me, Dale,' she said. 'I'd call that mad.'

'I didn't throw it at you. I threw it at the wall.' His voice was still low, but his eyes bulged like a bull's, and she feared that a good kick in the side was just a boot tip away.

'I can see that.' She felt herself cringe. 'I'm sorry. Why'd you have to go and do that, though?'

''Cause of you,' he shouted. Rena flinched and closed her eyes. 'You know I've got to go check on that job in Phoenix again today. And you know if I get it, I'll be there a week, at least. And Leighton Coulter just happens to decide he has to drive out here while I'm away.'

She waited for the blow, but it didn't come. Nothing came but silence. When she opened her eyes and looked up again, his face was that red-meat color.

'I'm your wife,' she said. 'I'd never do or say anything to bring shame to you. Besides, didn't you check on that job last week?'

'I told you I did.' He rocked back from her, as if he'd started to lose his balance. 'Now, I have to check on it again, since we sure as hell aren't making it on this outfit your old man left us. I just don't like the idea of Coulter coming out here while I'm gone.'

110

She rose to her feet. He'd simmered down now. She could always tell. He was like a roller coaster that had to fly out of control before it slowed and finally stopped.

'You don't have anything to worry about,' she said, and then slid the broken dish into the paper sack beneath the sink.

He moved beside her. 'You promise?'

'Of course.'

'If you're lying, the both of you are going to be in big trouble.'

'I'm not lying.' Nothing was going on with Leighton and her, nothing at all. 'Go see about the job, babe. You know I'm in your corner.'

'And you wouldn't hide anything from me?'

She knew where this was going, but she could handle him now. It would be fine if she just behaved. 'Of course not.'

'Then let's just go back to the bedroom,' he said. 'There's something I want to check out.'

'Sure, Dale.'

The hall felt too narrow, as if the anger and suspicion in the house had squeezed it together.

He stepped into the room, and as she knew he would, headed straight for her pillow.

'What are you doing?' she asked, her voice calm now, yes, calm, under control. 'What are you looking for?'

'Your little keepsake here, for starters.' He picked up her pillow and tugged at its seams. The whipstitch she'd done on it in the bathroom had been swift, but it held. Dale punched his fingers around both sides and bent the pillow almost in half. 'I saw something, I swear,' he said. 'You better not be playing games with me, little girl.'

Rena stood at the door to the bedroom, her hands folded in front of her, doing her best to look relaxed. 'I'm not playing games with you, Dale.' Her voice sounded a little too sing-song, and she could tell by his sudden shifty grin that he caught it.

'You ever try to, and you don't even want to know what will happen.' He walked up close to her, shot out his index finger and thumb like a cocked gun, then tapped his finger against her temple. 'Don't think you can trust Bryn either, just because she's Leighton's kid. She'll tell me everything that goes on here while I'm gone.'

'Nothing will go on,' Rena said. 'I promise.'

'If you do one thing—' He pressed his finger harder, and if she didn't know better she'd have sworn it was a gun. 'You do one rotten thing, and I'll take you out like that. It's a promise.'

She held her breath until he took his finger away from her head. Then she said, 'Good luck on that job. I sure hope you get it.'

He took one look back at the pillow and another one at her. Then he smacked her on the ass, friendly, though, not trying to hurt her. 'I swear, woman. You sure can screw up a good man's head.'

The smack turned into something more like a fondle. Not now, she thought as the fingers that had been tapping her skull a few moments ago began kneading her behind.

'Dale,' she began, but it was too late. 'Dale?' She looked toward the open bedroom door. Bryn had walked in on them once this morning. She could return any minute.

He kicked it shut and held out his big arms. 'Come here,' he said. 'I need me something sweet to remember on that drive to Phoenix.'

Fifteen

I had tried to call the Brantinghams several times after my talk with Luis. Each time, a rude woman cut me off, saying they were not at home and hanging up before I could leave a message. Farley and I discussed it and decided I needed to speak with them in person. Yet when I called the last time, the rude woman told me they were away.

'For how long?' I asked.

'For some time.' She sighed. 'For now, Mr and Mrs Brantingham are unavailable. Thanks for calling, though.' *Click.*

Meeting with Mayor Carla Brantingham was easy. Meeting with her parents again, not so much. I wanted to talk to them before I talked to her, but wasn't sure how. Thanks to Farley, though, I'd learned that her father played at a putting range by the river every Saturday. I didn't like acting like a stalker, but I didn't have much choice. Farley wanted to go with me, but I told him I wasn't sure what time I'd be going, if at all. Although he probably knew I was lying, he kept quiet.

Joseph Brantingham stood just outside the

course, talking to a guy about his age, both of them wearing the clothes that make sense only to golfers. He saw me, lifted his sunglasses, and moved away from his companion.

'Miss Doyle?' he asked with a squint. 'Kit?'

'Hello, Joseph,' I said. No one called him Joe.

'It's good to see you.' His smile was so innocent, so decent that I wanted to run in the other direction. 'I didn't know you played.'

'I don't.'

'Well, neither do I – not much any more. Just thought I'd come out and hit some balls around.'

'Joseph.' I nearly choked on my own voice. 'I've been trying to contact you, and no one knows where you are.'

'What do you mean?' he asked. 'We're home most of the time. At least you're helping solve other crimes. Knowing that, Bette and I are as much at peace as we can be under the circumstances.'

'But the person who answers your phone says you aren't available,' I said.

'Sandra?' He nodded. 'Our daughter is convinced we need a live-in helper, and we're putting up with the intrusion for now. I'm confused, though. Are you saying Sandra doesn't put through your calls?'

'The woman who answers your phone doesn't,' I told him, happy to tattle.

'Come to think of it, we've gotten very few calls since she joined us.' With each clench of his fist, his knuckles reddened. 'This is extremely disturbing. I need to go home now, call my daughter.'

'Before you do.' I reached out for his arm, but found myself unable to touch it. 'I don't know an easy way to put this, Joseph. I'm grateful for your funding my blog.'

'We're honored to do so.' He stared off at the horizon, as if trying to recall a speech. 'It's the most we can do for other families with losses like ours.'

'Someone has come forward.' I wanted to look anywhere but into his eyes, but forced myself to do it anyway.

'About Alex's . . .?' He couldn't seem to bring himself to say the word. I knew how he felt.

'His name is Luis Vang.'

His lips tightened. 'I know who he is.'

'Are you aware of his relationship with Alex?' I asked.

'Of course.' He lowered his voice, as if someone were close enough to hear us, but the other golfers had moved far away. 'I'm no fool.'

'Why didn't you tell me?'

'I couldn't,' he said. 'Bette has no idea. It would kill her.'

'That's your business, but I've been blogging about a death I knew little about, and a man may go to prison or worse because no one knows what really happened to your son.'

'What do his problems have to do with that?' he asked, all swagger and wealthy farmer now. 'Are you saying it somehow contributed to his murder?'

His attitude offset any pity I had for him. Yes, he had lost a son, and I had no doubt he'd trade any number of days on sunny, green-grass courses like this one if he could go back. But would he change what he had done?

'You thought you cured him, didn't you?'

He seemed to sink against the golf cart. 'What do you know about that?'

'That you sent your son away. That he was supposed to be turned around or whatever you call the process.'

'Conversion.'

'That's right,' I told him. 'Once he drank the Kool-Aid, he would never be attracted to anyone of the same sex.'

'No one said it was foolproof. We had to try though.'

His sadness upset me more than if he had lashed out at me the way I wanted to at him just then. 'What happens if this conversion doesn't work?' I asked. 'Do parents send their kids back for another jolt?'

'You can find that information on plenty of websites,' he said. 'I am very weary of this conversation, and I'm going home to my wife now.'

'Fine,' I said. 'I just wanted to hear it from you. I wondered how you could justify what you did, even if it were possible to stop human attraction.'

'I said it was a gamble, but even if they can't immediately eliminate the attraction, they learn how to develop the strength to abstain.'

'How easy would you have found that when you were his age?'

'That was different. I wasn't . . . . I wasn't like them.'

'You tried to change who your son was,' I said.

'I owed it to him.' His voice sounded as drained

as he looked. 'It's an even greater tragedy that he beat this demon and was killed before he could live a normal life.'

'You don't know?' Chills crept along my arms. 'You don't know, do you?'

His shocked, sad expression answered every question I had. He had honestly believed Alex was no longer attracted to men.

When I told Luis that Alex's dad had no idea that the conversion hadn't worked, he just shook his head.

'This isn't going away, is it?' he said.

'Not until we find out what really happened,' I told him. 'I need to talk to others who were in the camp when Alex was.'

'A guy named Jerry. He and Alex were friends, but when I asked him to speak to you, he said he's not sure.'

'Doesn't he realize what's at stake?" I said.

'There's a lot at stake for him too.' He handed me a piece of paper. 'Here are some numbers you can start with.'

Finally, I had a place to begin, even though the two sources agreed to speak with me by phone only.

A man who refused to give his name described the camp as torture, not treatment. He said he would die before he returned.

'All it did was convince me to be more of who I am,' a woman named Katherine said. 'They wanted to beat us into submission in that place.'

'And Alex?' I asked.

'Oh my god. Alex and Jerry were treated the

worst. I'm not sure why, but they seemed to get the brunt of it.'

I thanked her for her contribution and phoned Luis Vang again. 'I've got to talk to Jerry,' I told him.

'And I told you he's not sure.'

'Try to convince him,' I said.

He called me back and said that Jerry would meet with me. 'He's a pre-law student at the college and works part-time at a restaurant,' Luis said. 'Lives not far from here. I'll let him know to expect your call.'

When I called Jerry, I could hear the hesitation in his voice. 'Are you going to use my name?' he asked.

'Of course not,' I said.

'Then why don't you stop by Applebee's. I work there so I can't talk long.'

Even a short conversation was better than none. Farley and I met Jerry at the restaurant late that night. Once he got off his shift, he joined us in our booth.

As we stared at each other across the table, I thought that this tall, dark-eyed man could pass for straight if he wanted to. Apparently, he did.

'Order you a drink?' he asked and clutched a full glass. 'On the house, of course.'

'No, thanks,' I said, and Farley shook his head.

'I don't know if I should be talking to you,' he said, 'but Luis says you can help, and Alex was a friend of mine.'

'What happened to him?' I asked.

'That I don't know, I swear.'

'What can you tell us about Frank Vera?'

'Other than he's being charged with the murder, nothing.' His gaze was steady, dark eyes unblinking. 'Until this happened, I'd never even heard of him.'

From the back, a vacuum cleaner threatened to drown out his words. 'We're closing,' he said. 'Maybe we can talk again.'

'Can you at least walk out with us?' I asked him. 'Anything you can tell us will help.'

'I guess so.' He glanced over his shoulder, and I felt the hesitation set in. Still, we stood and walked toward the front entrance, where a smiling server, still in uniform, unlocked and held the door open for us.

Outside, a chilled breeze made me shiver. 'You met Alex at the camp?' I asked.

He nodded. 'And he was a good person. I don't know what I can say other than he didn't deserve what happened to him, and I hope whoever is responsible pays.'

'How was his relationship with Luis?' I asked.

'Well, considering that Alex wanted to change his life, not ideal.' He stood into the bright overhead lights, inching away from us. 'I barely know Luis, though, and I'm not trying to suggest he'd ever harm Alex.' He glanced around again, clearly nervous.

'Are you worried about someone seeing you with us?' I asked.

'No, not at all. Just my girlfriend.' His gaze bored into mine. 'She's coming to pick me up.'

'Oh.' I couldn't grab an easy answer to that.

'If you think of something else,' Farley told him, 'please contact us.'

We started to walk away just as a little red car pulled in front of the restaurant. Although I couldn't make out the features of the woman driving, I knew why she was there.

'Got to go now,' Jerry said.

'Wait.' I walked back toward him.

He flashed me a look of impatience. 'What now? We're in a hurry.'

'You knew Alex well,' I said. 'What effect do you think the camp had on him?'

He paused, sighed, and then wiped his brow. 'Not good. He really struggled.'

'Struggled how?' I asked, but he shook his head emphatically.

'That's all I can tell you. Alex was fighting a bigger, meaner demon than I was.'

'How's that?' I asked.

'Because I got cured.' His expression grew solemn. He nodded once, and then jogged over to the car.

Sixteen

Sometimes, she forgot things. Kendra had said that didn't make her crazy, and that was good enough for her. So maybe she could let herself forget what had happened in that sticky, sweaty bed with Dale less than three hours before. Yes. All that mattered right now was what Bryn had said, Leighton's wonderful news. She needed to figure out a way to tell Kendra.

I have something to tell you, Kendra. I don't know where it will lead, but I have some news about something that just might . . . No, that sounded too much like what her mama would call phoney baloney. She shut off the radio.

Kendra, honey. You've been there for me, and now I'm going to be there for you.

No. That kind of talk was more Kendra than it was her.

OK. OK. *Kendra. I love you like a sister.* That was the truth. *Kendra, I love you as if you were my own sister, and I've just learned something that I believe will be very important to you.*

Yes, that was perfect, because it was the way she felt. Even if Kendra had only just moved back, their friendship had started up where it left off all those years ago.

Rena parked the car in the back of Kendra's store and got out. *Kendra, I love you as if you were my own sister.* The pavement was already so hot that the heat burned through her flip-flops. *I've just learned something that I believe will be very important to you.*

Kendra spotted her from the back of the shop and waved. Her hair was pulled up, and the way the strip of sunlight lit her features, she looked as high-spirited and sure of herself as she had the first time Rena had ever seen her, back in high school. It seemed impossible that they'd ever been that young, but they had. Kendra Folger, a senior whose beauty and self-confidence gave her more friends than any one person needed, and Rena McCord, a scared little freshman.

When she'd seen Kendra walking down the

121

road that night she was driving home from church. The last thing Rena had wanted to do was pull over in her daddy's old rusted pickup and offer her a ride, but she couldn't just keep driving and pretend she hadn't seen her. Good thing she had stopped too. After Kendra jumped in, still wearing her green-and-gold cheerleader outfit, she didn't seem to mind the pickup and its tinny-sounding radio.

'Am I glad to see you.'

Her face lit up so fast that Rena almost missed the tears in her eyes. Then she noticed the torn skirt.

Months passed before they trusted each other enough to talk about that night. 'A bad date gone worse,' Kendra said, trying to make fun of it. But there was nothing funny about being out in a dusty field with a guy trying to grope you, even if he was the class president.

Rena had told her she should tell someone, go to the school counselor or her parents, but she didn't want to. 'I wouldn't know what to tell those people,' she had said. 'Nothing happened.'

But something almost had, and it might have if Rena hadn't shown up when she did. From then on, Kendra called that old pickup the Magic Pumpkin. Rena always felt like they should have warned someone about Phil. Class president or not, if he'd try to force Kendra, what would happen if he went after a girl who wouldn't fight back? They never knew because Phil's family moved away that summer, and they never saw him again. Even when her mind was at its worst, Rena never forgot that night on the road and the

122

way that, in spite of her torn clothes, Kendra seemed bigger than her problems.

That light that seemed to radiate from her was what Rena had noticed about Kendra the first day of study hall. Sometimes, after all she'd been through, Kendra still had that look. She had it now.

Rena tore across the room, walking toward that young Kendra as much as toward this one who was her best, maybe her only friend. 'Oh, Kendra,' she said, unable to remember the speech she'd rehearsed. 'Oh, honey. I have some wonderful news.'

Seventeen

My so-called week off never happened. Scott called and said they needed me after all. I thanked Farley, but he said that he couldn't take credit, and that Carla probably just wanted to scare me. If that was true, it wasn't working, especially after our meeting with Jerry.

'We need to talk to him again,' I said. 'He and Alex went through that together. I know he'll tell us more.'

The crazy woman looking for Edith Marie called again that morning. As usual, she was rude. And, as usual, she hung up in the middle of the conversation.

Tamera met me in the station lounge that morning. We had ten minutes after my show and before hers, and she was willing to spend that time trying to help me. The similarity of our situations had bonded us even closer than before, and every time we talked, I felt that I might really be able to find my mother.

I looked at the cheerful print on her aquamarine silk shirt and wondered if that's why she wore bright colors – so that she would have a little help lifting her spirits. Realizing that made me love her more.

'Any luck?' she asked.

I fought to keep the emotion from my voice. 'The detectives are following up on every lead they can find, but they don't know anything for sure yet. There are no listed telephone numbers under Trafton in Buckeye. No email accounts in her name either, and nothing I can find with my online searches.'

'So why don't we just go there?' she asked. 'Why wait?'

'Because of the ratings,' I said.

'You have the blog. Ratings won't make or break you. Farley's pushing to keep you here, isn't he?'

'Actually, he's been pretty supportive,' I said.

'Not supportive enough. Don't let him stop you, Kit.'

'Why are you so down on Farley?' I asked.

'Not him personally. It's just that he doesn't understand. He couldn't.' She shook her head, as if trying to escape a memory. 'We need to get you to Arizona right away. I'll go with you.'

'You're in ratings too.'

'I'll talk to Scott,' she said. 'He still feels bad

about making me work when my dad was dying.' She shrugged. 'Besides, it's only a job.'

One she was willing to risk to help me. 'You don't have to do this,' I said.

'You were there for me.'

'It's OK. I can handle the trip.'

She leveled her gaze and raised her eyebrows in a way that said she wasn't buying a word. 'Tell me the truth,' she said. 'You really want to go knocking on some stranger's door all by yourself, asking if she's your mama?'

She did have a way of making her point.

'Not really. But I will if I have to.'

She grinned. 'That's my point. You don't have to.'

'I'm glad.' I hugged her, realizing how much I meant it. 'I only wish you'd found your father while he was still alive.'

Tears welled in her eyes. 'So do I,' she said.

'He would have been proud of the person you are, Tamera.'

'Don't be talking that way, or I won't be able to get through my shift.' She managed to push me away so that she could look directly at me. 'You're my best friend, and I should go with you. Maybe I need to. It might be good for me.'

Farley came out and washed his hands in the aluminum sink beside the coffee pot. He did it every day, as if the show had left a residue he needed to scrub away. He probably wouldn't like what I was about to say, I thought, so I might as well not put it off, especially now that I had Tamera on my side. He and I had stood in for each other in the past when we'd had to. True,

125

we were in the ratings period now. And if he complained to Scott, the PD could force me to stay. A program director was the law, and I would have to follow that law or leave the job I loved.

As he drew closer, I caught a whiff of the scent left by the ginger-scented suds.

'Tamera's offered to come with me,' I said. 'To Arizona.'

'While we're still in the book?'

'I think I have to,' I told him. 'You know I'm not going to be any good on the air until I resolve this one way or the other.'

'Even on your bad days, the show's better than when you're not here.' The worried look in his eyes contradicted his calm tone. 'What about Tamera? Jimmy J will bitch to Scott.'

'She's talking to Scott herself.' I felt guilty and looked away. 'After the memorial service next Wednesday, I'd like to take a few days off to head over to Arizona.'

He looked as if I'd just turned in my resignation. 'And what did Scott have to say about that?'

'I wanted to talk to you about it first.'

'What's he going to think, so soon after Carla raising hell about you?'

'Farley!' I glared at him. 'My mom is dead. My mother may be in Arizona. Do you think I care about Carla? Or Scott, for that matter?'

'I'm not trying to be insensitive,' he said.

'And I'm not trying to be difficult. I figured we ought to talk about it first since you'll be the one who's affected.'

'We'll all be affected.' He sank down on one of the office chairs, as if I'd let the air out of him. 'And, yes, I know that shit happens without any regard to when the ratings fall.'

'You can carry the show.' I sat on the leather sofa across from him beside an antique clock with neon call letters from the station's rocker days.

'What about if you went the week after the memorial service?' he asked. 'Then you could take more time. It would be better all around.'

Tamera sat beside me. I glanced over at her. She looked away, but shook her head.

'I don't know, Farley,' I said. 'So much time has passed already.'

'But we're talking about it on the air! If anyone knows anything about your birth mother, they're going to call here or contact us through your blog or our website.' His expression grew animated as he began to warm up to this new tactic, and I realized Tamera was right. He was all about the ratings right now. 'This is probably the best place for you to be. You can see that, can't you, Kit?'

'For how long?'

'What do you mean?' His forehead began to glisten.

'For how long is this the best place for me to be?'

'Until we give it some time. Until we do whatever we can to get the word out.'

'Until after the ratings, you mean?' Tamera asked.

We were ganging up now, she and I. I knew it wasn't fair, but I needed help. 'That's exactly what he means.'

'Are you kidding me?' he said in a wounded

tone. 'I've tried to offer you support twenty-four/seven, and you think all I care about is the ratings?'

'It's your job to care. I get that. It's my job too. You were right about me changing though. My priorities have. And finding my mother means more to me than anything else in my life right now.' I started to apologize, and then thought, *No*. I meant what I had said. Unable to think of anything to add to that, I stood and started for the side door.

'Hold on just a minute.'

I stopped.

'You may not care about your job any more,' Farley said. 'But it's all I have, and I can't do it without you.'

I started to say that was ridiculous, but then I realized he was right. We were a team, and our chemistry made the show work. To the listeners, we came across as best friends trying to solve and heal what had been left unfinished. Without me, he would sound too cool, too laid back. Without him, I would sound too passionate and driven. Now that we were just getting the recognition and ratings we had worked so hard for, I had to admit that I didn't know what I would want to do once I found my mother. If I found my mother.

'I'm sorry,' I said.

'It's OK.' Farley stood with a sigh. 'I'm not completely thoughtless, and I hear what you're saying. You go, Kit. I'll just do the best I can.'

'Wait.' Tamera stood as well. 'Kit, if Farley needs you to stay here, why don't I just go?'

'Alone?' I asked.

'I've got the vacation time, and it's only Arizona,' she answered. 'I can scope out the place, and if your mother is really there, and we get some serious leads, you can be on the next plane out. You wouldn't have a problem with that, would you, Farley?'

'No, Tamera, I wouldn't have a problem with that.' He ran his hands through his surfer boy hair, a casual gesture, but I could almost hear him thinking. 'Scott might even give you extra time off if we say you're doing it so that Kit can stay here.'

Tamera raised her eyebrows. 'That's not bad, Farley.'

'Wait a minute,' I said. 'I haven't agreed to anything.'

'You don't have to, Kit.' She moved away from Farley and hugged me. 'I'm supposed to do this for you, I know it. And I want to. Besides, Jimmy J will love an opportunity to tear it up while I'm gone. Give him a day or two, and the jerk will probably fantasize that he can replace me.'

I felt myself relax. At least one of us would arrive there immediately. 'I don't know how to thank you.'

'I need to get out of this boring place for a while, anyway.' Her eyes glistened, and I knew she was remembering her own loss and the questions in her life that would never be answered in the way mine still might be.

'I feel like it's so much to ask,' I told her. 'It's not as if you have a ton of vacation time.'

'I think Farley's right. Scott will let me do it

on company time now that we're putting your story all over the place.' She wiped her eyes. 'But I'm on, like, now, and Jimmy J would like nothing better than to have to start the show without me.'

'Hurry,' I said, caught in mixed emotions. 'We'll talk about it later.'

She pecked my cheek. 'Consider it done.'

'I don't know,' I said to Farley as I watched her run toward the glass booth.

'It's the best way,' he replied.

'For us,' I said. 'What about poor Tamera having to fly to Arizona alone, just because we're slaves to the ratings?'

'She wants to do it.' He stopped, faced me, and placed a hand on each of my shoulders. 'Don't turn against me because of what's going on in your life, Kit. I'm your partner, and I care about you.'

His words hit home. I squeezed his hands with my own. 'I'm sorry,' I said. 'You're right. I've been all over the place.'

'I shouldn't have said that.' He let go of me, cocked his head, and gave me that grin. 'I know I'm being tough on you. In a way, I feel I'm losing you. Your friendship, I mean.'

'Just because I wanted a few days off at an inconvenient time?'

'If it's not just that, then . . .' He started toward the parking lot, and I followed. His black Corvette shimmered under the sun.

'Still the best car in the lot,' I said.

'Want to get a late breakfast? Lunch, maybe? There's an awesome new Mexican grill not far from here. The *cocido* stew will make you faint.'

130

'I wish I could, but I have to get hold of my mom's attorney in Washington. He keeps leaving messages, but we can't connect.'

'That's what I meant,' he retorted. 'We used to be a team. Now, you won't even have lunch with me.'

'Lunch?' I was angry now that he would be angry with me. 'You're worried about lunch when I have to go call my mom's attorney?'

'You stopped having lunch with me *before* your mom died. Something made you stop.' His gaze didn't change. And there was nothing I could say back because he was right.

I was still thinking about him after I got home. Why had I stopped having lunch with Farley? Why had I felt crowded? He was my partner, my friend. There'd never been anything between us, but after the divorce, I hadn't felt comfortable going out with him the way I had before. He hadn't changed. I had. But my life was too far out of control right now to try to figure out my conflicted feelings for Farley.

Matthew Breckenridge had left another voice message telling me to expect a letter from him. It arrived late that afternoon. I studied it and all the information about my mom's Trust, which was as conditional as she could be. My inherited amount increased substantially if I had children, while Mick's would decrease considerably. And if he had children, the money stopped. Although Mick had no desire to start a second family, I wondered if he would resent my mom trying to control his actions from the grave as much as I did.

I rushed through the rest of the attorney's letter.

131

She had taken care of all the tidy details, right down to her *resting place*, the attorney wrote, and I wondered if Breckenridge blushed at the cloying euphemism, or if he used it so many times that it seemed natural to him. I was surprised that she hadn't chosen Lake View, on Capitol Hill, where my grandparents were buried. But no. According to the letter, she had made *pre-arrangements* – another euphemism, but sadder – at Evergreen-Washelli Cemetery. I knew the place. In the old days, it was on the northern edge of Seattle. Now there was a Home Depot a block away. And a block beyond that, a Lowe's and a Krispy Kreme.

Still holding the letter, my hand began to tremble. Something about knowing her cemetery selection made her death more real to me. I could remember her taking me to my grandparents' graves and putting her arm around me when I stopped a few feet from them. I thought that if I got too close, a hand would reach out, snatch me, and yank me inside, and she must have understood my fear.

'They're not here, anyway,' she had told me in a soft voice. And, when she must have sensed my horror: 'No, that's a good thing.'

'Then, why do you come here?' I had asked, lip quivering.

'To remember,' she had said. 'Places like this give you somewhere to come and remember. Sometimes I even talk to them. You can, too.'

I couldn't recall the rest of the conversation, only that I hadn't wanted to talk to my dead grandparents that day and couldn't understand why she did. I also didn't understand what she meant when I asked if they could see the lake below the cemetery, and she said, 'They can see it wherever they are. The location is important to us, not to them.'

Now, her words came back to me. She had been dealing with the loss of her own parents that day, as I was now dealing with the loss of mine. And she was my parent, in spite of my anger and in spite of the questions she'd left me. I remembered her words – 'The location is important to us.' And I wondered if she'd chosen her *location*, as she called it, for me.

While she had tried to explain to me about death, my mom had neglected to mention that her parents were not my biological grandparents. *My mom. Elaine.* I didn't even know what to call her now. Nor could I sort out my feelings for her. Once more, I tried to put myself in her place, and again, I knew I could not keep such an important truth from someone I loved.

What my mom had done amounted to stealing. She had taken time I might have spent with my biological mother, my biological family, and I wasn't sure I could forgive her for it.

Eighteen

Matthew Breckenridge finally reached me that Saturday morning just after I'd watered the lavender, basil, and spindly but promising cherry tomato plants in my courtyard. Holding my phone, I jumped from stone to stone and turned off the sprinkler so that I could hear him better.

'Sorry we keep missing each other,' he said. 'How are you holding up?'

I wasn't up for small talk. 'I got your letter,' I said. 'I can meet with you later this afternoon, if that works for you.'

'This afternoon? Of course.' Then, he hesitated, and that sick feeling that had been with me since my mom's death returned. I sat down on a stone bench, not caring that I'd hosed it off moments before. 'We'll need to go over the Trust.'

That was the last thing I wanted to talk about. I felt as if I were on one of those moving sidewalks at the airport, and I didn't know when I'd get off. Meeting with Breckenridge was just part of the journey.

I forced myself to just breathe in the fragrance of the herbs and everything else living and growing in my garden and reminded myself that all of this would be over soon.

'Kit?' he asked. 'Are you there?'

'Yes,' I said. 'I'll see you then.'

Matthew Breckenridge was waiting in my hotel lobby when I arrived in Seattle about two hours later. I checked in and then joined him at a table lit by Swarovski crystal lighting.

We shook hands, and I was glad we were keeping our dealings formal. I didn't need anything to disturb my already unstable emotions. He was an ageing hawk-eyed man, who, in spite of his slight stoop and too-bushy eyebrows, was attractive in that way that came only with true self-confidence. His manner was relaxed, as if he had just come from the golf course, which, considering his polo shirt and casual pants, he might have.

Only the legal-looking briefcase attested to the fact that this was not a social visit.

'Cupcake?' He nodded toward a display on a nearby table. 'They serve them every day.'

'No, thanks.' I took a chair next to him. 'But you go ahead.'

He patted his middle. 'I'd better not.' Then he sighed, as if trying to decide how to begin. 'How are you doing?'

'Not very well,' I said.

'I understand, and I wish we didn't have to discuss business right now.'

'We don't have a choice. Please go ahead.'

'Your mother was a successful woman,' he began, 'and as you know, we were close personal friends.'

'No, I didn't know that.' I breathed in the sweet pineapple scent of the cupcakes and told myself I would not get sick. 'Unfortunately, I knew very few of her friends, Mr Breckenridge.'

'Breck,' he said. 'Please call me Breck.' He sighed, and then continued in a professional tone. 'Elaine had an investment account, something she started when you were born. No one knew about it, not even your . . . not even Mick Doyle.'

'My mom had money Mick didn't know about? Why? And if Mick didn't even know, why do you?'

'She had to tell someone.' He cleared his throat, and I realized this was painful for him, as well.

135

'The money was for you, so that if the time ever came, you could use it to help locate Kendra Trafton.'

That name again. I managed to nod. 'So you know about her too.'

'Yes.' Another sigh, heavier this time. 'And now, the funds Elaine acquired will be yours. She was certain you'd want to locate Kendra and possibly assist her financially if the woman's circumstances are as dire as we suspect.'

'How long?' I could barely get the words out. 'How long have you known about Kendra Trafton?'

'For some time.' He glanced away, as if deciding how much to share with me.

Mick had known. Breckenridge had known. But I hadn't known, because my mom hadn't wanted me to. 'Why did she keep this a secret?' I asked.

'She didn't intend to for this long,' he said. 'And she did give you the means to locate your biological mother and to help her. Kit, do you realize what Elaine has made possible? You can find this woman. You might even be able to change her life.'

'But she didn't tell me I was adopted.'

'She had every intention of doing just that. I know for a fact that she had already made inquiries. Most people don't get a chance to do everything they think they will in a lifetime.'

It was a feeble excuse.

'Well, I guess we'll never know what she would have done,' I told him.

'You heard what I said.' His tone turned cold. 'I know you're grieving, but I also know how

136

much your mother loved you. I had hoped I might be of some comfort to you.'

At that moment, I felt pity for this sad-eyed man who was trying to be strong. To tell him that he was the last person who could comfort me would be cruel. Instead I nodded at the folder and said, 'I'm really tired from my flight. Can we get started?'

My meeting with Breckenridge left me with an uncomfortable mixture of anger, gratitude, and more than a little fear. My mom had made arrangements for me to find Kendra, but she still hadn't told me about her when she was alive. All I got from him was the assurance that my mom had accumulated more money from her gyms and investments than I had realized. I'd known she'd done well. Her lifestyle had attested to that. But she had sold off all but two health clubs, and I'd assumed her finances were shrinking. Instead, they had increased. And now they were mine. Mine, Mick's and Kendra Trafton's. That's what I learned from Matthew Breckenridge. That, and the fact that he had been in love with my mother for a long time. Not that he told me that. He didn't have to.

Except for the rain, the memorial service was the way my mom would have liked it. At least, that's what I told myself. Photographs of her from childhood until only months before her death adorned the easels leading into the funeral home. Only Breckenridge, Doug, the young man who colored her hair, Mick, and I got to sit in the front row. I wondered at the significance of that and scanned the room, trying not to be obvious.

137

Mick leaned close to my ear and whispered, 'He's not here. We agreed it would be easier on you.'

How had he known I was looking for Richard?

With the groan of the organ, tears filled my eyes. Funerals did that to me, even when I didn't know the person well. Maybe it had something to do with my faith, or lack of it. As much as I wished I could celebrate the release of the soul from its earthly bondage, I could feel only the loss, the sadness, the pain of the people left behind. Now I was one of those people. I'd been left behind with questions as well as grief.

As I sat there, listening to the minister praise the woman I'd been raised to believe was my mother, a thought struck me so hard that I could feel the tingle in my fingertips. What if my mother, Kendra Trafton, were dead, as well? What if I had no mother? What if I were as alone as I felt at that moment, with no one and no connection, genetic or otherwise, to anyone?

I relived my fear when, at age four or so, I'd spilled fingernail polish I wasn't supposed to be playing with on Mom's Italian tile while she and Mick were out. When they returned, and I denied it, she had crouched until we were eye level and said, 'I love you very much, but whatever you do, don't you ever lie to me.' I burst into tears, and still in her dress-up clothes, she pulled me close to her, saying, 'It's all right. As long as you tell me the truth, it will always be all right.'

At that moment, and at that age, she smelled better than anyone in my small world and certainly on earth. Mystical, yet safe, and

138

somehow all-encompassing, although I didn't have words for any of that. I had only a sense of wonder and awe that this amazing, magical person was my mother. I'll never forget the smell of her perfume.

I remembered her driving me to preschool. 'You're going to meet lots of different kids today. I just want you to know that God made each and every one of you, and you need to love them.'

She was not much of a churchgoer, so I'm not sure how she came up with that speech. It worked, though. The only problem was trying to find kids that much different. The best I could do was Jeani, who was Japanese and whose dad owned a supermarket chain. When my mom came to pick me up, she found me holding Jeani's hand and announcing that I had invited her to lunch.

In the many times my mom repeated that story, I realized how proud she was that she'd conveyed, however awkwardly, one of her beliefs to me.

I wondered how she'd managed to pick me up from school every day while she was working as a trainer for the gym she eventually bought. Again, I ended up with the same question I always did. How could someone who'd been as good a mom as she had been deny me the one thing she could have given me while she was alive? How could the woman who taught me, from age four, the importance of honesty sustain such a big lie? I felt guilty thinking about these questions as I sat only a few feet from the urn that contained her ashes.

The soloist began 'Amazing Grace'. I thought of the building across from the station and its painted hymn. An audible sob escaped my mouth.

I couldn't help it. I was a rotten daughter to be so confused about my feelings.

Mick squeezed my arm. 'It's OK, Kit.' Tears filled his eyes as well.

We walked out together afterwards, arm-in-arm. I felt as if someone had beaten me. Every muscle ached. The rain had let up, and the sad faces and black umbrellas blurred together. People, many of them strangers to me, clustered around us. A woman in a hat hugged me. 'Elaine was like a mother to me,' she said. 'I'm so sorry.'

Fitness people, radio station people – some I'd met, others I hadn't – clasped my hands and expressed their condolences, one after another until their words and their touches blended into one.

Something stopped me, and I felt as if someone were watching me. I turned, and there he was. Off to one side, part of him shadowed by a tree, Richard McCarthy stood, in a suit and dark glasses.

His presence hit me with a jolt. My husband. My husband who'd left me and was in the process of divorcing me, because I didn't love him, he had said, because I didn't love him enough. My soon-to-be ex-husband. Tall as ever, mahogany-colored hair combed back from his high forehead so that he looked intelligent, interesting, and distant, all of which he was.

I stopped talking and returned the stare. He removed his glasses. I could feel the heat of him, even on this windy, rainy day. For a period of time I couldn't begin to estimate, we stood looking at each other.

Finally, Mick noticed and nudged me along. 'Sorry, Kit. He said he wouldn't show up.'

'It's all right,' a ghost voice that used to be mine replied.

Richard caught up with us at the family car. 'Kit,' he said, and I stopped in spite of myself.

'Richard.'

'I'm so sorry.'

'Thank you.' We traded word packages like near strangers.

'She was a wonderful woman.'

'Yes.'

Mick muttered something else, and we got into the back of the limousine.

'Honest, Kit,' Mick said. 'He told me he wouldn't be here.'

'Don't worry about it.'

From the day they'd met, Richard had been like my father's son, and I knew that Mick didn't want to give up on his dream that Richard and I would have the marriage he and my mom had missed.

Mick leaned back in the seat and peered at me. 'Can I ask you something?' And before I could respond, he continued, 'Did you know about Breckenridge?'

'No,' I said.

'Good.'

'Why?'

He tried to mask his emotions behind his dark glasses, yet the harder he tried, the more of himself he revealed. 'If he'd been important to her, she would have talked to you about him,' he said. Then, as if he were back in his studio in the motorhome, recording a commercial, he said, 'So, what do you think about the estate stuff?'

141

'That Elaine was being controlling. Like, you lose money if you choose to have kids with Rachel?'

The cloud lifted, and for a moment, his hair sparkled in the sun, so glossy that if it weren't for the silver at the sides, I would have guessed he had it colored. 'You know that's the last thing either Rachel or I want,' he said. 'And that was just Elaine's way. You need to understand that.'

'Maybe I would have, if I'd been given a little truth to factor in.'

'I told you my feelings on that,' he said.

'That's right. You did.' Hurting him would only make me feel worse. It wasn't his fault that I'd never known my biological parents, my biological mother. We both knew whose fault it was, but we didn't dare discuss that now. How could we? I began to realize that death required an exercise in manners. Everyone was in pain. The last thing we wanted to do was inflict more.

He squeezed my hand. 'You'll understand better when you have kids of your own.'

Yeah, right. I didn't dignify his statement with an answer.

'I love you, Kit. I want such good things for you.'

Translated: *I want Richard for you.* But it was way too late for that.

'Love you too,' I said, 'and I do understand.' I hugged him and kissed his cheek. This was what children did to parents in situations like this. Hugged. Kissed. Said they understood, even when they didn't, when they couldn't possibly.

* * *

142

On the plane trip home, I did something I was rarely stupid enough to do. I drank. Short little drinks of straight Tanqueray, with a squirt of lime to kill the first sharp taste. They worked. I got home with little memory of plane fear or the music I'd forgotten to play because I hadn't needed the distraction.

The fist beating my head from the inside out and my dry mouth the next morning reminded me why I seldom opted for alcohol as a painkiller. Yes, I'd gotten through the flight. Sure, I'd momentarily forgotten the conflicting emotions yanking me through an emotional tug of war at the memorial service. I had even swallowed, right along with the gin, the memory of how my body froze when Richard had looked at me like that – the same way he had when he'd told me he wanted a divorce. But as I opened my eyes and tried to avoid the reality of even my own breath, all of those memories, all of those ghosts, were all too happy to step into my morning and remind me, in living color, that I hadn't missed anything, only postponed it.

Back in his boozing days, Mick used to say that drinking vinegar would prevent a hangover and even derail one already in progress. He and his buddies laughed about how he'd stumble in and grab the vinegar bottle, spilling most of the contents all over the sink.

Looking out over my safe little courtyard, while I felt a raging war in my head, I stood at the sink and tossed down a shot of Bragg's Organic Apple Cider Vinegar the same way I'd tossed that gin on the plane.

143

I hated the taste, the sweet-harsh, throat-scalding swallow. But darned if it didn't seem to work. The day shifted into focus. I took another shot. Same fiery taste. Same burn in the throat and the stomach. But I felt better still. A final shot, and, in spite of my watering eyes, I felt ready to face the shower.

I parked in the station lot about four thirty in the a.m. and escaped into the safety of the studio and its somehow welcome scent of scorched coffee left on the burner all night.

'There you are. It's about time.' I jumped as Tamera stepped beside me, although it was way too early for her to be here. Her hair was hidden under a stylish straw hat too vivid and red for dawn. 'I prayed for you,' she said, and I believed her.

'Thanks.' I poured some of the coffee into my mug. 'It was tough. I even drank on the plane coming back.'

'Some drinker you are. What'd you have, a beer or two?'

'Gin,' I said. 'Enough to give me a hangover. I had to drink vinegar to get rid of it; one of Mick's old tricks from his bad-boy days.'

She made a face, as if she could taste it. 'I'm so sorry, Kit.'

'I'll be fine. Everyone has to deal with loss.' Something about the wary way Tamera was watching me made me feel uncomfortable. 'What is it?' I asked.

Then, I realized her eyes were different. Glassy and kind of scared, as if she was the one with the hangover. 'This is a terrible time to tell you, right before you have to go on the air.'

My skin tingled. 'Tell me what?'

'Tamera, wait,' Farley called from the control room. He strode toward us, frowning. 'I told you to wait, damn it.'

'And I told you I wasn't going to.'

The tingle spread. Feelings of hope and fear buzzed in my brain. 'What is it?' I demanded, my gaze fixed on Farley.

Farley pushed sun-streaked hair off his forehead and smiled. 'I wanted to be the one to tell you,' he said.

'It's about your mother,' Tamera whispered, her eyes soft and dark as shadows. 'Oh, Kit, a woman phoned yesterday from Arizona. I took the call myself.'

'A woman?' *Arizona.* She'd said Arizona. 'Kendra Trafton called here?'

'No,' Farley said. 'Not Kendra Trafton, but someone who says she knows who Kendra is. The caller has been following the story on the air and on our website, and she just got back from visiting her son in Arizona. She claims her son knows Kendra. He recently just saw her and another woman in a market in Buckeye.' Tamera's fingers on my arm seared my frozen flesh. 'It sounds like it could be the real deal, Kit.'

Nineteen

Mick and Rachel were staying at a nearby Hyatt where they had left their motorhome. I had planned on meeting them for a late breakfast, but the time got away from me. At least that's what I told myself. The memorial service had left me with too many mixed emotions to short out this soon.

As I left work that morning, Scott followed me to the parking lot. I hadn't seen him for a couple of days, which was unusual for such a micro-manager. Not that he was a bad program director. I hadn't minded him until recently. Now I cringed at the sight of him.

'Kit, do you have a moment?' As if I could say no.

'I know you've got a full plate right now,' he began.

'I'm doing the best I can.'

'Now that the memorial service is over, I think it's best if we drop references to your other situation as soon as possible,' he said.

'My search for Kendra?'

'Kendra. Right.' He smoothed a wrinkle out of his T-shirt. 'You write an unsolved crimes blog, and I think we're off course. As soon as Mother's Day is over, we need to get back to crimes. Murder.'

'That's fine with me.' I didn't care, and I let him know it. 'You'll need to notify Farley. Send a memo, or whatever. Is that all?'

His cheeks turned red. 'The real reason I wanted to talk to you was about some things you've been doing . . . which I'm sure are because of everything you're going through.'

Now my cheeks were hot. 'What kind of things?'

'Joseph Brantingham,' he said. 'Carla is furious.'

146

'I didn't do anything to Joseph. His family sponsors my blog, and I had information that might help them find out what really happened to Alex.' As I spoke, he nodded with a set smile, as if waiting for me to stop speaking, so I did.

'In the future, do not speak with any member of the Brantingham family unless you run it by me first.'

I started to ask what would happen if I did, but we both knew the answer to that, and I was too weary to fight.

'OK.'

He looked surprised. 'We have an understanding then.'

'Yes, we do. Anything else?'

'Nope.' He shook his head. 'You have a good day, Kit. I know things will get better for you soon.'

As horrible as Carla was to me, I felt something close to sorry for her. Not because she was a nice person. Far from it; she wasn't. Yet I knew that she had been raised with a lie as big or bigger than the one with which I'd been raised. Yes, she knew who her biological parents were. In my family, though, a gay brother would not have been a source of shame so great that anyone could even consider sending him away for a faux cure.

I sent Rachel a text and asked if she and Mick were still at the Hyatt.

We'll wait, came the reply text.

They were waiting in the lobby on an oversized sectional. Mick looked apprehensive, and Rachel was just Rachel, so calm and supportive that if you didn't know better, you'd miss her strength.

'Glad you could join us,' Mick said and patted the place beside him. I realized that he had done that as long as I could remember.

'Mick, I . . .'

'KWEL are screwing with you, aren't they? Because you're the only one willing to tell the truth. How many of those cowards will even try to do that?'

'I got it from you.'

He shot me that stiff grin that meant he hadn't heard me correctly.

'Honesty,' I told him. 'I don't know how you did it, or how I absorbed it, but you're the one who taught me the importance of telling the truth. You used to say that people who lied all day would wake up one morning and decide to say the sky was green because they could no longer tell the difference.'

'I did?' He made a face, but he couldn't conceal his pride.

Rachel stood. 'I need to go pack.'

'You packed hours ago,' Mick said.

'You see?' I told him.

'Yeah, I see.' He smiled and patted the place beside him again.

I sat.

I hadn't yet found Kendra Trafton, and I had no idea when, if ever, I would know the identity of my biological father. But I knew now I would not give up. Just as important, after all these years, I had my dad back.

'I'm going with you,' he told me.

'Later,' I said, 'and then you definitely will. I need to see Kendra alone first.'

148

Twenty

The last person Rena expected to see that morning was the first one she saw. Debby Lynn Glover, big as life, snaking her way up the drive in her little Honda and stepping out in a pair of white cut-offs almost as tight as Bryn's jeans.

She left the car door open. Something about that ticked Rena off. How dare the past just march up her driveway like this, as if it owned her? Especially on the day she had to go with Kendra to Tucson and meet the contact for Kendra's daughter. At least Leighton would be picking up the woman at the airport and driving her to her hotel. Later that afternoon, the four of them would meet up. Rena didn't need Debby Lynn barging in like that, but she had no choice.

Debby Lynn. Rena had envied her once. Not so much her beauty, but the way she wore it. Back in high school, it was Debby Lynn's eyeliner Rena had really envied, her slithery clothes, the hair that fluffed above her narrow forehead. Today, though, that blond-streaked hair wouldn't distract anyone for long from her stretched, tan face and the little lines around her mouth.

Since she was already looking, she might as well try to see if Debby Lynn was still wearing a wedding ring. There was a big old rock flashing on her left hand, all right, but it didn't look as if it had anything to do with marriage. Cocktail

149

rings? Wasn't that what they used to call them? *Wonder if she stole it.* The thought bubbled up before she could stop it, and then she almost laughed when she realized why.

Debby Lynn had always been the high school klepto. Leighton used to joke that when Debby Lynn Glover walked down the aisle in Sears, the displays would disappear, everything from electric carving knives to portable TVs. Of course, that was before he married her, and before they had Bryn. Remembering that made Rena feel better about standing here in her church skirt while Debby Lynn slunk up in her cut-offs, cropped top, heels, and red shoulder-bag, the same color as her toenails.

Why was she here now? It was as if Rena's past had started to catch up with her present. Maybe overtake it. As she walked on to the porch and headed down toward Debby Lynn, she decided that, even though more than twenty-five years had passed between high school and now, she still didn't want this woman in her house.

Soon, they stood face-to-face. Whatever scent Debby Lynn was wearing hadn't changed since high school. In it, Rena could smell the rain of her youth, the skirts and sweaters, the cool, anxious air of football games, her throat raw from cheering for Dale.

'Well, hi there, Rena. How're you doing?'

'I'm on my way out to the garden,' she said. 'I've got chores to do.'

'That's the only greeting I get after all these years?'

'Sorry, Debby Lynn,' she said. 'I'm sure you're

150

here to see Bryn, and you're welcome to do that. You'll find her back there in the store.'

'I'll get to Bryn soon enough. Right now, I want to talk to you.'

'Sorry, but I'm too busy.' Rena's heart started to beat faster. 'You should've called first. I'm trying to finish up my chores. Then I've got an appointment in Tucson.'

'Don't mind if I tag along, do you?' As she moved closer, Rena realized she was about two parts perfume to one part woman. Something was driving her, though. Something had always been driving Debby Lynn. 'You look good, Rena, a whole lot better than you did when we were young. Nice shoes, too.'

Debby Lynn had spotted the ribbon in Rena's hair right off, and her off-the-shoulder top and matching black sandals. Rena was embarrassed, knowing that she'd put them on because she'd be seeing Leighton. But at least the shoes weren't gold. At least she didn't have nail art on her toes the way Debby Lynn did.

She stood by the decorative gazing ball Kendra had given her for the garden. Silvery green and calming, it balanced on the fence post. Some days, it looked like a cheap steel globe. Other days, it could reflect even the hottest, most hopeless moment into something cool and magical. Rena liked to look into it and imagine it was a crystal ball, even though she knew it was almost as tasteless as those elf statues and pink flamingoes some people had. Tacky was just fine in a garden, though, if it made you happy.

'What's this?' Debby Lynn marched up to the

151

ball, but she seemed to be looking at something else. She reached into the shallow basket on the ground next to it. 'Have you been smudging, Rena Pace? You know that's the work of the devil.' She lifted out the bundle Rena had placed there.

'Your mama doesn't think so.' Rena couldn't help enjoying the way Debby Lynn's eyebrows shot up. 'From what I hear, she still buys her white sage at the shop.'

'She buys candles, that's all.'

'If you say so. It's a nice shop, though. Maybe you should go with your mama sometime.'

'I've been there, and I won't be going back any time soon. Everyone knows what they do there.' She gave Rena a thin-lipped smile with no friendliness in it. 'And everyone knows Kendra isn't really an herbologist, or whatever they call it.'

'Herbalist. And, Debby Lynn.' She made her sigh heavy. 'You're here to see Bryn, not give me the third degree.'

'It's not your way to be snooty.' Debby Lynn pushed her hair behind her ears and squinted so that her face looked narrow and mean. 'You're not still mad at me for marrying Leighton, are you?'

'Of course not,' she said. The sun seemed to bear down on her. 'What's past is past. We were in high school.'

'He's a cold fish,' Debby Lynn said, 'and a spiteful bully. He lets Bryn stay with him for six lousy months, and all of a sudden, he's trying to tell her she should be in community college. She's not cut out for college. She's already proved that.'

'I guess it's up to her to decide,' Rena said.

'You and I never went to college,' she said, as if their lives were anything that Bryn or anyone else would want. 'Barely got out of high school, did we?'

'I went back for my GED,' Rena said, embarrassed to be proud of it, but having to say it anyway. 'Got a secretarial certificate from the JC, too.'

'But you never had to use it. Dale didn't make you work a single day.'

'I work at the store.'

'But you own it, you and Dale. That's different.' Debby Lynn sat down on a stump beside the tomatoes, her legs stretched out and so smooth looking that Rena figured she must have had them waxed. 'Leighton still hates me for what happened when he was in law school, and he's trying to get even by making Bryn think I didn't raise her right.'

Rena stayed standing. Easier to spot the snakes that way. 'What happened when he was in law school?' she asked.

Debby Lynn chuckled. 'You mean he didn't tell you?'

'We don't talk,' she said. 'I mean, we didn't talk until he called to ask if Bryn could work the summer here. I couldn't see that it would do any harm. Wasn't trying to start any trouble with you two.'

'Trouble's already there,' Debby Lynn said. 'As far as you and Leighton go, I don't care what happens.'

'Well, I do,' Rena said. 'I am a married woman.'

'So was I.' She winked at Rena. 'Men,' she said. 'They think they can do anything, and then if we try it, they have a fit.'

Rena bent down and pretended to check the tomato leaves for worms, trying to figure out what Debby Lynn meant. Had Debby Lynn been playing around? Was that why she and Leighton got divorced? Had she fooled around on him when he was in law school? Rena couldn't wonder and didn't dare.

'Will you be taking Bryn home, then?' she asked, and looked up from the plants. Maybe something good could come from this visit after all.

'Not yet,' she said, a little too quickly. 'Maybe working here is good for her. I always gave her too much. She thinks she can have anything she wants without doing anything for it.' She stood and brushed the stump dust from the back of her pants. 'So what's Kendra doing back in town?'

'She's in Tucson,' Rena said. She couldn't look Debby Lynn in the eyes.

'I wonder why she'd want to come back here after what happened. You think there'd only be bad memories, wouldn't you?'

'No telling. She seems happy enough.'

'Divorced.'

'A lot of people are,' Rena said.

'You aren't.'

'No.' She looked down at her wedding ring, her hands. In the harsh sun, they looked older than she was.

'It never changes,' Debby Lynn said.

'What do you mean?'

'No matter how much time goes by. No matter who gets married or whose kid disappears, nothing around this place changes. We are just the way we were twenty-whatever years ago, all of us.'

'I don't know,' Rena said. 'I don't mean to be rude, Debby Lynn, but as I said, I have an appointment. Why don't you go on in and spend some time with Bryn? That's why you came by, isn't it?'

'Sure is,' she said. 'But I've got to run an errand first. I'll be back in a little while, because, believe me, I'm not going to let that conniving ex-husband of mine turn my daughter against me.'

Rena watched her make her way to her car with the same arrogant strut. She stood there as she heard Debby Lynn start the car and take off. They'd had Bryn together, Leighton and Debby Lynn, and all Debby Lynn could do was call Leighton names. No time to worry about that, though, or to wonder why, after all this time, they were all meeting up again, like it or not. All that mattered right now, today, was helping Kendra meet with the Californian woman who claimed to know where Kendra's daughter was.

She started back to the house, and then she stopped. What was different? The fence post stood there, dusty, cracked, and bare. The glass globe was gone. Rena moved closer. The white sage bundle of branches had disappeared as well. First, she was angry. Then, she couldn't do more than shake her head. Debby Lynn was right – about herself, at any rate. Nothing had changed.

Twenty-One

Friday arrived with a drop in temperature. Since I'd gotten the news about Kendra Trafton, and spoken to my private detective, I couldn't sleep. All I could think was how lucky I was, how very, very lucky. I called Breckenridge, who told me to be careful. This woman might not be my mother. But I knew.

I'd underestimated Mick and how much he had loved my mom, and my loss was deepened by the knowledge that I was part of the reason they hadn't been able to share more of their lives together. I spent much of that night mourning all of the Micks, all of the Elaines, and, of course, all of their children.

Somewhere, right now, Tamera was flying close to the town where Kendra Trafton lived, meeting the lawyer, Leighton Coulter, in Tucson, Arizona. Then Mr Coulter would bring her to Kendra. I couldn't think about that, couldn't wonder how my mother's face would look when Tamera handed her my photo and the letter I'd written to her. She had wanted me enough to give birth to me. Surely, she would want to meet. My only regret was that I couldn't be there with Tamera. Soon, though.

The nameless rude woman trying to find her mother Edith Marie had phoned again twice that week. Even though she hung up on me both times, I couldn't help relating to her. We were on the same journey, only she dealt with her pain differently than I did. It was still pain she didn't deserve.

Farley and I worked out at the gym and met back at the station. Although we usually talked between sets, we hadn't done so today, and I wasn't sure why. Maybe because I didn't feel as close to him as I had before my separation. Maybe because it was Farley who'd come up with the brilliant idea that Scott could give Tamera a week off as long as I would agree to stay and work the Mother's Day show.

A compromise was better than nothing at all, and that's what I'd done – compromised with Scott and Farley, taken up Tamera on her offer.

So, Tamera went, and I remained. And leaving the gym, I had little to say to Farley.

'I always knew,' the female caller whispered into the studio that day. 'Even though my parents didn't tell me, I just had this feeling.'

'What do you mean?' Farley turned to grin at me and pointed to the board full of blinking green lights. We were going to have a great hour. At that moment, I couldn't help wondering how my own story would end.

Before our caller could answer, I said, 'I do know what you mean. The rest of them are together. You're kind of apart.'

'Oh, yes,' she said. 'They're part of a family. You aren't. And you never can be.'

As she spoke those words, I realized that I was mouthing them. *You never can be.* Regardless of how hard you try, *you* never can be. Was that true for me? I thought of Tamera again, who had put her own loss aside to try to help me. I'd had a good mom, a great and caring mom, but I'd been denied this very important part of my life.

Farley took another call. Moving too fast, almost erratic. Just when this first woman was getting to her point, he cut her off. But now, he'd snared another woman, her voice strident. 'I'm adopted like you, Kit, and I don't spend a minute of my day worrying about who my biological mother is. You shouldn't, either.'

'Why do you say that?' I asked, realizing the pain I was feeling registered in my voice.

'They gave me away, girl. *She* gave me away. Your mother gave you away, too. Why should we care about them? You just tell me that.'

Sitting there next to Farley, in our cage of a studio, I wondered if she was right.

Farley cleared his throat. 'Because they're your history and your future, too, if you have children,' he put in.

'Children?' I could almost hear the caller gasp. 'I'd never have children.'

'And why is that?' he said.

She sounded stymied. 'I just wouldn't.'

'I understand,' I said.

Farley gave me an odd look, part question, part answer. 'Being adopted would make you not want to have children?' he asked.

'Not being adopted,' the caller said. 'Having no roots.'

'But you have roots,' I said. 'You just don't know where they are.'

My being adopted wasn't the reason I didn't

158

want children, at least right now. Long before my mom died, something uncertain in my life made me believe I didn't know how to create a safe place for a family. Richard had taken my reluctance for something else, and that had been, as my dad said, the beginning of the end. But it wasn't because of roots or lack of them.

Before I could think more about it, another woman called in. She said she went by Jules and was from Florida.

'I never had a problem the way you folks have,' she said. 'I was raised with the knowledge that I was adopted for as long as I can remember.'

'You're lucky,' I told her. 'Very lucky.' I felt more than saw Farley's scowl. I'd made a meek comment. Not great radio.

'My biological mother was always extended family,' she said. 'Some people call it first mom, but I don't like that because it would make my mom second, and she's not.'

I felt, as well as heard, her words, all the way through me. 'I hope I can one day achieve even a little of your understanding,' I said, close to losing it.

'I hope so, too, Kit,' she replied in a soft Southern voice that sounded as if she meant it.

Before I could reply, Farley cut her off with a hasty goodbye and got a man on the line. Ratings, I realized. *We're in the book*, as he had said. The Arbitron book. This was what he wanted. To demonstrate the wide audience; to show that men listened, too; to show that everyone listened to Gnarly Farley and sidekick Kit. I couldn't blame him for it. I'd been where he was, with a contract

159

floating toward me, so light and tenuous that it could sprout wings at any minute and fly away.

'Tucson, Arizona,' Farley said. 'You're on the air.'

'You say Kendra Trafton is your mother?' the new caller asked, in a voice made hoarse either by the connection or because the speaker – male, I'd presume – was trying to disguise it.

The abruptness of it surprised me, but I managed to get out a: 'Yes.'

Farley gave me the raised-eyebrow look that was his way of asking me if I thought the caller might be a nut. In my current state, I couldn't begin to know.

The caller cleared his throat. 'And you were adopted at birth, correct?'

'Yes, I was,' I said, my mouth so dry that I could barely speak. I reached for my bottle of water.

'Well, that's impossible,' he said, his voice louder and harsher now, 'and this is some kind of hoax you're pulling.'

I couldn't reply. Farley leaned into the mic. 'Kit was adopted,' he shot back. 'How can that be a hoax?'

'Because of Kendra Trafton. Her daughter wasn't adopted at all.'

I suddenly felt uneasy, unsafe. Even in these familiar surroundings, with Farley an arm's length from me, the beginnings of fear spread over my skin, as if someone were breathing down my neck.

'What happened to Kendra's daughter?' Farley asked in the aggressive tone he used when we got crazies on the air. 'Suppose you tell me.'

160

'She wasn't adopted,' the man said. 'Kendra's daughter. She was kidnapped.'

My shudder was almost audible. Dead air, loud as an explosion in its suddenness, filled the station. We couldn't have it; one of us had to say something. I fought to speak, but I couldn't find my own words with the caller's voice echoing in my brain.

'You're going to have to prove that one, friend,' Farley said, bailing me out again. The shine on his forehead made it look as if his skin were melting. 'Right now, an associate of ours is traveling to Tucson, to meet with Kit's birth mother.'

'What are you talking about? I just told you what happened to Kendra's daughter.'

'We'll have to find out for ourselves,' Farley said. 'In the meantime, our colleague is on her way there right now.'

'That's right,' I managed to add. Then I flashed Farley a look that I hoped conveyed my gratitude. It wasn't just the ratings now. He was trying to protect me from this troublemaker. I thought what Farley said would shut him up. I hoped it would.

'You can tell that associate, colleague, or whatever you call her to head on down to the newspaper in Phoenix and do some checking,' he said. 'The kidnapping was pretty big news over here. But this wasn't any newborn they took. The girl was almost three months old when it happened. And it was Kendra's fault, too.'

Almost three months old. Kendra's fault. My dream of finding my mother began to dissolve. 'Why are you calling?' I said, angry enough to shake off my fear now.

161

'Just trying to help, ma'am. Just trying to help.'

'If you're really trying to help, give us your name,' Farley demanded and wiped a handkerchief across his face. 'I mean it, man. Tell us who you are and what you know.'

'Check those old newspapers, and you'll find out.' And then the connection was broken.

I looked at Farley and pointed at the lights. He shook his head and faced the mic. 'That's it for today, folks. We end today with a caller too cowardly to give his name claiming Kit's biological mother had a child who was kidnapped. We have our own Tamera Flowers heading for Arizona as we speak. Most of all, we have callers from all over the country willing to share their stories with us and with our listeners. You keep calling, and we'll keep sharing. Thanks for being here with me, Gnarly Farley, and *Perp Talk* founder, my partner, Kit Doyle. Tune in tomorrow to hear more about Kit's search for her biological mom, and to share your own stories of adoption and reunion.'

We exited to the sounds of Paul Simon's 'Mother and Child Reunion'.

I winced. 'Tell me you didn't pick that music, Farley.'

'I think Scott did,' he said.

'Subtle.'

'As a sledgehammer.' He couldn't resist adding, 'I heard that Simon named the song after a chicken-and-egg dish he'd seen on the menu of a Chinese restaurant.'

'Well, Scott will be having second thoughts now that Carla has told him we need to drop my search for Kendra on the air.' I leaned back in my chair, as if the breath had been knocked out of me. Farley had saved the show. He had saved me.

'Thanks,' I said, 'for everything.'

'No problem, partner.' The tone of his voice told me all I needed to know.

'Tell me that last caller was a nut. Tell me he made up everything he just said.'

He shoved the hair from his forehead. 'He might be a nut,' he said, 'but I don't think he was lying. He might just believe he's telling the truth.'

We walked out together. I wanted to ask him, ask someone, if what the caller said could mean that Kendra Trafton wasn't my mother, because I'd already engaged in numerous fantasies where she wasn't. I had already checked all the newspapers. There were no stories of kidnapping that I could see. I needed to go back, check more, and maybe spend a little more money on the online investigators. Or maybe I should give up the hopeless online search and hire a real flesh-and-blood investigator.

'Don't look so lost.' Farley nudged me with an elbow. 'Even if he's right about Kendra's daughter being kidnapped, that doesn't mean you aren't her daughter.'

'But it does complicate things. You know what, though? Mick has to know how old I was when they adopted me.'

'We're going to have to ask Tamera to check out the newspaper files,' Farley said.

'I hate to tell her. She wanted to make this

163

happen for me because she couldn't make it happen for herself.'

We stood in the parking lot together. He kind of choked on his voice for a moment, but then he bounced back, all Farley blond with attitude. 'Let's get something to eat. Then you call your dad and Tamera.'

For the first time in a long time, I wanted to go out with him the way I used to. But I couldn't get the caller's raspy voice out of my mind.

'Mick's with a client.' I fumbled in my bag for my phone.

'I'll call her.' Farley punched numbers into his phone, and I could hear the musical tones, even from where I stood. I waited, but then there was nothing. Just flat dead air.

'She's not answering,' he said.

'So I hear.'

'Maybe she's driving,' he said. 'Or out of range.'

'Yeah, maybe.' As we walked to his car, I tried to remember another time I'd called Tamera and not been able to reach her. I couldn't. The woman's life was attached to her phone. He opened the car door and waited for me to climb in. Instead, I stood there and said, 'I don't like it, Farley.'

For a moment, I thought he was going to argue with me, maybe tell me I was overreacting. Instead, he shook his head in a way that conveyed both helplessness and something else I couldn't read.

'Neither do I,' he said. 'I'm going to try to find a number for that lawyer in Phoenix.'

Twenty-Two

From the outside, the hotel looked south-western, but on the inside, it just looked old. The blush of pink on the taupe wall was like a cosmetic that failed to disguise its age. Sheets of clear plastic covered the stairs. Tamera Flowers, their contact person from the California radio station, had found the hotel on the Internet. Rena hoped the woman wasn't too disappointed. Maybe the rooms in the newer construction, past the glass door and the swimming pool, were better.

'Are you nervous?' she asked Kendra as they approached the front desk.

'No,' she said. 'Not after everything I've been through. This could be a wild goose chase, remember. I just want to hear what this Tamera lady has to say.'

'Is she bringing photos?' Rena asked.

'I think so. And a finder's fee for Leighton. He's already turned it down, of course. They're insisting, and he says if push comes to shove, he'll ask them to donate it to one of his causes.'

'That sounds like him,' Rena said. And then, quickly, 'I'm glad you're not scared.'

'I'm not anything,' Kendra replied. 'That's the best way. Just go into it expecting whatever and know it will work out, one way or the other.'

'I could never be as calm as you.'

'Sure you could. You could be anything you want to be.'

'Debby Lynn says we're all just exactly the same as we were in high school.'

Kendra's head whipped around. 'When did you start listening to her?'

'I'm not saying I listened to her, but she and Leighton are in some kind of war about Bryn. Debby Lynn stole that gazing globe you gave me right from under my nose. My sage wand too.'

'She didn't.'

'Swear to God.' They both laughed. 'I'm going to make her give them back, though.'

'Good luck with that. I already ordered another Buddha. What do you suppose she does with all that stuff? Does she even know she takes it?'

'She knows, all right,' Rena said. 'The woman's mean, but not crazy. Being one doesn't mean you're automatically the other.'

'I know.' Kendra squeezed her arm. 'And you aren't either one.'

The desk clerk drifted over toward them. She reminded Rena of Bryn – not her appearance as much as her age and attitude.

'Could you call Tamera J. Flowers' room?' Kendra asked, her professional tone masking her feelings. If she didn't know better, Rena thought, she'd think this was strictly business for Kendra.

The clerk looked at the computer in front of her and typed in a couple of keys. 'Flowers, I remember the name,' she said. 'Tamera Flowers. She left about an hour ago. Are you with Mr Coulter's office?' The expression on her face said if they weren't with Leighton's office, all bets were off.

'Yes,' they said, almost in unison.

'All right, then,' she replied, without looking up long enough to even pretend to check them out. 'Ms Flowers left you a message. She said to tell you she's on her way to Saguaro Park, as per your instructions, and she'll see you there in about twenty minutes. She'll be driving a black SUV.'

'Thanks,' Kendra said. Her voice sounded shaky now, and Rena noticed her nails digging into the counter. 'When did she leave that message?'

The clerk looked down. 'Just before she left. About an hour ago.' Then, her face scrunched up, and she gave them the once over for the first time. 'You do work for Mr Coulter,' she said. 'Right?'

Rena nodded. 'We're working with him,' Kendra said. 'Is there a problem?'

'Jason,' she called out to the other desk clerk, who'd just gotten off the phone. 'It says here that this message for Mr Coulter was already delivered. Is that correct?'

Jason came over, gave them a professional desk-clerk smile, and then looked down at the computer. 'That's right,' he said, tapping the screen. 'I gave the message to Mr Coulter myself.'

'On the phone?' Kendra asked.

'No, he came here looking for Ms Flowers. I told him where she went.'

'Hey.' The girl squinted, as if the sun were in her eyes. 'If you work for him, why don't you know that?'

'With him,' Kendra said. 'We work with him.'

'Terry, you can't be giving out information to anyone who asks for it,' he said.

'I didn't.' Her voice rose, and Rena could see they were ready to go at it.

Kendra nudged her. 'Come on.'

They arrived at Saguaro National Park in fewer than fifteen minutes, give or take. Why here? Rena wondered. The flat land began to slope, and the scrubby Palo Verde trees and saguaro cacti blanketed the brown flannel ground. That's how this place looked, like something created on fabric.

Some called the saguaro majestic. To Rena, they were defiant, and more so than usual today, as if to say this was the way you had to look and this was the attitude you had to have to survive the desert.

Kendra wasn't talking. Nervous, Rena guessed. She appeared composed as always and just as grounded, but Kendra could be secretive, and she was keeping what she was really feeling far away from this drive. *Please let Kendra find her daughter.* She deserved some happiness. That Flowers woman had come, just as she promised. Leighton was probably already with her. For a moment, Rena almost forgot her own problems. Her heart was full of hope for Kendra.

The Rincon Mountains rose ahead of them. But with more than one hundred fifty miles of hiking trails, how were they going to find Leighton and Tamera Flowers?

Then they saw it – a black SUV parked on the right side of the road.

168

'There,' Rena said, but Kendra had already pulled over. Her hands on the wheel looked as if they belonged to a stranger.

They got out of the car and went over to the SUV.

Kendra peered inside, then ran her finger over a transparent decal on the driver's window. 'Rental,' she said.

'Why here?' Rena looked around at nothing but sage-colored cactus, the dry, scrubby hills around them. 'Why set up a meeting out in this place?' Nothing about this was right. She felt as if they had walked into a trap.

'I don't know. It doesn't make any sense.' Kendra shielded her eyes with her hand and looked up the hill. Only one small structure, some kind of historic stone building – Rena could tell from the plaque beside them – sat on top. It would be a tough climb, but people did it every day, just to look out on these sucked-dry plains the way people in other places gazed out on the ocean. Even the breeze was hot. It would be worse up there. 'We either go looking,' Kendra said, her eyes harsh as the sunlight, 'or we wait down here for her to come back.'

'Call Leighton,' Rena said.

'I tried in the car.' Kendra reached into her bag and put in his number once more. 'Nothing. There's no reception out here.'

'Then we have to look,' Rena told her. 'How do we do it?'

'You take one side, and I'll take the other,' she said. 'Go as high as you can, no higher, and if you see her before I do, call out.'

'I don't like it.'

'Neither do I. We don't have to do this.'

'But she came here to help us, Kendra. We at least have to be sure she's not out here alone.' Rena looked at the hill and felt sick. 'It just doesn't seem right. If someone's willing to pay a five thousand dollar fee to find you, I don't get why she'd make it so difficult for you to find her.'

'But Leighton knows where she is,' Kendra said. 'She might even be with him right now. Maybe they're in his car looking for us. Only a lizard would climb that hill in this heat.'

She was right about that. 'Do you have a phone number for her?' Rena asked.

'Sure do.' Kendra dug it out and dialed as they stood there in the sun. They'd put on their good clothes, Rena realized as she looked at Kendra's turquoise sundress and jewelry to match, and then at her own green top, as if she was on her way to church. Their good clothes, as if doing so would put them in better favor, find them a happy ending to their story. Kendra's face didn't look happy, though. 'No answer,' she said. 'Not even voicemail.'

'So, what do we do?' They were this close to possible news of Kendra's daughter, and now they'd hit a dead end. Rena had one foot in hell and the other in purgatory. That's what her dad would've said, and she hoped that wasn't blaspheming to think so.

'Back to our original plan,' Kendra said, not looking any better. 'I'll keep trying Leighton on my phone. Let's just look around a little.'

'Are you sure?' As Kendra bolted up the hill, Rena walked around the bottom of it: brown and green, mostly brown, mostly dirt, mostly dead. This Flowers lady would be just fine. She was probably signing papers for Kendra's daughter right now. This would turn out to be a day of miracles. They'd all be happy. It could still work out.

A noise stopped her. A softer version of the nail gun. Rena froze. Something was there in one of those green clumps. A snake. Oh, yes. It was the sound of a rattler. She wanted to run, but she didn't dare. *It's as frightened as you are*, Kendra would say. *Just pretend you don't see it.* She couldn't see it either. All she could do was just stare in the direction of the sound.

She reminded herself that snakes moved slowly unless they were striking. Yes, unless. She pretended to be part of the environment, a tree, a flower, and wait until the snake moved on. Another rattle. She forced herself to stand still. Slowly, she turned toward the bush where she suspected the snake hid. She couldn't get a glimpse of him, though. Something else shown through the brush, something sparkly. God, it looked like a bracelet, a fancy woman's bracelet. But what was it attached to? She moved closer and saw it then, a long arm partially covered by dirt.

'Kendra,' she screamed, before she could think better of it. 'Kendra, come quick.'

A living whip lashed out and struck her. A snake, with four rattles, slapped against her like a wet rope, its fang puncturing the flesh of her foot.

She screamed again and fell to her knees, inches away from the lifeless arm, the bracelet. A woman, she could see that now. It was a woman, her bright-blue dress torn, her face nothing but blood. 'Kendra, help.'

'I'm coming. Where are you? What's wrong?'

Her voice sounded muffled, far away. Rena had to do something, had to get someone out there. Most of all, she had to get out of here before the snake struck again. She tried to lift herself, but the throbbing hole in her foot was draining her energy. Her arms collapsed, and her head struck the ground, face first.

'No!' She spit out dirt and fought to stay conscious.

'Rena, my god.' Kendra. Finally, she was here. Rena tried to warn her about the snake, but her voice came out a sputter. She couldn't hold on any longer. She drifted away, toward the horrible noise echoing in her head, the rattler again. Or was it the nail gun? Or both?

Twenty-Three

Farley didn't think I should fly to Arizona. Too much of a long shot, he said. Too many loose ends still unresolved. I should wait until I knew more, wait until I was sure I wouldn't be hurt. Farley was all about waiting, and as much as I appreciated his concern, I knew I need to be in the one place where I might actually find my mother.

We debated the issue on the way to a late breakfast as I sent yet another text to Mick. I needed to know how old I'd been when he and Elaine adopted me, and I couldn't blame his silence on his commitment to his job.

The top was down, and the breeze, relatively unpolluted at this hour, ruffled Farley's hair and made him look far more mellow than he was.

'What good will your going out there do if we can't get in touch with Tamera?' he asked.

'Maybe it won't matter, but I just want to be there,' I said. 'If only to see what's going on.'

'At least wait until you hear back from Leighton Coulter, would you?' His voice rose above the wind with a certainty that reminded me of the way he had confronted the caller who claimed that Kendra's daughter had been kidnapped.

'That's another reason I want to go,' I told him. 'I want to see what I can find out at the local newspaper about the kidnapping.'

'You can do that right here,' he said as he pulled into the restaurant parking lot.

'The Internet had nothing.'

'Do you really think you need to go all the way to some little hickville newspaper office in Arizona to find out if the story is true or not?'

'Well, it was so many years ago, and it seems like it never went national,' I said. 'How can I possibly find out anything here? How can you?'

'Have you forgotten?' He gave me one of those disarming smiles that were his specialty. 'I drink with cops.'

What I had always considered one of Farley's few flaws had blossomed into a huge asset. While we ate omelets I barely tasted, he made phone calls to people he addressed as, 'Hey, man.' Most of all, he reassured me.

'My buddies are going to do everything they can, Kit. We're going to get to the bottom of this, I promise you. We're going to find out the truth, maybe as soon as today. Do you realize that? As soon as today?'

If he were a preacher, I'd be saying the amens. Instead, I just kept repeating, 'Thank you.'

We drove to his place for coffee and to wait for news from his contacts. The wind had tangled my hair into knots, but it didn't make any difference now.

Farley patted my knee. 'Why so glum?' he asked in that way of his.

'Not glum, just worried about Tamera and nervous about hearing back from Mick,' I said. 'I appreciate your trying to help.'

'Purely selfish motives, ma'am.' He glided the car into the underground parking place for his building and sat there in the cool, dusky garage without moving.

'Selfish? How's that?'

I could sense him turn his head and knew he was watching me. 'I want my partner back.'

'I haven't really been gone,' I said, trying to feel indignant, but suspecting he was right. Our eyes met, and I felt a flash of something – recognition, connection, that nameless thing we used to have before Richard left, before my mom died, before I discovered that my mom wasn't really my mother. 'I think we'd better go get that coffee,' I said.

I'd been to his apartment numerous times, but not recently and never alone. I felt awkward in the elevator and more so when I stepped inside and smelled the combined scents of leather, sandalwood, and something I could only describe to myself as tranquility.

'I see you still have the same maid service,' I said, as a way to break the ice. The dark leather and ebony wood that filled the room dared anyone to as much as run a finger along it and find dust.

'You know me,' he said. 'Sometimes, I throw out the newspaper while I'm still reading it.'

Still, I knew he was proud that his apartment, with its balcony, mirrored dining room and adjoining kitchen with stainless-steel appliances, wasn't the typical DJ crash pad. No, this was a home where anyone who visited felt compelled to linger. He headed for the back, and I started to follow.

'No way.' He held up a hand. 'Farley's maid service didn't make it back to my office today.'

'I don't care,' I said.

'But I do.' He gave me that disarming look again. 'I'll go check my email. You wait here. Put on any music you like.'

'I'm not sure I can wait,' I said.

He closed the louvered doors behind him, and I sat on the leather sofa. I did not play any music. I looked at the window leading to the balcony. I didn't think about anything except why we were here and what I hoped Farley would be able to find. I heard him before I saw him again. 'Bingo.'

I'd heard the word *palpitate* all my life, but I never felt it until Farley shouted out like that. He

175

burst through the door, all smiles and sheets of paper.

'May first,' he said. 'That's when it happened. Look at this.'

In that heart-pumping moment, I felt as if he held my future in his hands. Like gleeful children, we spread the papers out along the leather sofa – newspaper stories, several of them. *Child Reported Missing* was the first headline I spotted. I grabbed it and read it aloud:

> Jillian Trafton, three months old, was reported missing yesterday by her mother, Kendra Trafton. The Buckeye resident said she left her daughter in her car around noon, while she stopped at a phone booth to make a call. Approximately fifteen minutes later, she reported Jillian's disappearance to an officer.
>
> 'There are no suspects at this time, and no signs of a crime,' said Sergeant Ray Nolan of the Buckeye Police Department. 'No family members are under suspicion at this time.'
>
> Jillian's father, Edward, a teacher at Lowell Elementary, has organized a private search party.
>
> However, Nolan asks that anyone with information contact the police department. He also reminds parents not to leave children unattended, even briefly. 'This wouldn't have happened if the mother hadn't stopped to make that call,' he said.

Farley took the paper from me. 'What a hatchet job,' he said. 'They weren't trying to find her child. They were trying to hang the blame on her.' He stared at the paper. 'She doesn't look much like you, does she?'

'The mother?' I asked. 'Or the daughter?'

'The mother,' he said. 'I guess.'

I shook my head and moved close so that I could take another look. Kendra Trafton's haunted face stared back at me. She had to have been younger than I was now. Either her hair was very short, or it had been pulled from her face.

I tried to recognize myself in her, to see that she was my mother and know for certain that I was the missing Jillian. I couldn't, though.

Her eyes looked dark, but maybe that was the fault of the blurry copy I was viewing. Her cheekbones were high and strong. This was a woman of big bones, not at all my body type. That might not matter, though. I didn't know what Jillian's father, the Edward of the newspaper article, looked like. Maybe the Lowell Elementary teacher, who'd organized a private search party for his daughter, was smaller, curly-haired, and fair. I still had a chance.

Then, I took a good look at Jillian Trafton. It was a baby picture, but even so, I felt little connection to it. She was a beautiful baby, which I had not been in those early pictures taken with my mom. Jillian's head looked shadowed, as if the soft hair growing in there was dark. For one long moment, I tried to believe, to pretend. It was as if I were some kid at an orphanage, resorting to any trick to be selected.

'How are you doing?' Farley asked. 'All right?'

I nodded, no longer knowing. Then, I remembered what I'd been searching my mind for: the first photo I ever saw of myself. Only frizzy blond curls. Elaine had laughed and said she'd had to stick the bow to my head with tape.

'I'm not sure I'm that girl,' I told him. 'She doesn't look like me.' Tears appeared from nowhere. I couldn't stop them. I felt orphaned then, for the first time since I'd read my mom's letter.

Farley's expression turned sad, and his smile couldn't disguise that he felt the same way I did. 'You can't be sure,' he said, although I knew he was as certain as I. 'She's only an infant. Besides, we're going to find out.'

'It's not me. It's not my hair.' My voice, my sobs weren't mine. They were the voice and the sobs of a child.

'Kit.' He put his arms around me and patted my back, awkward pats but sincere, if only because they were so self-conscious. I dove for his shoulder and buried my sobs there. 'Please don't, Kit. It breaks my heart to see you like this.'

His words sank in. My outburst subsided, then stopped. The storm had passed. Farley said it broke his heart to see me hurting. Farley cared about me, cared about my feelings. Someone cared. Farley did. I lifted my head from his shoulder, which was drenched now, thanks to me. His face was close, his expression no longer scared, but his lashes looked wet. 'I didn't want to cause you more pain,' he said. 'I wanted to help.'

178

'You did. Farley, you've helped me more than you know.'

'I'd do anything.' His voice was warm. 'I'd do anything for you.'

Then, his lips settled on mine. And it seemed the most natural thing in the world to lace my arms around his neck, to fall into the kiss and into him. In that one movement, I slipped into the sensations of taste, smell, the clammy feel of his leather sofa on my bare arms. I tried to pull away, but he seemed to take my squirming for passion.

'It kills me to see you like this,' he whispered. 'I want you back the way you were.'

'I will be,' I said. 'I will.' Then, somewhere in me, a brake screeched my body to a halt. My hands went to his chest. I pushed, and then pushed harder. 'I can't do this,' I said.

'I hear you.' He froze, and I knew he was processing, deciding how far to take it. 'Do you want to go home?'

'I need to,' I said. 'I'm sorry, but I don't have any idea what to do next. Tamera is out in Arizona meeting with some woman who doesn't even look like me. Mick's not returning my phone calls, and that little girl in the newspaper photo . . .' I couldn't go on.

'You wanted Kendra to be your mother,' he said. 'Maybe she still can be. Maybe you're wrong about the photos.'

'I'm not wrong, Farley.'

'You could be. You're upset. These are rotten copies.'

'*Farley.*'

'All right.' He stood suddenly and put out his hand for me to do the same. 'I'll take you home,' he said. 'I'm sorry about that.' He waved at the sofa. 'I don't know what got into me.'

But it wasn't him. It was us. He was just giving me an out. 'There's too much going on with me right now,' I said, as a weak attempt at apology.

'I know it hasn't been that long,' he said, and I knew he meant since my separation from Richard.

We stepped on the elevator that still smelled of his cologne.

'Don't give up. For all we know, Kendra is your mother. You can't base everything on one old photo.'

'Do you believe that, Farley?'

'It's possible.' The door opened, and he was Radio Farley again, making his way through the dim, chalky-smelling rows of cars as if he wasn't concerned about anything more important than if he'd remembered his sunblock. His carefree gait and calm, deceptive smile hid his true thoughts, I knew.

I wanted to give him more, but I was stuck back in that spotless living room of his, looking into the dark eyes of that beautiful little girl with all the hair. A little girl I never could have been.

Twenty-Four

We drove to my place in silence. He turned on the radio, and some Norah Jones floated in. I studied his profile and that tight smile he sent into the wind and wondered how well I knew him. Although we were close, neither of us had ever crossed that line of mutual attraction before. Farley had just gotten out of a relationship when we had met, and I had sworn I would never get involved with anyone who worked in radio. Yet we had kissed back there in his apartment as if we'd meant it. We'd come close to doing more. I tried to figure out why. The closest I could come was that, although I didn't know him as well as I should after two years together on the air, there was something about Farley Black that made me feel safe.

For that reason, perhaps, when he stopped the car in front of my house, I leaned over and kissed him on the cheek.

He moved his lips to mine. I let the kiss linger, and then touched my finger to his face. 'Thank you,' I said, 'for trying to help.'

'I wish I could have done more. Let me know the minute you hear from Tamera.'

'I will.'

He leaned over to open my door, and on the way back, his lips brushed mine again. That was one time too many, I thought, but it didn't matter. I was going inside now, anyway.

I slid out of the car seat and looked back at him. I don't know what I was planning on saying, because I didn't get a chance to say anything. Approaching the car, walking a little too fast, came Mick and Richard. No, it couldn't be my father and my ex-husband, marching up to us with the conviction and self-importance of two cops who'd just discovered a crime in progress.

181

'What are you doing here?' I demanded, realizing I was directing the question to Richard.

'Trying to help you out,' he said. He looked ridiculous, still wearing his white veterinarian coat with tennis shoes and a baseball cap. He pulled the cap down over his eyes in a nervous gesture he probably wasn't even aware of. 'We didn't plan to interrupt a love scene.' Richard looked at Farley with such disdain that I almost expected him to spit. Then he turned his fury on me. 'I can't believe you'd pull something like this.'

'Lay off her.' Farley got out of the car, slammed the door, and went eye-to-eye with him. 'What you saw was friendship, man, all right? And if you don't know the lady any better than that, maybe you ought to get the hell out of here before someone knocks you on your sorry ass.'

Richard met the challenge. 'That someone had better be a whole lot bigger than you, Farley.'

'Easy,' Mick shouted, as if giving a command to a dog.

'Out of respect for you and for her, I won't press it,' Richard told Mick. Then, with a look at Farley: 'You're lucky.' Richard looked ready to charge, and then stopped, the way I'd seen him stop in the middle of too many arguments with me. Logic kicked in, and he slowly adjusted his baseball cap.

'Will you cut it out?' Mick wedged himself between the two of them like a squat little referee between two towering boxers. 'I understand that you two have hard feelings, but we can't deal with that now. We've got to help Kit.'

'I don't have hard feelings,' Farley said. 'I just

don't like him accusing me of something he knows nothing about. Kit doesn't care about anything except finding her mother, and I'm trying to help her. If he cared about her, he'd understand that.'

An impassioned speech, but still my cheeks burned as I remembered what had happened and what almost happened up in Farley's apartment. I looked from him to Richard. Farley was bright as sunlight, but with a secret side I was only just beginning to sense. Richard was guarded, moody, and brilliant. If I had to choose right now, could I? And why would I have to choose? Richard had already left me.

'How crazy is this?' I started laughing. 'All four of us wearing dark glasses. We're having this heated discussion, and we can't even look each other in the eyes.'

'You can look me in the eyes.' Farley yanked off his glasses. His eyes were his best feature. He couldn't hide the emotion brimming there, and that only increased his appeal. I didn't want to, but I took off my own glasses and met his gaze.

'You know, Farley,' I said. 'You don't need to stick around for this soap opera. It's not in your contract.'

'Don't be harsh, Kit,' Mick said and took my arm. 'I know you're hurting, and so am I. Richard came to see me yesterday, damn near yanked me out of the motorhome.'

'Why?' I asked. 'And why haven't you answered my text?'

'Work's been a killer.' He looked down.

'Well, you're here now. How old was I when you adopted me?' I asked.

'I don't know.' he said. 'You were a baby. Elaine would have known. It's probably written down somewhere.' He avoided my eyes.

'What is it?' I asked.

'This isn't easy for me to talk about,' Mick said, 'but Richard made me realize what I'm about to tell you will come out sooner or later, and it will hurt you even more then.'

I couldn't deal with any more confessions. I felt my legs threaten to give out. I couldn't balance. It was as if they were not made of flesh and bone, but something insubstantial. Farley seemed to sense it, and his arm shot out around me. Richard glared. I glared back. He'd been the one to leave. He had no reason to play the broken-hearted victim now.

'What?' Farley demanded. 'Just tell her.'

Mick took off his glasses, too. In his pale eyes, I saw something I'd never glimpsed there before. I saw fear. And that fear ignited my own.

'Please tell me,' I said.

He looked around at the sunlit sidewalk, the kids across the street with their Frisbees. 'Don't you think we should go inside?'

I broke free of Farley's grip. 'Tell me, Mick, and tell me right now.'

He looked down, then up at me. 'This might be the most difficult thing I've ever done,' he said. 'I told you that we adopted you, remember?'

'That's right.' I nodded and felt my head move up and down through the air. 'I'm adopted. I know that.'

184

'You aren't adopted,' he said. 'Not really.'

My body and mind froze to a standstill.

Farley, however, leapt to life. 'What do you mean she's not adopted? What are you trying to pull now?'

'Settle down, please.' Richard stiffened, and even behind the dark glasses, I could feel the fire in his eyes. 'She's not adopted. That's why Mick's here. That's why I went to see him. I knew something was wrong, even when we were married. She couldn't locate her birth certificate.'

'But if I'm not adopted—' I began.

'What is she?' Farley finished, his arm tightly around me now. 'Whatever it is, you owe her the truth.'

'Her mother, Elaine, moved heaven and earth to get her,' Mick said. 'She wanted a baby. She wanted this baby.' His gaze lingered on me.

'Tell her the rest,' Richard said. 'Just tell it, Mick.'

'Kit, honey, it's not as if we stole you or anything. The mother, Kendra Trafton, wanted you to go to a good family. But we didn't adopt you at all.' His eyes bore into mine, full of tears, now, full of remorse. 'We had to pay.'

'You had to pay? You *paid* for me?' I echoed, trying to keep myself separate from the chilling words. 'What does that mean?' But I knew. I knew.

'Kit . . .'

'Leave me alone, Mick.'

'We had to. It was the only way we could be sure we'd have you. There was another couple behind us, and if we'd waited even a few hours, we might have lost you.'

185

The betrayal I had experienced in the past couldn't begin to touch this.

'Forgive me,' he said, 'for not telling you sooner.'

'So how'd you do it?' I shoved the glasses into my hair, no longer caring that they could see my tears. 'Where do you go to buy a newborn?'

Mick looked at Richard, who nodded. 'I think an attorney handled it,' Mick said. 'We signed papers. It just wasn't a legal adoption.'

I still couldn't process this news. The idea of being purchased like a sack of flour was more than I could handle. 'How much?' I demanded. 'A hundred? Five hundred? A grand?'

'Twenty, I think,' he choked out. 'Twenty thousand.'

It sounded like a lot, which made me feel even worse. Apparently, I didn't feel I was worth as much as a moderately priced automobile. 'And my birth certificate?'

'I don't know, honey.'

'What about my name?' I moved closer and forced him into eye contact. 'Was I really named after a great aunt, or was that a lie too?'

'I'm not sure,' he said. 'I'm really not. And Kit, Richard's right. You need and deserve to know anything I can tell you about your life. I'll answer any question you have from here on out.'

A decision he should have made more than twenty years ago. I needed to call Tamera and let her know what I'd found out. I needed to research how people bought babies, back when I was born, and maybe I should even consider writing another post for my blog. Most of all, I need to cry.

'Thank you for this information.' I said it as if speaking to a stranger. All I could think of was getting away from this man who had lied to me my entire life, and from Richard, who had left me, and had then decided to try talking my dad into sharing some version of the truth. 'I'll need some time to digest all this.'

'I understand, Kit,' Mick said. 'Richard and I will be going now. You just let me know when you want to talk again.'

'Kit, wait.' Richard took off his glasses. 'Could we discuss this for a minute? Alone?'

I hated that he and Farley had heard Mick's confession. Even more, I hated that I felt ashamed and embarrassed, as if this family secret were somehow my fault.

I shook my head. 'It will have to be later, Richard. I don't want to talk to anyone right now.' I looked directly at Mick.

Slowly, he turned. After a moment, so did Richard. I watched as they walked down the sidewalk, blurred watercolor shapes through my tears.

Twenty-Five

My parents had paid for me. I couldn't deal with that much more now than I had been able to when Mick informed me of the fact. Another couple was 'behind' them, he'd said. What would have happened if they had come up with the

187

twenty thousand before Mick and my mom had? My history would be different, but maybe not as dishonest as it had been until now. Yet my family's secrets were minor compared to what I now suspected the Brantinghams were hiding.

I couldn't put off what I had to do, regardless of what it cost me. Yes, I had told Scott I wouldn't contact Carla or her family without his permission, but nothing he or anyone else said would stop me now.

I found Carla trying on dresses at the bridal store where her assistant had told me that Carla and her mother were shopping for her parents' renewal of wedding vows. A narrow shop lined with more merchandise than square feet, it ended at a wall of mirrors with a curtained dressing room on each side. Bette Brantingham sat in a moss-green wing chair. A flute of champagne along with a silver platter of cheeses gleamed on the round glass table. The platter appeared untouched. The flute needed refilling.

Just then, a brunette who must have been in charge of arranging this little tableau appeared with a full bottle.

'Refill?' she asked in the perpetually cheerful voice of one who catered to the rich. Bubbles fizzed into the glass.

'Lovely. Thank you.'

The brunette turned from her toward the dressing room. 'Do you need any help?' she called out. Clearly, she was not addressing Bette, who had already clutched the glass in her French manicured nails.

'I'm fine.' Carla joined them in front of the

mirrors in a fitted pink dress, part prom queen, part sex kitten. She frowned and put on a matching sequin jacket. 'What do you think?'

'Very pretty,' Bette said, 'isn't it, Monique?'

'Beautiful,' the saleswoman gushed.

I cleared my throat, and they turned toward me. Pressed by lace and ruffles on all sides, I felt even more claustrophobic as Carla marched toward me.

'Whatever you need, it could have waited,' she whispered. Her shoulder-length helmet of yellow-blond hair didn't move.

'I'm sorry,' I said. 'If I could wait, I would have.'

'Carla,' Bette called from the wing chair. 'Is everything all right?'

'It's fine, Mama. Why don't you and Monique look at a gown for you? Kit and I need to talk for just a moment.'

'Hurry back. We have work to do, don't we, Monique?'

'Indeed we do.' The brunette lifted the bottle of champagne once more.

Still wearing the pink dress, Carla walked ahead of me to the front of the shop, where the forest of white dresses grew even thicker and seemed to close in on us.

'Mind if we step outside?' I asked.

'Not a bad idea.'

We went out into the relatively fresh air. Carla inhaled deeply, as if taking a drag of a cigarette. 'This had better be good,' she said.

'I wish it were,' I told her.

'What then? And please make it fast.'

'I spoke with your father,' I said. 'As you know.'

She gave me a bitter smile. 'And yet here you are doing what you were told not to do.'

'He was under the impression that Alex returned from that place you sent him to after one week and with no desire or at least no willingness to move forward as the person he truly was.'

'Perhaps Dad needs to believe that for now,' she said.

'Why?'

'Because he's old, and he doesn't need any more heartbreak.'

'And Alex?' I felt as if I were spitting out the words. 'Why would you want to do that to him?'

'Alex is dead,' she said. 'Can you imagine what that did to my parents? To my mother?' She glanced back inside, where I imagined Bette lifting her glass yet one more time, her eyes blurring against a future she didn't want to comprehend and a past she didn't dare to remember.

'I'm sure it hurt them,' I replied. 'And I'm sure it hurt you as well.'

'I'm the resilient one.' She squared her shoulders in the pink monstrosity and stood even straighter, as if to make her point. 'I always have been.'

Another time, I would have believed her. Another time, I had believed her.

'He was your brother, Carla.'

'My best friend.' She nodded. 'Alex meant the world to me. I miss him every day.'

'Yet you convinced your dad to send him to conversion whatever-you-call-it therapy. You paid for more treatments your father didn't know about, didn't you?'

She lifted her chin, but said nothing.

'Do you deny it?'

She shrugged and glared at me. 'Go on.'

'You say he meant the world to you, yet you subjected him to horrendous treatment. And you lied to your father about it.'

'I'm devoted to my family,' she said. 'The more I learn about you, Kit, the more I realize how unqualified you are to examine and bring to light stories about victims like my brother.'

'Why are you really trying to hide the truth?' I stepped back and took in the whole of her, every artificial, tragic detail. 'And why are you willing to let an innocent man be prosecuted for a crime he didn't commit?'

She took a step toward me, and then apparently thought better of it. In spite of the heavy make-up, her skin was the color of chalk. 'I've had enough,' she said.

'So have I. Is your public image that important to you? Or is it the election?'

'You're delusional.' She flounced to the glass door, where her reflection shimmered.

'Take a look at that and tell me who's delusional,' I said.

She gasped and hurried inside, and I knew I had stirred the proverbial hornet's nest. She could buy prom-queen-from-hell gowns. Her parents could renew their wedding vows. But now, at least, she was aware that someone knew that her concern about Alex's murder was really just a cover-up of his orientation so that she could continue to run for office on her family values platform.

When I arrived home, I spotted Farley parked outside my house. We hadn't spoken after that humiliating moment with Mick and Richard, and it wasn't like him to just show up unannounced.

I got out of my car and ran around to the driver's window, which was down, as it always was on any day with even bearable temperatures.

'I've been waiting for you,' he said, and we hugged.

Then he took off his dark glasses, and I saw his eyes.

'What happened?'

'I haven't been able to settle down,' he said. 'So I decided to check back with one of our interview subjects.'

'Which one?' I asked.

'Jerry. I went back there.' He started the car. 'It's worse than we thought, Kit.'

'I can't imagine anything worse than what we thought,' I said once we were on our way.

Farley didn't answer.

Finally, I asked, 'Where are we heading?'

'Jerry doesn't want to talk where anyone can overhear,' he said and pulled off the freeway. 'There are a bunch of storefront restaurants over here by the bank. The area behind is more like a park.'

Farley still seemed stiff, and I knew he was holding back something. That wasn't like the guy I knew, whose life mantra seemed to be 'what you see is what you get'.

The area wasn't the little mall of restaurants I had pictured. It was small storefronts, many of them vacant, with sun-proof glass and names like Mr Pickle and Pita Man. The area between them, the bank, and a museum of some kind wasn't a park either. Yet, on a webbed chair in a shaded grassy area, holding a paper cup of coffee, sat Jerry.

His dark hair had been shaved to the skull, making his square jaw and large eyes even more prominent. In khaki shorts and T-shirt, he could be mistaken for a college student, except for the pain in his expression, even when he tried to smile.

I pulled up the only remaining lawn chair, and Farley squatted beside me.

'How much did you tell her?' Jerry asked him.

Farley shook his head. 'That's your job, man.'

For the first time, he seemed to genuinely smile. 'Well, you do know that Farley popped in on me unexpectedly, correct?'

'Right,' I said.

'He made me realize I have to tell the truth to someone, and he convinced me that someone is you.'

'Go on,' Farley said.

'Well, Kit,' he said. 'I owe it to Alex to tell you some things.'

'And those things are?'

He glanced back to Farley, and then met my eyes reluctantly. 'The treatment didn't work on me.'

'Because it's not treatment,' I said.

'They mean well.'

'Are you kidding? Camps like that aren't even legal in this state.'

'But they believe what they're doing.' He forced a smile. 'They're the first to admit that they don't have a perfect success rate. I guess I fall into that other percentage.'

'Because you're normal, Jerry,' I said. 'You do know that, don't you?'

'This isn't about me,' he said. 'It's about Alex. I lied to you before. We were both having problems being cured.'

'Neither of you needed curing.' I knew he didn't hear me, but tried anyway.

'Alex's problems were different than mine. He was already in love when they brought him there.'

I nodded. 'With Luis Vang.'

'That's right. Sometimes I pretended to the others, just because I was so miserable. I can't explain it, only that it almost felt better to act like I was this way because I loved someone, not because something was wrong with me.'

'What did they do to you?' I asked.

'They tried to help. They . . .'

Farley shot to his feet. 'Tell her the truth.'

'I can't even think about it.'

'Did they beat you?' I knew nowhere else to begin.

He seemed to stare into space, into a situation I could not see. 'It's about self-control. In order to stay strong, you have to learn control, how to resist temptation. I did try, and so did Alex. I know he did.'

'You're avoiding my question,' I said. 'What did they do to you?'

'It was tough.' He glanced down at his empty cup, or maybe just his feet. 'Alex and I got the

194

tests at the same time. We needed to control our impulses.'

'Farley?' I asked.

'Jerry didn't tell me this part,' he replied.

'Because I can't.'

'Because you're ashamed?' I asked.

'Yes.' Tears filled his eyes. 'Fuck, yes, I'm ashamed. Alex got through it, and I didn't.'

'The so-called acclimation films?' I asked.

He shook his head. 'They were easy compared to the body wrap.'

I glanced over at Farley and realized this was clearly as new to him as it was to me.

'I read a little bit about it,' I said.

'Did what you read say that they wrap those wet sheets around you until you feel like a mummy and then let them dry on you?'

Nothing I had read was at all that direct. 'That's suppression and torture, Alex.'

'It is supposed to help you conquer urges and grow stronger. Only third-weekers get it.'

'Third-weekers?' I felt so sick that I could barely meet his eyes, where he could barely hide what had been done to him.

'Those of us who fail the first tries. If those who care for you can afford it, they send you back.'

'Why did you go along with it?'

'I told you before about my family, that I'm the only son. They have money, and I'm supposed to pass along the name and everything that goes with it.'

I didn't bother trying to tell him he could do that as a gay father. I just wanted to let him know there was nothing wrong with him.

'First, you have to be who you are.' A few yards from us, the freeway noises drowned out my words, but I knew he heard me. 'Your family is in denial,' I said. 'They are the ones who aren't normal.' His eyes brightened for a moment, so I pressed on. 'You didn't fail the test. The test failed you.'

'I really wanted to be OK.' He looked away, and then back at me. 'I'm just not.'

'Please don't believe that about yourself,' I told him. 'Just as they have fake cure places like the one you and Alex went to, there are caring people who can help you open up instead of shut down.'

'I'm a lost cause.' He drained his coffee and sat the cup on the ground. 'I hope what I told you today helps Alex's family, because nothing I do now will help mine.'

'You actually went willingly to this torture?' I asked.

'Of course not.' His eyes widened. His smile could be that of a child. 'We soon realized that they meant the best, though.'

'If you didn't go willingly,' I asked, 'how did you get there?'

'How does anyone go where they don't want to go?' His eyes gleamed with unshed tears. 'You're out walking one day. Or, like Alex, you're playing tennis. Someone taps you on the shoulder. You turn around and realize there are other some-ones standing behind them.'

I felt myself jerk from my chair. 'You were kidnapped?'

'Goes with the territory.' He spoke slowly, as if trying to explain a term to someone who didn't speak the language. 'That's how we say it in treatment.'

Twenty-Six

Rena woke slowly, and for a moment, she thought she was still struggling to get to her feet. But, no. She was in a bed now, not sprawled on the ground. Her skin was chilled, and she remembered occasional words and images from her fitful nightmares. She could hear her name spoken in a whisper that turned into a hiss. She saw the snake, fifteen inches, maybe longer, the four rattles on his tail. She felt the strike, her fall, the dirt in her mouth.

Her sandals, she thought, her silly sandals. As she eased into consciousness, the shadows dimmed, and she saw Leighton's face, the young Leighton from high school, his blazing, determined eyes, and his taffy-colored hair curling around his ears. This was a guy determined to escape his world, regardless of what stood in his path.

'Leighton.' She forced the word through numb lips. 'I can't feel anything.'

'You're going to be fine, Rena. We took you to the emergency room.' His voice sounded as if he were speaking through fabric. 'I kept your foot in an ice bath, and they think the venom didn't travel any farther.'

'But my hands.' She didn't know how to

describe the numbness that had overtaken her whole body. 'My fingers. Where did you get the ice?'

'It's all right. They gave you the anti-venom. You're going to get to go home.'

Home. She closed her eyes. Home. No, she wasn't going anywhere. She was going to die. Just like that woman out there in the desert.

She jerked with a gasp. 'The woman, Leighton,' she said. 'There was a woman in the bushes.'

'Stay calm.'

She saw the blur of his hand move to her shoulder, but still she felt nothing. 'I know I'm not making it up. You have to go back there. You have to try to help her.'

'Easy,' he said, and she felt the pressure now.

'I mean it. You've got to go back there.' She could feel her heartbeats, and she could begin to smell the medicinal room.

'You're coming out of it, I can tell. You rest. Then we'll take you home. We can talk about it on the way.'

That wasn't good enough. She had to know at least that one thing. She had to know about the woman in the bushes. Light edged out the shadows of the room. She heard a voice growing louder in volume.

'I need to talk to my friend.' Kendra's voice overcame every doubt in her mind. 'Please let me talk to her. Where *is* Kendra?' Rena asked, looking to Leighton for the answer. In the time she'd closed her eyes, he'd aged back into himself. He was right, though. Her body was beginning to free itself from the venom's hold.

His gaze had shifted from her to the still-shadowed space where she thought Kendra's voice was coming from. He shook his head, and Rena imagined something secret in his eyes. The look on his face made her want to cry. In fact, she was crying. She hadn't even known it. In fact, she didn't know how long the tears had been running down her face. All she knew was that something horrible had happened, and she was never ever going to be the same.

Rena drifted in and out of consciousness, opening her eyes when they helped her from the wheelchair into the car, then sliding down in the back seat, barely aware of movement. She heard music as they drove, the music of voices, full of the word *her*, the word *she*. People were talking about her, whispering about her in the front seat. Leighton's voice floated back. 'I'm glad you had the courage to return,' he said.

Who was he talking to? Who returned? Slow laughter followed his words. Rena forced her eyes open. There, above the back of the passenger seat, was a shiny gray-streaked ponytail. 'Kendra?'

The laughter stopped, as if someone had snapped off a radio.

'We're almost there, Rena. You rest.'

The car went strangely silent, which helped her wake up and clear her head. She looked down at her foot, the small black mark the doctor had made around the red bite. Yes, she remembered the doctor with his white coat and his marking pen. She put her hands over her face. No, please don't let her crumble. Don't let Dale win. She could not survive another breakdown.

'How are you feeling?' It was Kendra's voice now, a different voice than she'd used with Leighton, lilting and friendly.

'I'm going to be fine.' Rena forced herself to sit upright. 'I'm going to be myself again, Kendra.'

The landscape around them slowly turned from black and white back into color. Mustard yellow, deep, dusky greens, brown. Snake colors. Snake country. She hadn't been thinking right to walk through that brush with sandals on.

She could feel her strength returning. She saw Kendra and Leighton clearly now. They seemed to be sitting close together on the seats, but that was crazy. The seats were where they always were. It was just that her vision was different, watching from behind them like this. It reminded her of study hall her freshman year, how Kendra and Leighton, both seniors, sat side by side like that ahead of her, heads always close.

That was before that night she had stopped in her daddy's pickup for Kendra. It was before she'd known them, even before she'd known Dale.

'Dale?' She hadn't meant to shout, but it came out that way. 'Does he know what happened?'

'I called,' Leighton said. 'Bryn told me he got that job out of town. She doesn't know how to reach him, so no, he has no idea what happened to you.'

'Good. That means he'll be gone a week.' She looked into the rear-view mirror and caught Leighton's solemn gaze with her own. For a moment, she thought he was judging her, but that wasn't what his eyes reflected. He just looked sad. 'I mean, it's good he won't be there to worry,' she said.

'And it's good for you, too,' Kendra cut in, with the same firm voice she had used on the doctors in the hospital. 'You just need time to heal.'

Yes, she did. She needed lots of healing, all right.

They pulled into the drive, and Rena's vision returned as if it had never left. There it was: her life until now, her property, thanks to her parents. It always made her think of that folk song, 'A Penny to My Name'. Had it been five years since her mama died? A rare kind of cancer, they said, until a year ago when her daddy died of the same rare type, and the doctors stopped guessing. Much as she missed them, she knew there was nothing for her daddy here without her mama. She used to dream of a marriage like that back when she still had dreams. She used to dream of Leighton and her together.

Her parents left her the gas and convenience store, just like in the song. Like that song, she often wished she was alone with a penny to her name. The older she got, the better alone sounded, especially now, with Dale off on that job, with her life handed back to her like a gift.

Leighton and Kendra were scary silent in the front seat. As she looked out on the only thing she owned, Rena realized she didn't really know either of these people entrusted with her care. No, that wasn't right. Of course she knew them. They had grown up together. They had shared the best and worst of their pasts.

'What is it?' Kendra's voice was high-pitched. When she swished that ponytail around to look at Rena, her eyes had an odd cast to them. Maybe it was the moonlight and its eerie glow that seemed chilling, even on this parched, hot night.

'Nothing.'

'Are you feeling better, Rena? Can you get out of the car if I help you?'

For a moment, she was afraid – scared to stay in the car, scared to leave it and go into that place that was hers. It didn't look like much, with just the one little sign and the stucco front painted that fake adobe color that, in the moonlight, looked like dried blood. Her daddy had built it up, though. He'd been able to make a good life there after the cotton went bad, and she could make a good life too if Dale could help out a little more when he wasn't on the construction jobs, and if they could just get some reliable workers.

'Rena?' Kendra said again.

'Give me a minute.'

Rena felt sick. Maybe it was the medication they'd given her, although she couldn't remember any medication, couldn't remember anything. No, the doctor, she remembered the doctor with the black marking pen and the white jacket, the way he'd drawn on her ankle around the area where the bite was. So that they could locate it, he had said to someone, as if they needed any help locating the hideous wound the snake had left. Rena looked back at the store. It was just the way it always was this time of night, huge bugs silhouetted by the lights in front. In back, her house would still be the same, and she'd be safe there, even without Dale, maybe safer.

'I'm ready,' she said, to Kendra's unreadable eyes.

'If you're sure. You're not supposed to walk on that foot, so Leighton's going to take one side, and I'll take the other. Just keep your left leg from touching anything.'

Almost before Kendra finished speaking, Leighton had opened the car door. 'Here,' he said, reaching in for her. 'Be really careful, Rena. Usually, people with bites like yours have to be hospitalized overnight. You were lucky, and we have to keep you that way.'

Rena told herself to reach up to him. If she couldn't trust Leighton, even with these weird effects from the drugs, she couldn't trust anyone in the world. She reminded herself that she and Leighton had loved each other once. Lately, when she caught his eye, she wondered if they still did.

But that was before today, before all of that whispering in the front seat. Maybe the anti-venom had made her paranoid, but she didn't think so. Even now, with Leighton reaching out for her, and Kendra's shadow behind him in the moonlight, she knew she didn't know either one of them. Maybe they were saying the same things Dale did. Maybe they believed she had lost her mind again. Tears filled her eyes. That was ridiculous. Something to do with the venom. She had to believe in these two. If she didn't, they'd all be lost.

'Come on,' Leighton said. 'Just slide across the seat. We'll help you the rest of the way.'

'I'll make some chicken noodle soup,' Kendra said, still in shadow. 'That's what you need now. That and lots and lots of water. You've got to flush out those toxins.'

Kendra made sense. It was probably the right thing to do to just slide out of this sweltering car and get to her own bed, with or without help. She had to be careful this time. It was a sudden movement that got her bit on that hill out there.

That hill.

That sparkle. That watch.

'Wait.' She perched on the edge of the car seat, ready to let Leighton lift her out.

'What is it?' Kendra answering again, not Leighton.

'Kendra? Where are you?'

'Right here, Rena. You know where I am.' Warm hands folded over her cold, numb ones, and, yes, Kendra's face appeared right beside Leighton's. 'Are you ready to go inside now? Do you want us to stay?'

Us?

Kendra's widow's peak looked like a dark arrow against her forehead. Rena turned away from it.

'I just want to go inside, go to sleep. I don't need either one of you.'

'Are you sure?' Leighton's voice now.

'Very sure.' She was angry. Why was she so angry? It didn't matter. She had to ask the question that had been burning through her since she

204

regained consciousness. 'Kendra?' she began. Better to start with Kendra. She didn't dare take on Leighton.

'Come out first,' Kendra coaxed. 'Let me help you get out of here.'

She didn't budge. 'I'm not doing anything, not going anywhere, until you tell me the truth, Kendra. I have to ask you something, and I want you to know that I can take the answer.'

'I'll tell you anything, but just come on out. At least get some fresh air.'

Rena let them help her then, and Kendra was right. Rena didn't realize how much she needed the fresh air until she stood outside the car and began gulping it in. They balanced her one on each side, human crutches, each with an arm around her.

'That woman with the watch,' Rena said, looking up at Kendra. 'Right before the snake got me. Is she alive or dead?'

'Oh, Rena,' Kendra whispered.

And to Leighton, 'Did you call that guy at the Sacramento radio station?'

'I haven't been able to reach him,' Leighton said. 'I gave the police his contact information, though.'

'Police?' Rena asked. 'No!' But of course she had known all along that the woman was dead. Then she stumbled, fell into the darkness. And she couldn't be sure which one of them, if either, blocked her fall.

Twenty-Seven

I couldn't get Jerry's tortured face out of my mind. Worse, I continued to hear his voice, twisted with guilt. The answer had been clear all along, and I would have seen it sooner if I had only known where to look. Now I had to act before I lost my courage. Before leaving for Luis Vang's, I tried to phone Tamera again, but my call went straight to voicemail. If I didn't reach her soon, I would book a flight to Arizona immediately.

Luis answered the doorbell moments after I rang it, as if he had been waiting for me. Maybe he had been. Perhaps he knew as well as I did that the partial truth is still a lie.

'What a surprise,' he said. 'I was just leaving for work.' His T-shirt and shorts were as immaculate as his glasses, but he looked dressed more for the tennis court than the classroom.

A racquet leaned against the wall as if confirming my suspicion.

'School's out today, Luis.'

'Student teaching is different,' he said. 'I have some administrative work to take care of.'

'Even if you leave, I'll just come back.'

'You have no right to do that,' he said.

'I have a right to the truth.'

'Meaning?' He glanced at his wrist, but I saw no watch there. 'Come on. I have things to do.'

206

'I know why Frank Vera didn't kill Alex,' I said.

'You don't know anything for sure.'

'Alex killed himself, didn't he?'

His sigh was as much an admission as anything he could have said. 'Come in.' He didn't attempt to hide the sudden tears.

We sat at a breakfast nook that looked like a booth in a retro diner. Luis, no longer the thoughtful host, put his head in his hands. Finally, he wiped his eyes. 'There is no point in lying.'

'No, there's not,' I said. 'My partner Farley and I have been interviewing people who went to that camp. So far, only one claimed that the cure worked, and his reason is that he doesn't want to lose his family.'

'Sounds like Alex,' he said. 'That's why you can't let his parents know the truth.'

'I have to,' I told him.

'No, you don't.'

'What happened, Luis?'

'I thought we were broken up, but once he came back, we got together again.' He turned away from me and stared out the window. 'That's when he . . . when it happened. His sister.'

'Carla found you together again?'

He nodded. 'She must have been following us or had us followed. She told Alex he was sick, a pervert, and that she would make sure he got sent back to that place. They would try every cure, she said, as many times as it took.'

I stood up and looked out the window of this peaceful home in this neighborhood of tradition.

207

The trees, most of which had arrived long before the safe structures of Tudors and bungalows, canopied over the rooftops, as if to say no storm could touch the homes for long. Yet harm had come to this neighborhood. Alex Brantingham had killed himself. And his family, maybe others in his community, seemed content to let Frank Vera take the blame.

'It's time to come forward.' I put out my hand to Luis. 'You've got to tell the truth.'

'But my parents!' he said. 'My dad is from Vietnam. My mom is Mexican. Can you imagine how many ways Carla will ruin their lives?'

'She can't have that much power.'

'She's managed to keep even me quiet all this time.'

'Not entirely quiet. Now you can do more than make anonymous calls, Luis. And you might be able to help other people like Jerry. He really believes the so-called treatment failed because there's something wrong with him.'

'I thought Jerry came out thinking he had been helped. I heard he was dating some woman he works with.'

'He did whatever he thought he should. Did you know they wrapped Alex and Jerry in wet sheets in that place? Did you know they let those sheets dry around them so that he could learn control over what they thought were unnatural impulses?'

'I never knew.' Luis reached across the table for my hand. 'Now I have a better understanding of why Alex did what he did. Thank you.'

'They destroyed him,' I said. 'Now, if you are

208

able, I would like you to help me tell the truth about that.'

'I'll need time.' He reminded me of myself, always putting off that uncomfortable, maybe life-changing decision.

'Take as much as you need.' Yet the conviction in his voice encouraged me. 'I do have a favor to ask,' I said.

'You're full of favors.'

'This isn't for me, and it is important.'

'Important like your next story?'

'You know better than that.' I pulled back so that we were eye-to-eye in the booth. 'Life-and-death important.'

'How?'

'Jerry's in trouble. He was kidnapped by family members and sent to that place the way I'm sure Alex was. He's despondent and miserable.'

Finally, Luis seemed to hear me.

'Does Jerry have the same contact information as before?' he asked.

'Yes,' I confirmed. 'Right now, he sounds as desperate as Alex must have been. Help him if you can.'

I left Luis, convinced that he would reach out to Jerry, and that maybe by coming forward, he and Jerry would help many more people in similar situations. Now I had to deal with my own family secret. I waited until Richard's office was closed. I knew he would be there. He always was. Once we were face to face, I would make him tell me the truth about how he had known I hadn't been officially adopted. Just as important, I wanted to

209

know why he hadn't told me any of this while we were together.

Trish Stevenson's Harley was parked outside McCarthy & Stevenson Animal Hospital. She came out just as I arrived and gave me a hug. She had as much energy as the animals she loved, and she was the perfect business partner for Richard. Since I had seen her last, she had spiked her short blond hair.

'Oh, Kit,' she squealed. 'I'm so glad you're back, babe.'

Her glow was natural, a combination of genetically blessed skin and a level of activity that always kept color in her cheeks.

I returned the hug, and then backed away. 'I'm just visiting, Trish,' I said, unsure how else to make her understand.

'Oh. Got it.' She scowled and shoved her hands into the back pockets of her jeans. 'I mean, I'm sorry. You know how much I love you and Richard.'

'It's good to see you,' I told her. 'There's no reason you and I can't still be in touch, you know.'

'That's right,' she said. 'We'll do that. I was so sorry to hear about your mom, Kit.' Her face turned red. 'I mean, about Elaine. She was a good person.'

'Yes, she was.' I couldn't say more.

I watched Trish jump on the Harley and took a moment to compose myself before going inside.

The hospital hadn't changed since the last time I'd been there, the day Richard had let me know our marriage was over. I walked through the

210

entrance, where an elegant Grecian-looking stone tile sign was painted with the word 'Cats'. On the other side of the building was an identical entrance and a sign that read 'Dogs'. Richard and Trish had taken a risk when they'd moved their practice into this pricey shopping center in an upscale community, but it had paid off. Richard liked to brag that, for the first time since he was in college at Davis, California, he was as busy as he wanted to be, which was very busy.

As I stepped into the front office, Chantelle, a former stray and one of two office cats, jumped on to a pillar that was used to hold sign-in information.

'Hey, there,' I said, and stroked her mottled fur. 'You're getting to be quite the fat little princess cat, aren't you?'

'Hello, Kit.' Richard came into the room. 'I've been expecting you.'

'You have?'

He nodded. 'And, by the way, Chantelle is at optimum weight for her build.' He leaned down and slid his index finger under her chin. 'Aren't you, pretty girl? So are you ready for your treats?'

Chantelle wasn't the brightest, but *treat* was one of the three or four words in her vocabulary. She looked up at him as if he were God, the look I'd seen from animals since the day I'd met him. It hurt to recall how that memory made me feel. It hurt to see Chantelle, who obviously remembered me. And, yes, it hurt to be close enough to smell Richard's scent, a sharp whiff of citrus. I knew it well.

He had left a partially full bottle behind when

he moved out. Some nights, when I was especially lonely or scared, I'd spray some on my pillow and instantly smell my marriage – the best parts of it, at least. I didn't do that often, and only at night. Everyone has a trick to get through those hours – alcohol, drugs, television, sex, food. So, I had men's cologne, but now that I smelled it again, on Richard, I was embarrassed, as if I'd been caught, as if somehow he knew.

'I had to come,' I said.

Again, he nodded. 'Because you want me to level with you, right? You want to know how long I knew what Mick told you.'

'Am I that transparent?'

'I can understand how you might wonder, but no, I didn't know for sure. Do you really think I'd keep something like that from you?'

'I don't know, Richard. It's just weird you'd be so certain there was something strange about my parentage and never mention it to me.'

'I couldn't. I didn't know anything for certain.' He leaned against the pedestal. 'I always sensed I was looking at a puzzle with a piece missing.'

'Thanks,' I said, pretending to joke.

'Not you, Kit. Your situation. You know how close I've always been to Mick.'

As different as they were, they seemed to bring out the best in each other. Mick's openness had helped Richard open up; Richard's reserve had made Mick more thoughtful.

'What did he say to you?' I asked.

'It's what he didn't say. Mick has always been guarded about you, and as you know, he is not a guarded kind of guy.'

'And that's what made you suspicious?' I didn't buy it.

'It made me curious,' he said. 'And then there was our wedding, our honeymoon. Don't you remember the problems we had with your passport?'

'Of course. No one could find my birth certificate.' A memory I had misplaced returned to me. I stood hand-in-hand with Richard in the middle of November in a crowded post-office line, not caring about the wait or the cold because we were together. 'You're right. At the time, I just blamed it on the inefficiency of the system.'

'Once all of this stuff about your birth mother began, I put it together,' he said. 'I went to Mick and made it very clear that he'd better be ready to tell the truth.'

'You did that for me?' My lip trembled.

'You wouldn't expect less from me, would you?'

No, I wouldn't. I had counted on Richard, believed we would be together forever. Even now, apart as we were, I knew he was there for me. I would bet my life on it. And I owed him the truth as well as I knew it.

'What I've found out about my parents has hurt me,' I said. 'It's devastated me. But what hurt me more was *not* knowing and yet still not feeling complete. If that is part of what drove you away from me, I'm sorry.'

Richard scooped up Chantelle and put her on her padded perch. Then he faced me, eye-to-eye, the way he did when he demanded complete honesty.

'Kit.' His voice was level, almost stern. Although we didn't touch, I felt his strength as if he were holding my shoulders. 'I miss you.'

'I miss you too, Richard.'

'You haven't moved on?'

'God, no.' I knew he meant Farley and felt myself blush.

My cellphone began to vibrate. 'I'm sorry,' I said. Farley's number glowed on the dial.

Richard frowned.

'I should take it,' I told him.

'It's Farley Black, isn't it?'

'He's my partner, Richard. This could be business.'

'*Could* be,' he repeated as the phone continued its insistent rattling. 'You've made my point for me.'

The vibrating stopped. I felt I'd just lost something valuable. Chantelle leapt on the table and shoved her head under my hand. I stroked her fur and wondered again how a man who could be so good with small creatures could be so poor at communicating with his own wife. Make that separated, soon-to-be ex-wife.

'Happy?' I asked him.

'What do you think?' He put the cat treats into Chantelle's food dish. 'I go with Mick to try to shed some light on your past. Instead, I find you kissing the guy when I drive up. How would you feel?'

'I was hugging him, and even if we were involved, which we're not, it's none of your business.'

'You're right,' Richard said. 'He was always

interested in you. I knew that, but I didn't think you'd turn to him so soon after we split.'

'I did not turn to him, as you put it,' I said, 'and we split, as you put it, because you left me.'

'I asked for a separation because I didn't like where we were headed,' he said. 'But I still care for you, and I'm worried about you. Oh, Kit. You know I still love you.'

If he meant that, if he really did love me, then maybe there was hope for us. Love should be enough, but I had learned the hard way that a couple needed more. Mick and Elaine certainly had.

'Why then?' I continued to stroke Chantelle, but kept my gaze fixed on him. 'And don't you dare start that baby thing.'

'It's not a thing. It's a lifestyle.'

'You said it didn't matter. I spelled it out on our first date.'

'I know,' he said. 'I couldn't believe your gall to make those demands on a first date. Then, later, I thought I could do it. I really did.'

'What changed your mind? Your dad's death?'

He pulled out a chair and sank into it, looking beaten. 'You'll never know how tough it was,' he said, 'but I couldn't lie to you. It's not as if I didn't try to discuss it.'

I felt myself clench up inside, trying to keep his words from touching me. 'I told you how it had to be. I'm not cut out to be a parent. It's not a risk I'm willing to take – at least, not right now.'

'Well, I am,' he said. 'Once I lost my dad, I knew that's what I wanted.'

'More than you wanted me.'

'That's not true.' The anger finally reached his voice, raising it. 'I wanted you more than anything. I couldn't understand why you wouldn't even discuss it. Couples do, you know. They might start out one way, and then change their minds later on.'

'I told you.' I felt as if he were betraying me all over again. 'I *told* you I wasn't ready and wasn't sure I ever would be.'

'But why, Kit? You didn't know about your mother then.'

'But I knew that, as wonderful as my mom could be, I didn't fit into that family. I sensed there was something that they knew about me and I didn't. To want a family, you need to know what a family is, what it is you're passing down.'

That was true. I'd *felt* deceived, even before I realized that I had been. And even now, I wasn't sure I had anything to pass on to anyone else. As the caller on the air that day had said, I had no roots.

My phone went off again, and this time, I knew I couldn't ignore it. 'Sorry,' I told Richard. He stood without moving.

'Hey, Farley,' I said.

'Where are you?'

'With Richard, at the animal hospital.' For a moment, I felt a flash of guilt.

He paused and then said, 'Good.'

That had to be a first. 'What's going on?' I asked.

'It's bad news, Kit. Very bad news.'

I sat down on a cold wooden bench. 'My mother? Kendra?'

'No.' He sighed. 'And the police don't have a positive identification yet.'

'What kind of identification?' I demanded. 'What's happened?'

'They found a body in Arizona.' Another pause, and I knew he was crying. 'They think it's Tamera.'

'God, no, Farley.'

'That's all I know. I'll get in touch with you as soon as I hear more.'

We ended the call, and I rose from the chair.

'Kit.' Richard came to me. 'What happened?'

'Tamera.' I reached up for his face and held it in my hands, the stubble of his beard gritting against my palms. His scent was part of me now. I could smell our marriage, remember the trust, and for this moment, that was all I needed to do. 'They think she's dead.'

'Oh, Kit.' He pulled me close.

I wrapped my arms around his neck and let him hold me.

Twenty-Eight

At first Rena did nothing but sleep. She opened her eyes on occasion to swallow soup or some other tasteless concoction held to her lips, but mostly she slept, trying not to replay what she had seen. Images and voices danced on the surface of her consciousness. A murmur, a whisper slipped into her brain. She was never far away from the scary, conspiring noises on the outskirts of her dreams.

She must have slept with her mouth open. Her tongue felt parched. Her body throbbed with pain. Dim light turned the room to shadows. She turned her head on the pillow, carefully, in case someone were watching her. Dale's side of the bed was empty. That was good. He was still away on the job. How long had he been away? What day was it?

She turned her head to the other side. A man sat in the rocker beside her bed, reading a book. She gasped, and then put her hand to her mouth when she realized it was Leighton.

'Don't be afraid,' he said.

'What day is it?' she asked.

'Friday night.' He put the book on the nightstand. 'Don't you remember? Kendra came over and made soup for us?'

Rena didn't remember any of it. She was going crazy, or he was lying to her. 'Are you sure?' she asked.

'Don't let it bother you.' He turned up the bedside lamp, and she could see his face, his sharp nose and chin line. He leaned down close to her, and his hair gleamed gold where the light hit it. 'Your eyes don't have any more red in them,' he said. 'You're getting rid of the poison.'

'Tell me who that woman was,' she said without moving.

Leighton's eyes met hers. 'They think it's Tamera J. Flowers from Sacramento, California, the radio talk-show host who was supposed to meet with Kendra.'

218

'God, no.' Rena had known it, but to hear it from him brought back that moment of the wrist-watch, the bare arm, the strike of the snake. 'What happened to her?'

'Crushed skull,' Leighton said. Rena cringed, and he put his hand on her arm. 'They don't know who did it.'

'Weren't you out there with her?' she asked.

'No. After I picked her up at the airport, she was going to wait at her hotel until it was time to meet with Kendra. Instead, she left a message with the front desk that she'd gone out to the national park. I followed her there. She must have been killed right before I arrived.'

'Who did it?'

'They don't know.'

'Wasn't anyone else out there?'

'Just you and Kendra. You were the only ones. You must have been right behind me.' His voice had an odd echo, or maybe it was just in her head.

'You know we didn't have anything to do with it.' A shudder crept along her arms.

'Of course not,' he said. 'That's not what I meant.'

'What did you mean then?' She couldn't help it. Her memory had been stolen from her. She had to know what he knew.

'Only that you and Kendra were the only ones there,' he said.

'And you,' she said. 'You were there, weren't you, Leighton? When did you come?'

'I don't know. I wasn't looking at my watch.' She caught the annoyance in his voice, although his expression remained calm. 'My only concern was you.'

'Did you see it?' she asked. 'Did you watch that snake bite me?'

'No.' He looked down, and she couldn't tell what he tried to hide in his eyes.

His words jolted back her memory. She could feel the hot air sucking the breath from her, could see that woman, exactly as she'd seen her in that moment that she'd known she was dead.

Rena shuddered, cold on the surface of her skin, blazing inside. 'Why would anyone want to kill her?' she asked.

'I don't know, Reen.' The word sent her spinning. He hadn't called her that for a long time, not for years. He realized it, too. She could tell from his shocked, sheepish expression. 'I'm sorry,' he said. 'Old habits die hard, I guess, if they die at all.'

'Don't apologize. I know you didn't mean anything by it.'

'It's been so long. I don't know what to call you.'

'Rena will do.'

'Yes. Rena.' He held out his hand. 'Let me help you out of bed. You'll get even stronger once you can walk.'

She looked down at her nightgown. It covered her up pretty well, but she still felt funny hobbling around in it. 'My robe's hanging behind the bathroom door in there,' she said. 'Would you mind getting it for me?'

Leighton stepped into the bathroom and returned with her terry-cloth robe, a dingy pink she'd never really looked at until that moment. Slowly, they walked the house together, and Rena could feel the strength return to her legs. They even walked on the porch, but then she heard a twig break somewhere and insisted that they go inside. With every step they took together, with every helpful gesture Leighton made, the question that had been torturing her was answered. In spite of her earlier doubts, she trusted Leighton.

'Why are you smiling?' he asked. They'd finished off Kendra's soup and were sitting on the love seat while a song Rena had never heard played.

'I'm just thinking how good it is to listen to music again,' she said. 'Who is that?'

'Delbert McClinton. A little rowdy, but he knows about the blues.'

'Don't we all?' she said.

He gave her a lazy grin. 'What do you know about the blues, Reen?'

'As much as anyone, I guess.' Her mouth went dry again. She had almost died. Leighton and Kendra had helped her survive. It seemed normal – even right – to have Leighton in the house like this with her alone, and it seemed just fine to tell him what she knew about the blues.

'Does he hurt you?' he asked.

'Leighton.' She jumped up from the love seat. Her foot exploded into needles of pain, and she collapsed back down.

'I'll kill him if he does. He was always a bully, even back then when he called me a wimp.'

'He was just jealous of you,' she said. Here they were talking about Dale, her own husband, and they weren't even using his name, as if he was a thing instead of a person. 'A bully,' she said. 'Yeah, he was. But it didn't get bad until he knew he'd never be the athlete he'd hoped to be.'

'Why'd you marry him?' He moved his face so close to hers that she could smell his warm, sweet breath.

'Why'd you marry Debby Lynn?'

'I've given that a lot of thought,' he said, 'and the best I can do is to say that, for one brief period of time, she made me feel like a man.'

'I didn't make you feel like a man?'

'You were out of the picture by the time I got together with Debby Lynn.' He looked away toward the wall of shadows. 'I'd seen it happen to other guys in the service. First the letters slowed. Then, the big goodbye letter hit. You never even did that. You didn't give me the courtesy of a goodbye, didn't even care enough to do that, Reen.'

'I did care.' She had buried the memories of how it ended, but now they all bubbled back. She knew Leighton must have hated her for it, and she knew she owed him the truth. 'It was a crazy time,' she said, 'and I don't just mean the war.'

'You married someone else. You married Dale Pace and never told me.'

'I cried,' she said, as if she were still that girl, hugging her pillow and hoping for a miracle. 'I cried for you.'

'And that's supposed to make it all right?' His voice was rough, and she hated herself for making him carry that anger and pain all of those years.

222

'You cried, so that makes it fine that you didn't bother to mention that you married our high school star athlete while your boyfriend, the class nerd, was in the Army?'

'I had a breakdown, Leighton.' She couldn't believe she'd said the words, but it was too late to go back. 'I had a breakdown, and Dale helped me. He stood by me, even when they thought I might be losing my mind. It was only later that he got so bad to me.'

The music had stopped now, and her voice was the loudest thing in the room. She glanced down at her foot, the pink wound puckered like a kiss. She looked up at him, the fury and disbelief in his face, still harsh in the lamplight.

'Why didn't you tell me?'

'I don't remember,' she said. 'That's the truth. For a while, for a long time, I think, they didn't let me talk to anyone.'

He put his arm around her shoulder. It felt warm and right. 'How did you get well?' he asked.

'I'm not sure I did.' Her voice cracked.

His arm closed in around her. 'Why do you say that?'

'I still forget things sometimes,' she said. 'And I'm scared a lot.'

'Everyone's scared.' He made a noise that didn't sound anything close to laughter. 'Everyone sane, that is. I'm glad you told me, though. I never could figure out why you'd leave me for him. I mean, I know he was good-looking and athletic, and I realize he could probably have any girl he wanted, but I didn't think that you would do that.'

'I didn't.' She said it before she thought. Then she motioned for him to help her out of the chair. 'Come on,' she said. 'I want to show you something.'

They walked back into the bedroom, and she settled herself into the rocker and removed the pillow from behind her back. 'Remember this?' she asked.

He shook his head. His expression had changed. He looked lighter and years younger, the lines of doubt erased. 'Should I?'

'Tri-Hi-Y,' she said. 'While the class brain was studying in the library, his girlfriend was sewing this pillow for her hope chest.' She handed it to him, and he ran his hands over its furrowed surface.

'I don't remember it, but if you say it's important, it is.'

'It was purple and white squares,' she said. 'You just stitch the tops of two squares together. That's what makes the smocking.'

He sat on the bed and took a closer look at the pillow. 'I can't say that I remember it exactly, but it does look familiar.'

'Work your fingers inside those stitches on the side,' she said. Her heart sped up, and her breath came fast. Let this be the right thing to do. Let her be right about Leighton. She could see by his eyes that he'd found the new stitches in the pillow.

'There's something buried in here, an envelope.' He pulled it out slowly.

Rena hadn't taken it out since the day she hid it before Dale could find it. She watched as

Leighton lifted it from the pillow, opened it, and took out what was inside.

His face filled with the realization of what he held. 'It's us.'

'At the fair, your senior year.' She choked on the words, and she could see the tears in his eyes. She rose from the chair so that she could see too, and then hit the floor with her foot. She moaned.

'Hold on.' He helped her on to the bed, and they looked at the short string of photos, the two of them in a fair booth, laughing, kissing, and holding their fingers in Vs over each other's heads. Five shots in all. 'We were beautiful,' he said. 'Why didn't I know we were so beautiful?'

She looked hard at the faces of the two young people who had been Leighton and Rena. Time had robbed them of everything except memories. Maybe that's why she had kept the photos and risked what would happen if Dale found them. As painful as the memories were, she wanted them now, and she needed to fill in the blank spaces in her mind. They sat beside each other, Leighton holding the photos. She looked up at him, until he returned her gaze.

'You asked if I cared?' she said. 'There's your answer.'

'Reen.' His voice broke. His arms went around her. She pressed her face against his shoulder. 'How could we screw it up like that?' he said against her hair. 'How did we ever get from there to here?'

'I don't know. Leighton, there's so much I don't know any more.'

He continued to hold her, stroking her hair. 'I'll never let you go again,' he said. 'No matter what.'

'No,' she whispered. 'You know what he'll do.'

His steady hand on her hair quieted her racing heart. 'He's not going to bully you any more,' Leighton said. 'He's never going to bully you again. It's you and me now. It's us, Reen.'

A faraway part of her wanted to believe him, but the part that could think knew it was dream talk. She and Leighton had been given their chance. They couldn't go back.

The needles in her foot relaxed and let up. She felt as if she'd had a cup of one of Kendra's night-time herbal teas. She let herself drift, as if she and Leighton were on a safe little boat together. She slid down on the bed and felt him follow along side of her. Then, she knew what the sensation was, something she'd almost forgotten.

'I feel safe,' she told him.

'I want you to.'

She was lying on her bed, her bed and Dale's, with Leighton. She didn't want to lead him on, but she was so light-headed that she didn't know how to tell him. She pressed her hand against his chest. 'I can't, Leighton. I wouldn't do anything wrong.'

'I know. Don't worry.' He lifted her hand and kissed her fingers.

'Could we just stay here like this for a while?' she asked. 'Would you mind?'

'I'll stay as long as you want me to,' he said, and drew her closer.

And she did want him to stay, just like this, his breath soft and easy on her. She was sleepy, but she wasn't scared any more. She knew Leighton would be here, and she knew he'd take care of her in whatever way he could, until she got stronger. And, Lord, she really did want to get stronger now. Maybe he was right and they really did have a chance.

She felt the terry cloth slip from one shoulder and didn't care. She didn't have to protect herself from Leighton. She wanted just to float on this dream with him as long as she could.

'Safe,' she told him again. 'You make me feel safe.'

'You are safe with me.' He pressed her head against his shoulder, and she knew he would hold her like that all night. 'I won't let anyone hurt you,' he said.

She shuddered just a little, then let herself drift off. Only one person wanted to hurt her, and they both knew who that was.

Rena woke up to the sound of the shower in the morning, and she knew without thinking that it was Leighton. Sure enough, he came out a moment later, in his jeans and the shirt he'd had on the night before, his face pink and soft looking. Her head felt clear, and she couldn't remember any dreams. She did know every word they had said to each other, though. She knew she had shown him the photo strip, which was still on the bedside table.

But what about her? Rena looked down and realized she was still wearing her robe. Good. They must have slept on top of the covers. 'Thank you,' she said.

Leighton came over and sat down beside her on the bed. He smelled of soap and her shampoo. She wished she could bury her face in the smell. 'Let me see your eyes.' He lifted her chin and stared at her. 'Not a trace of red. That's perfect.'

She still felt weak, and she still cringed at the thought of having to deal with Dale when he got back. But she was better, she knew. 'I'm going to be all right,' she told Leighton. 'Thanks for taking care of me. I'm going to be fine now.'

'You sure?' She could tell from the way his eyes stayed on her that in his mind he was still seeing those pictures. She was too.

'I am.' She patted his shoulder. 'Tell Kendra to go take care of her shop. I can get around just fine, and I can feed myself. You guys have already spent too much time taking care of me.'

'I'll tell her.' He moved closer.

'I don't know how to say this, Leighton, but something in me started to heal last night. It was because of you.'

He reached for her, and she turned away from his lips.

'I understand,' he said. 'You're going to be yourself again. Just let me hold you for a minute.'

His chin pressed hard against the top of her head. 'You helped me last night,' she said. 'I think you turned it around, whatever I was going through.'

'I hope so, Reen.' They both laughed.

'Go on, now. And thank you for staying with me.'

He took her shoulders in his hands. 'There's a

lot going on right now, but I'm going to figure it out. Then, once it's behind us, I'm coming back here, and we're going to have a real talk.'

Last night, she would have been afraid, but she was starting not to be. 'You do that,' she said. 'You find out what happened to that poor woman who tried to help Kendra.'

'I intend to,' he said. Then, he leaned down and let his lips brush hers.

'Leighton.' Memories shot through her. Other kisses. Other days, other nights. Promises, wishes. She thought she'd had only one strip of photographs. Instead, she had a whole lifetime locked in her mind. 'Come back soon.' Wasn't that what she'd said before he'd left before? Was she really saying it again?

'I will,' he said, and kissed her again, a little longer this time, and Rena had to be the one to pull away. He squeezed her shoulder. 'But this time you'd better be waiting for me.'

Twenty-Nine

Tamera was dead. I couldn't forgive myself for letting her go to Arizona on my behalf, and I tried to make sense out of her death. After losing my mom, I had felt numb. Now, I realized how raw that pain still was.

Despite my own grief and guilt, the airport that day had an optimistic feel as I waited with Richard for my flight to Phoenix. Richard wore jeans and a sweater, and his hair was smashed down from the baseball cap.

'Mom and I were in an airport the last time I saw her,' I said. 'I just assumed there would be a next time. Now, she's dead, Tamera has been murdered, and—' I couldn't finish. 'Tamera,' I managed to get out. 'I let her go in my place so that I could do my stupid radio show.'

'Don't, Kit.' Richard put his arm around me, and I tried to control my trembling. 'She wanted to go. You didn't make her.'

'How do you know that?' I asked, and then I realized the truth. 'You were still in touch with her?'

'We talked sometimes,' he said, his voice guarded.

'Of course. You were good friends.' How self-centered I had been to assume that Richard would break off his relationships with my family and friends just because he'd broken off his relationship with me.

'Tamera was protective of you,' he said, 'and because of what happened when she tried to find her father, she was determined to help you find your biological mother.'

And she had died trying.

'I never dreamed anyone would kill her,' I said, forcing myself to keep my voice low. 'Why would anyone want to harm Tamera? I never should have let her go to Arizona.'

'Maybe it has nothing to do with you,' Richard said, as if trying to convince himself. 'Maybe it was random. Drug-related; a robbery, maybe.'

I felt the strength drain out of me. 'I don't

believe that. Something's going on. Somehow this is all connected.'

'Let me get you some coffee,' he said.

I nodded and wondered what he was doing back in my life. One minute he never wanted to see me again. Now, he was offering to fetch my coffee. It was temporary, though. I knew that, too. We had too many differences to give each other more than momentary comfort. 'Coffee would be great,' I said. 'Black, no sugar.'

'I haven't forgotten.'

He said it lightly, but I felt a twinge I couldn't identify. Maybe it was just the surreal quality of the airport. Maybe it was the confusing chemistry between us – two people who'd once been a couple, but who were now somewhere between that and being the polite, very separate individuals divorce would render us.

I watched him walk away, the easy gait of a man who looked a lot more open than he was: a man who let in very few people.

I started to phone Farley, but before I could, I realized there was someone else I needed to call. Matthew Breckenridge, the man who had apparently replaced Mick in my mother's life, had tried to contact me, as he had promised, regarding my mom's autopsy. He was the one who had dealt with the doctors and, unlike Mick, knew the details. I needed to know more about how she died, why her heart stopped. Surely there was no connection between her death and Tamera's murder, but I couldn't take any chances.

Breckenridge's voice registered surprise when I announced myself. 'I didn't think you would

231

return my call,' he said, 'but I'm glad you did.'

Richard returned with the coffee, and I took the flimsy cup from him, gesturing with the phone. He nodded and stood behind me, as if protecting me from an invisible attack.

'I need to talk to you about my mom,' I told Breckenridge. 'About her death. I don't know how to ask this, but are you sure, are the doctors sure, that she died of natural causes?'

'Oh, my, yes.' He seemed shocked, but I was the one who slopped coffee on to my hand.

'How are you so sure?'

'You don't know,' he said. 'Do you?'

I wiped my hands on my jeans and listened, afraid of what he was going to say next. I felt Richard's fingers on my shoulders and realized how tense I was. 'Don't know what?' I asked.

'I'm sorry. Elaine was so private, so proud. I'm not surprised she hid her illness from you.'

'I didn't know anything about an illness,' I said. My thoughts flew haphazardly. I remembered that she'd always seemed to spend an inordinate amount of time on doctors' visits. I'd even wondered if she were a hypochondriac. Then, there were those hospital stays. But they were for cosmetic surgery. At least, that's what she'd said.

'She had a difficult time with it, especially because she was such a perfectionist,' Breckenridge told me. 'We were lucky to have her as long as we did.'

'She never told me,' I said.

'I'm sorry. You know how she was. If she didn't speak it, then it didn't exist. Besides, it was an extremely rare blood disorder. I can send you details if you wish.'

'Did Mick know?' As I asked, I remembered that Mick had tried to tell me, but I was too overcome with grief to believe that he knew more about my mother's health than I did.

'Of course he knew,' Breckenridge said.

'She told him but not me?'

'It wasn't like that, Kit. Before they married, Elaine told him that they'd never be able to have their own biological children. Mick – your father – is a good man.'

'Yes,' I repeated. 'A good man.'

'My relationship with Elaine started out as purely business, so I already knew everything before we . . . before . . .' His voice faltered, and then broke.

And he had still fallen in love with her. There was more to Breckenridge than I'd guessed.

'I'll want to talk to you again,' I said, 'but I have a plane to catch right now.'

'Contact me anytime, Kit.' I could see why my mom had trusted him. His manner exuded strength. 'I'm only sorry I didn't get to know you when Elaine was alive.'

After we ended the call, I sat there holding my phone in one hand, my coffee in the other. Richard came around from behind me and sat on the seat next to mine. 'What's the matter?' he asked.

I had to board, which was good because I couldn't stay there any longer. 'My mom died of a rare blood disorder,' I said. 'It's as if everything I believed in is a lie.'

'It's not,' Richard said. 'We're not. And your

233

mom wanted to be superwoman. That's probably why she didn't tell you. She thought she could conquer anything, and she did, for years.'

Part of me was furious, but part of me understood what he and Breckenridge had tried to say. In any case, I needed to go to Tucson and try to find out what had happened to Tamera. 'I need to go,' I said. 'The lawyer, Leighton Coulter, is supposed to meet me at the Tucson airport.'

He put his arms around me. 'Why don't I try to get on the next flight and meet you there? I don't want you to be alone.'

As much as the idea appealed to me, I shook my head. I'd have enough to deal with without trying to sort out my feelings with Richard. 'I'll be all right,' I said and gave him a peck on the lips, the first kiss we had exchanged since our nightmare began.

The short flight to Phoenix was fine, as flights go, especially since I'd been trying to digest the information about Elaine's illness and trying to sort out how Tamera possibly could have been killed.

Once I got on the plane from Phoenix to Tucson, however, I was lucky I hadn't eaten lunch. The plane bucked and twisted all the way to Tucson. Several passengers said it was because of the weather, because of the heat. I didn't know. I just wanted to be out of that sky.

Leighton Coulter met me at the gate. Although he had to be close to fifty, it was clear from the sloping muscles beneath his blue denim shirt that he worked out. His faded blond curls fell on to his neck. Only on a second look could I see the gray ones blended in.

'How was your flight?' he asked.

His voice wasn't what I expected. Southern, serious, and studied, it was a country-lawyer voice, and this man no doubt used the soft drawl to mask his motives and anything else he wanted to hide.

'Not the best,' I said. 'But I'm not here because I enjoy flying. What can you tell me about my friend's death?'

'Not much.' He sighed, as if remembering something too terrible to speak of. 'I'll share what I do know in the car.'

'Where are we going?'

'To see Kendra Trafton.'

My mouth went dry. 'Yes. I mean, thank you.' Nothing I could say seemed sufficient.

I sat in the seat beside him and realized I was finally going to meet this woman who was supposed to be my biological mother. Maybe the newspaper photos of her daughter were misleading. Maybe I'd really be seeing my mother in less than an hour.

'Did Tamera meet with Kendra?' I asked.

'She never had a chance to.'

'What happened?'

'She left her hotel to meet with someone. When Kendra and her friend found her . . .'

'Go ahead,' I said.

'It's grisly.'

'I can handle it.' I shoved up my dark glasses so that he couldn't see the tears in my eyes.

'Kendra and her friend Rena Pace went to Tamera

235

Flowers' hotel. The desk clerk told them Ms Flowers had gone to Saguaro Park. When they got there they found her. She had been bludgeoned.'

I gasped.

'I'm so sorry. There's no other way to say it.'

'Who was she going to meet?' I asked.

Leighton's face settled into sadness. 'Me.'

'Why you?' I managed to ask as we bumped along the narrow road.

'Because she asked me to meet her there, and because I'm Kendra's attorney.'

'Do you think she's my mother?'

'I don't know anything about that.'

'With all due respect, Mr Coulter, I think you do.'

'Why would I? She was living in California a long time and only just moved back.' Beneath his cool demeanor, I could sense tension. 'I've told you I don't know anything. I'm just trying to facilitate the meeting. If you want to go head to head, we can do that, too.'

'I don't want to go head to head.'

'Good.'

'I'm just nervous,' I said.

'I know.' His voice went soft, gentle. 'It might have been better if you hadn't come.'

'I had to. Tamera was killed trying to meet Kendra on my behalf.'

'I know. I met your friend's plane. I was there right after her body was found.'

I looked at him again, trying to read beneath his stony features. 'How, exactly, do you fit in here? In my story, I mean? The detective agency contacted you, I assume.'

'I'm sure they contacted numerous attorneys in Arizona,' he said. 'I just happened to be the one who knew Kendra. And, of course, I knew about her daughter Jillian's disappearance. Kendra still lived in Buckeye when that happened.'

We began to approach Tucson, but the landscape didn't change much. It reminded me of home, except for the cacti, which looked artificial, almost as if it had been placed there to enhance the ambience.

'I read how Jillian disappeared,' I said. 'Kendra had stopped to make a phone call. Was she ever found?'

'Not a trace,' Leighton said. 'It ruined Kendra's life. She hired detectives, psychics, went off on one wild goose chase after another. It ultimately broke up her marriage.'

'I wish I could be that girl,' I said.

'So do I.' His voice sounded wistful.

'But I saw her photo, and she didn't look anything like my own baby pictures,' I told him.

'Photos can be deceiving, especially at that age.' He glanced over at me, as if trying to imagine me in one of those shots of Jillian Trafton. 'One thing's for sure – Kendra didn't put her baby up for adoption. If you're Jillian Trafton, you were taken.'

'How does she feel about my coming?' I asked.

'It's hard to know how Kendra feels.' His smile lacked joy. 'But she's been through so much that she knows not to expect anything.'

'You're friends, then?'

'Since high school.'

A question had been nagging me since we'd

started talking. Finally, it found words. 'Do you know who Kendra was calling?' I asked.

'When?'

'That day when her daughter disappeared. She stopped to make a phone call and left the child in the car. Who was she calling on that phone?'

'What difference would that make?' He pumped the brake, and we came to a sudden stop at a red light. His lips were tight, and he swallowed, as if suddenly thirsty.

None, I thought, and almost wished I hadn't asked. But I knew what he was going to say before he spoke, and I knew I'd have to go forward.

'She was calling me.'

'Why?'

'I don't remember. It was a long time ago.' He parked along a sidewalk lining old-fashioned shops that now housed an aromatherapy soap store, a shiatsu treatment center, a boutique, and what looked like a head shop. 'This block is our San Francisco,' he said. 'Come on, let's go inside.'

Although I believed he had lied to me about the phone call, I didn't have time to question him further. I got out of the car, and then realized someone was standing in the doorway of the store. As we drew closer, she moved into the light. She was a large-boned woman, her dark hair pulled back from her face. She wore a long, sleeveless black-and-white print dress and dark glasses, which she removed as we approached.

There was something magical about her, an energy that bordered on charisma. Her eyes were accepting and friendly, yet the way she studied me made me want to squirm.

'Kit,' she said, 'I'm Kendra. I'm so sorry about your friend.'

'Did you meet Tamera?' I asked. 'Were you there?' I could barely move my lips while I was searching her face for any similarity I could find. 'Do you know how it happened?'

I could see that she was searching my face as well. 'No more than Leighton knows,' she said, and then she wiped her eyes and stepped back from me. 'This is the last thing I expected. It did cross my mind, but I didn't believe it could be true.'

I bit my lip, well aware what would come next, realizing I'd wasted my hopes and my time to chase a story that wasn't true. 'You're not my mother,' I said. 'Are you?'

'No.' She smoothed her hair and kept her gaze steady on mine. 'I wanted to be. I hoped you'd be my Jillian. But I can see it now.' She hugged me, a warm, good hug, full of the scent of herbs. 'I'm not your mother, little girl,' she said. 'But I know who is.'

Leighton gasped. 'What are you talking about, Kendra? What do you mean you know who her mother is?'

Kendra linked one arm through his and her other through mine. 'Come on. I've been doing a lot of thinking, and I know what we need to do.'

'You know my mother?' My voice was shaking. My mind filled with images, words, hope. Most of all hope. I was a child again, giddy with

239

wonder. 'Who is she? Where is she? Does she know I'm here?'

'She doesn't even know you're alive,' Kendra said. 'Kit, she thinks you're dead.'

Thirty

Rena had tried to walk Leighton out when he left, but her foot felt numb and full of fluid, and he insisted that she stay in her bedroom. That was what she did, lying against the pillows that still smelled of him, trying to put the pictures together in her mind. She really wanted to remember now everything she'd forgotten, and she wanted to forgive herself for everything she remembered. She needed to.

The front door slammed shut like a gunshot. Rena managed to get to her feet. Leighton wasn't a door-slammer. He must have forgotten something.

'What is it?' She stepped into the hall.

'What the hell do you think it is?' Dale stood like a bull between the front door and her. He seemed to grow bigger each time she saw him, and now he looked ready to explode.

'What are you doing back?' she asked, barely able to get the words out. 'Did you hear what happened?'

'I know what happened, all right.' Dale started toward her, his eyes a milky blue, the way they were when he'd been drinking, but she could tell

240

he hadn't been. This wasn't drink that distorted his features. It was anger.

'I was bitten by a rattler,' she said. 'I almost died.'

'Maybe you should have.' He came closer, and she could smell his sour coffee breath. No, her husband hadn't been drinking. This meanness was all him. Her mind was clear. Something had happened to her last night, and she wasn't afraid any more.

'A woman was murdered,' she said.

'Maybe she deserved to die.'

'What are you talking about? She was trying to help Kendra find her daughter. I found that poor woman's body, and when I screamed, a rattler struck me.'

'Keep talking,' he said. 'Nothing's going to get you off the hook.'

'What do you mean?'

'I mean this.' He slammed his fist into the wood lining the doorway.

She'd forgotten how strong he was. But she couldn't think about that right now. She had to think about Leighton. She had to think that she was safe and that she didn't have to be afraid any longer.

'Don't, Dale,' she said. 'I've been through too much.'

'Too much with Leighton?' His face loomed close now, and his expression was twisted and evil. 'I didn't get the job in Phoenix. In fact, I've been parked behind the store, and I've been watching the house. I know he stayed here. I watched him drive away.'

Something wasn't right about Dale. He was lying, maybe, or not telling all of the truth. She refused to draw back from him and forced herself to meet his hateful eyes.

'You've been watching since when, Dale?'

'What business is that of yours?' he demanded, his eyes bulging.

'You say you've been watching. I'm just curious why you didn't see Kendra and Leighton drag me in from the hospital and sit by my bed until I could swallow food. Where were you then, Dale?'

'None of your business.' He tugged at his shirt, and she glimpsed something on his neck, something too purple, too blotchy to be a regular bruise.

'What woman's been kissing you on your throat?' she asked. Lord, had she gotten that brave? He'd slap her for sure now.

He pulled his shirt collar up higher. 'Don't start pointing fingers. You aren't as pure as you pretend. You never were.'

'That's not true.'

'You're the one with the guilty conscience, Rena. I know what went on in here with you and Leighton Coulter. I knew that wimp would come back some day and try to mess up our lives.'

'He didn't try to mess up anything,' she said, 'and he doesn't want to.' Maybe there was still a way to calm him down. She wasn't sure, though, not any more. 'The memories are starting to come back,' she said. 'I'm getting it all back, Dale.'

'Well, goody for you.' He ran his hand through her hair the way he did when he was ready to grab it too hard and pull her up to him. 'Just know that I'm the only reason you didn't end up in the crazy house.'

'What do you mean?'

'Just that.'

His smirk reminded her of how much she'd feared him. She would never fear him again.

'I never belonged in the crazy house,' she said.

'You don't think so?'

'No. Of course I didn't. Why would you even suggest that?'

'Because I know about you, the real you. I know about all the stuff you forgot.' He moved closer to her. 'You are losing your mind again. You know that, don't you?'

'I'm not.'

'Then tell me why I leave the house to find honest work, and you have a new guy sleeping here.'

'He's not a new guy. He saved my life. He and Kendra.'

'Yeah, right.' He moved closer to her, his eyes so watery that there was barely any color at all.

She thought of the snake again. She hadn't seen its eyes, but imagined they couldn't have been more terrible than these. 'Leave me alone, Dale. I mean it.'

'I'll leave you alone when I'm good and ready. I might just leave you altogether.'

'That's fine.' What had taken control of her? Somehow, she actually had the nerve to talk to him like this – without fear. 'That's just fine, Dale.'

Color rushed to his face. His huge chest heaved.

Then a strange smirk twisted his mouth, and he looked away toward the chair. 'What's that?'

She turned, but before she could see what he was talking about, he shoved her away and grabbed the pillow. Rena stepped back and edged toward the door. She'd left the photos out on the table. *Oh, God, don't let him find them.* 'You're crazy,' he said. 'You know you're crazy. And you tried to kill yourself once before.'

'I didn't!' She realized she'd screamed it.

He snatched up the strip of photos from the table, and his mouth fell open. She'd seen that look only once or twice, and only when they were very young. 'So it *was* him,' he said. 'It was that wimp Leighton all the time.'

'I didn't see him in all those years, I swear. I've been faithful to you.'

'You've been faithful to him,' he shouted. 'That's why you kept his picture.'

He ripped the photo strip in half, and she screamed. Then he started toward her.

Rena ran, still screaming, through the house, through the back door. She'd flag down a car, do anything to get away from him. She hit a rock, and pain jabbed through her foot. She fell and scraped her hand. No time to think about the pain. She struggled to her feet.

'Don't try it,' Dale yelled. She looked up in time to see a boot tip connect with her side. It felt as if it had cut her in half, and she caved into her stomach, trying to roll away from him.

'No, Dale.'

Another kick. She tasted dirt. Dale stood over her, holding his gun. He shoved it toward her.

244

She cringed and drew back. He couldn't do this, not to his own wife. A car pulled up, and a woman's shriek broke through the buzzing in her head.

'Dale!' Bryn's voice. Yes, there she was, hair flying, her expression as full of terror as her voice was. 'Are you crazy?' she screamed. 'What are you doing?'

He moved his aim away from her, but continued to hold the gun. 'Go inside, Bryn. We're on the same team, remember?'

'I'm not going anywhere.' She stepped between him and Rena, and then looked down at her with wide eyes that didn't seem able to focus.

'I told you she's crazy,' he said. 'She's right on the edge, ready to crack.'

'I'm not,' Rena whispered. 'He's trying to push me over the edge, but I won't let him. He's not strong enough.'

'Inside, Bryn,' Dale said again. 'Let me take care of this out here.' It was the voice that had always sent Rena running, but Bryn didn't budge. She raked the hair out of her eyes and continued to stare at Rena.

'Help me,' Rena said to her. 'Please.'

'You didn't tell me you were going to hurt her,' Bryn said, her voice rising. 'You said you were going to leave her!'

Rena's tears dribbled into the dust. Dale had wanted her to have another breakdown so that he could be with Bryn. 'It won't work,' she told him. It wouldn't work. He would never be the boy he wanted to be again, even if he did go off with Bryn.

'Shut up,' he said. 'Go on in, Bryn, honey. I need you in the store.'

'*My* store,' Rena said.

He turned around from Bryn, and Rena could see the jiggle beneath his T-shirt. He wasn't just big any more. He was soft, too.

'It should've been mine,' he said. 'Just like your two-faced father to leave it to you, after all the help I gave him.'

Beside him, Bryn began to sob softly. 'I'm going to call my daddy,' she said.

'Don't even think about that. You know Leighton's always hated me. He'll try to stop us from being together.'

'Then leave Rena alone,' she said. 'Let's go inside and talk, Dale. Help me understand what's happening.'

'He's trying to kill me.' Rena knew with a shudder that this was what was really happening out here. Her vision began to blur. She needed to clear her head and get back on her feet before Dale hurt her again.

'That's insane.' Dale leaned down and whispered to Bryn. Rena could make out the words 'breakdown' and 'suicide'.

Bryn finally stepped away from him. 'Well, all right,' she said slowly. 'But don't do anything to her.'

'Please,' Rena moaned to her. 'Please stay.' Bryn was Leighton's daughter. She had to have some of his decency. She couldn't just walk off like this.

'Hurry up,' Dale said. 'Get back to the store. Come on, get going.'

Bryn turned, and Rena watched, drained of hope as the girl hurried off toward the store.

'Now, then,' Dale said. He smiled at her and then at the gun.

'Please.'

'You were in love with him,' Dale said, and moved closer to her. 'I was the football star, but you wanted him. I took you anyway, even though I knew it was his baby, not mine, you lost.'

Nothing could help her now. 'I'm not ashamed of it,' she said. 'I'm only sorry I let them talk me into marrying you.'

'So am I.' He crouched down beside her. 'I took care of that one bitch trying to poke her nose in our business. You'll be easy.'

'Bryn will tell.' What did he mean he took care of that bitch? Was Dale responsible for murdering that poor woman she had found?

'You're right.' He cocked his head, as if thinking through what she had said. Then he nodded. 'Bryn will tell, all right. I just have to take care of her too.'

Thirty-One

We rounded the desolate corner that Leighton Coulter said would lead to the gas and convenience store. No, I shouldn't say Leighton Coulter. I should say my father. I could see the resemblance now in our hair color, the shapes of our faces. His eyes were still blank with disbelief.

Kendra's news had almost flattened us both. Now, we sat side-by-side in the back seat as Kendra drove down the narrow, dusty road. I squinted at the stark landscape and attempted to find a structure.

Leighton looked at me again, as if trying to make sure I was who Kendra had said I was. 'It's going to be a few more minutes before we're there.'

I nodded, knowing I already trusted those eyes. 'I can't believe this,' I told him.

'Neither can I. They told me our baby died.'

'She almost did,' Kendra said, and met my eyes through the rear-view mirror. 'You were so early, they didn't think you had a prayer. Rena's folks didn't know she was pregnant, so when she went into labor, I signed her into the hospital under my name, thinking we could keep them from finding out.'

'But they did find out,' Leighton said. 'What happened, Kendra? Not even Gerald and Anna could be so unforgiving that they'd get rid of their own grandchild.'

'I think they must have convinced themselves that it was best for all involved,' Kendra said. 'Rena was fragile. After they told her she lost the baby, she just shut down. Dale stepped in to save the day, and all of a sudden, Gerald and Anna had enough money to buy the gas and convenience store.'

'Twenty thousand,' I said, trying to make a joke of it. 'That's how much Mick and Elaine, my parents, paid for me.'

Kendra met my eyes in the mirror again. Hers

were luminous, full of goodness. I knew the kind of person Rena, my mother, had to be to have her for a friend. 'I'd hoped and hoped you might be my Jillian, but the minute I saw you, I knew who you were,' Kendra said. 'And I knew who your parents were.'

'You look just like your mother, Kit,' Leighton said.

'And you, Leighton, too,' Kendra said. 'She has your eyes.'

And in this vehicle of strangers plowing through the desert, these strangers talking about my eyes, my family, my genes, I just laughed, bubbling with joy unlike any I had ever known. I belonged somewhere, I really did. I had a past and a future. My life wasn't just present tense. For the first time, I was able to release some of my anger. How could I be angry when I had a family, not only a mother, but a father?

Tamera should be here for this, I thought. She had died for no reason, trying to help me.

At that moment, I wished I could tell Elaine how grateful I was to her for leaving me the letter and the name Kendra Trafton. Without that, I would not have found this place and these people. She must have known that her health was failing, and she wanted to finally give me the truth.

Kendra's gaze continued to flit up to the mirror, as if she were checking my reaction.

'You're watching me,' I said to her reflection.

'Because I'm happy. I can't tell you how happy I am that you found us.'

I leaned forward and touched her shoulder. 'I'm

sorry it didn't work out the way you'd hoped. Your daughter, I mean.'

She sighed and shook her head. 'It was my own fault. I'll pay for it the rest of my life.'

'It was not your fault,' Leighton said.

'I never should have left Jillian in the car, not even for a moment.'

'You were trying to do the right thing,' he insisted. 'You did do the right thing. The moment Rena told you she was pregnant and giving birth, you drove to the nearest phone booth and called me. It was just too late for me to do anything. I was already headed for boot camp. The next thing I heard—' He turned to me and touched my face with fingers so light that I could barely feel them on my flesh. 'But it was a lie. You're here now, and we will be a family, I promise you.'

'There it is,' Kendra said.

The structure I had been seeking suddenly appeared: a tumbledown country store with an old-fashioned gas station in front. Its odd-shaped pumps looked as if they belonged in some fifties monster movie. A battered sign in front, black on a white background, announced 'Gerald's Gas'.

'It's not much,' Kendra said quickly, 'but the house is nice.'

'Is Dale still out of town?' Leighton asked.

'I'm not sure for how much longer,' Kendra told him.

They pulled into the drive. I didn't know how I should feel, didn't know how I should look. I wore only a black tank top and faded jeans. Was this how I was going to meet my mother?

'I'm scared.' I realized the fear wasn't new, but something I'd buried for many years, maybe my whole life.

Leighton put his arm around me. 'You're beautiful,' he said. 'You are going to change Rena's life, maybe even save it.'

'One thing's for sure,' Kendra told him. 'Rena leaves with us, today. I should have insisted on that sooner.'

'You just got back this year,' Leighton told her.

'I still should have.' Kendra's voice rose as she spoke, and I figured she was thinking about her daughter.

She pulled to a stop right outside the store. I started to ask where Rena was, but the words didn't get out. A young woman with long blond hair ran from the back, screaming. Kendra opened the door and started to get out.

'My daughter,' Leighton told me, then did a double take as he realized what he was saying. This girl, then, this shapely, young and very, very scared girl, had to be my half-sister.

She ran to the car and grabbed Leighton. 'He's going to kill Rena,' she said. 'Oh my God. He's going to kill her. I pretended to go along with it so I could call you.'

'Dale?' Leighton asked.

'Yes. Oh, Dad, I screwed up big time. He wanted to go away with me, get rid of her. He said divorce, that she was crazy. But she isn't.' She choked out tears and clung to Leighton. 'Hurry, Dad,' she said. 'He has a gun.'

Leighton shot through the drive leading to the back. Kendra followed. I did the same as I looked

251

at this young woman who resembled me so completely.

'What's your name?' I asked.

'Bryn.' She drawled it out. 'Who are you? Why are you here?'

'Bryn,' I said, 'I think I'm your half-sister.'

'No. How?' Then she looked at me, grabbed my shoulders, and pulled me closer. 'Oh my God,' she said. 'Rena Pace, that lady out back there. She's your mother, isn't she?'

'Yes.' I could barely speak.

'She hates me,' Bryn said. 'But I didn't realize what I was doing to her, how wrong it was.'

'Don't worry about that now. Come on.'

'My dad will stop it.' Bryn looked in the direction in which the others had fled. 'Our dad, I guess,' she corrected herself.

'Yes.' Our dad.

'Do you have a phone with you?' she asked.

I nodded. 'We need to call for help.'

'I don't know. I thought I loved Dale, but what he's doing, it's not right.'

'Who's Dale?' I asked as we ran up the drive.

'Rena's husband. He always said she was crazy.' Bryn shouted the words over her shoulder. 'He thought she'd go nuts, and we could be together. That's not what's happening, though. He has her on the ground.'

My mother, on the ground. I had to do something. I fumbled for my phone. 'We've got to call the police right now,' I said. 'Do you have a gun? Any kind of weapon?'

Bryn shook her head. 'Dale has the only one.'

I looked around frantically. Against the side of

the building, next to the faucet, I spotted several garden tools stacked in a neat row. Hoe, rake, clippers. And next to them, a tire iron. It wasn't much, but it was better than nothing. I picked up the tire iron and followed Bryn.

I wasn't ready for what I saw in the backyard. A large man stood poised with a gun in his hand. Beneath him, in the dirt, a small blond woman in a pink robe cowered. My mother. Rena Pace, her dusty face streaked with tears. I started to run to her, but Kendra held me back.

'Let Leighton settle this, and don't worry. Rena's going to be fine.'

'What the hell is going on?' Leighton demanded as he marched toward Dale.

'Butt out, Coulter. This is between me and my wife.'

'Leighton, be careful,' Rena called out.

I was terrified for her, afraid I'd lose her after I'd come all this way.

The big man's boot shot into her side, and she screamed. So did I, as if he'd kicked that steel toe into me, as well.

Leighton jumped him with an animal noise that sent chills through me. I called emergency, and when a voice answered and tried to confirm our address, I gave as much information as I could. Then I added, 'We need help out here. A man is trying to kill a woman, and the woman is my mother.'

Leighton was thinner but in better shape than Dale Pace. They struggled on the ground, and for a moment, I thought Leighton had him. Then, Dale got on top of him as Rena squirmed away.

'He's strangling him,' I shouted.

'Stop him,' Rena called out.

Kendra tore across the distance and attached herself to Dale Pace's meaty shoulders. He screeched, and I realized she'd jammed her fingernails into his flesh. I could see the blood. He rose, shook her loose, and in one slow, horrible moment, as she tumbled to the ground, he grabbed Leighton by the neck and placed the gun to his head.

'No,' I shouted. Before I knew it, I was there, the tire iron in my hand. I struck Dale Pace over the head with it, gagging at the sound it made, yet unable to stop.

Blood running down his face, he wrenched it away from me. As I stood there, ready to attack again, he fired the gun, and Leighton fell.

'You killed him, Dale,' Bryn shouted. 'You killed my father.'

'It was an accident. Self-defense. You saw what happened.' Dale dropped the gun. Blood dripped down his face. He tried to wipe it away. 'Start the car. We're getting out of here.'

'No. You killed my father.' She flew at him, and he tried to push her away. 'I wouldn't go anywhere with you.'

For that distracted moment, Dale didn't realize how close I crouched to the gun. I reached out for it, knowing what I must do. Someone had to stop him. Before I reached it, another hand snatched it up like a claw.

'You killed that woman, Tamera, didn't you?' Kendra, her shirt torn and bloody, tried to take aim.

Dale Pace spotted her, pushed Bryn away, and

tried to wrestle the gun away from Kendra. 'Tamera thought she could come mess up our lives, try to tell some kind of truth that would hurt more than anything,' he shouted.

'How'd you kill her?' Kendra danced just far enough from his grasp. 'A rock to the head? A gun butt?'

'A rock. And the gun butt. You happy now, bitch?'

For a moment, it looked as if they were dancing. Dale Pace had Kendra in a bear hug, pulling her tighter. Then the gun fired. Kendra screamed. Dale staggered back, his features twisted, his hands on his throat. Then he dropped to the ground a few feet away from Leighton. Kendra stood alone, staring down at the gun.

Thirty-Two

Rena lifted herself from the dirt. Leighton lay before her, his head bleeding. The blond girl crouched over him.

'He's breathing,' the blond shouted.

Where had this girl come from? Her long, curly hair was splashed with blood, yet she didn't seem bothered by it. And she was right about Leighton. Although still unconscious, he was taking in shallow breaths.

'Somebody call the police,' Rena said.

'We did.' Bryn knelt beside her, tears streaking her face.

Kendra stood over Dale's body. Slowly, she put one hand over her mouth. Then, her gaze met Rena's, and she shook her head. 'I'd do it again,' Kendra said, and then she collapsed into tears. Bryn began to sob as well.

'You're going to be all right now,' Rena said, stroking Bryn's hair. 'You didn't know about him. Neither of us ever knew about him.'

'I'm the one who should be shot,' Bryn said. 'I brought all of this on. Please, please don't let my daddy die.' She begged it as if Rena had the power to make that decision.

'He's not going to die,' she said. 'He can't.'

How much later was it? A few minutes? An hour? How long had this other girl been standing there watching her? Rena had been so concerned about Leighton and Bryn that she hadn't been aware of anyone else.

Rena looked over at her again. The girl started crying, not a sound, just a steady wet stream of tears streaking through the cuts on her face. The black top she was wearing had been torn down one side. She was a fighter for such a tiny thing, but now she looked like a little girl, standing there as if not sure what she should say.

Rena moved closer to her. Her foot felt as if it had been seared. She wanted to cry, too, but she wasn't exactly sure why any more. There was something about this girl that was so sad. The girl worked her mouth, as if trying to find her voice, as if trying to tell Rena something important.

'What is it?' Rena asked.

'I can't believe it,' the girl finally managed to say. 'I just can't believe it.'

Rena couldn't turn away from those eyes, pale yet cloudy, strange but familiar. She stepped closer until they were face-to-face, until she could smell sweat. Her own or the girl's? She wasn't sure any more.

'Where did you come from?' she asked. 'Who are you?'

The girl smiled and put out her arms. 'Don't you know?'

Thirty-Three

Leighton survived his wounds. Dale Pace did not.

Kendra was not going to be charged, as her shooting Dale was a clear case of self-defense. He had died almost instantly. Through a daze, Rena had asked if he'd suffered and seemed to relax when someone told her he had not.

Dale had been willing to do anything to get rid of Rena, and he'd been convinced that Leighton had made up the story of Kendra's daughter as a way of getting back in Rena's life. Besides, he couldn't afford to let anyone get too close to Rena. I also suspected that Dale had been the one to phone our station with the news that I could not possibly be Kendra's daughter.

Soon after I'd tried to introduce myself, Rena had collapsed and was able to focus on what was happening around her for only moments at a time. She was dehydrated, they said, and weak. But other than the injuries sustained from

Dale, she would be fine. My mother would be fine.

Bryn and I sat together in the hospital waiting room. Neither of us had showered or changed, but we had encouraged each other to share a dry tuna sandwich an hour before. I couldn't imagine what in Bryn's life had forced her to seek what she perceived as strength in Dale Pace, but I couldn't judge her. In the time we'd sat there together, she had told me how she was raised, and I thanked every god who tended to such matters that I'd had the relative stability of Elaine and Mick.

'What are you thinking?' Bryn asked me just then.

I looked into her slate-blue eyes and knew I could never lie to her. 'Relative stability,' I said. 'I guess it's about the only type there is.'

Here I was on a well-worn tweed sofa, looking at this young woman who bore such a resemblance to me and to her father that anyone could pick us out of a crowd as family. And to think we almost never met.

'Do you think Rena's going to be all right now?' Bryn asked in a shaky voice. 'I mean, in her head.'

'I hope so.' At this point, I wasn't sure of anything. 'According to Kendra, most of Rena's problems were brought about by Dale's abuse.'

'And I just added to it.' She tried to blink back tears. 'I hope she makes it, Kit.'

'So do I. And just from what I saw of her, I can tell my mother's tough.' I covered my lips with my hands.

'That's the first time, isn't it?' Bryn asked me. 'The first time you called her that?'

I could only nod.

We picked up magazines, but I couldn't focus on the articles or even the photos. World news, celebrity gossip, and recipes seemed to have no place inside our tiny world. I thought again of Tamera. She should be here with us now.

Sometime later, Bryn nudged me and gestured across the room. 'Do you know that guy?' she asked. 'He's acting as if he knows you.'

I glanced up in disbelief. Richard flashed me a smile, waved, and covered the lobby in his wide gait. I was glad to see him. I couldn't believe how glad.

'How'd you hear?' I began.

'Farley, how else? He called and filled me in on what he knew. I couldn't just stay home, so I thought I'd come out here and do the hospital wait with you. If that's all right, I mean.'

I nodded my gratitude. 'It's better than all right,' I said. Then, aware of Bryn watching this exchange in utter confusion, I said, 'Richard, I'd like you to meet Bryn. My sister. I have a brother, too. Daniel. He's on his way.'

His eyes registered shock, then something else so honest and warm that I had to turn away. He took Bryn's hand and put an arm around me. 'I'm so glad to meet you, Bryn,' he said. 'I'm Richard McCarthy. I'm your sister's husband.'

Thirty-Four

Rat-a-tat. Roar. Rat-a-tat. Roar. Would she always hear that gun? Would she always see Dale, striking like the rattler, trying to kill her? Trying to kill Leighton? She was feeling more like herself now, trying to figure out what to ask the white-uniformed nurse holding the back of the wheelchair.

Was Dale really dead?

Was Leighton really going to live?

Was the girl here not just a wish Rena wanted so much that she appeared as real as life?

'I'm feeling much better,' she said, not knowing how else to start.

'I know. You're ready to go home.'

Home? 'Yes.' There was no way she could ask her questions. Instead she looked at the wheelchair and said, 'I don't think I'll need that.'

'Oh, come on,' the woman said. 'Your daughter wanted to come get you herself, but it will be easier on you if we just wheel you out to her.'

Your daughter. She hadn't imagined it. 'What does she look like?' she asked.

The nurse chuckled. 'You know what your daughter looks like, don't you? Curly blond hair, petite figure, very pretty.'

'That's right,' Rena said. Yes, this was the same girl.

'In short,' the woman said, 'she looks just like

you. Now, into the chair, please. You don't want to make her wait.'

All the way down the long hall, Rena thought about her daughter. Would she be embarrassed that Rena wasn't married when she got pregnant? Would she be able to accept Bryn after what happened with Dale? Would she like Daniel? Would she like *her*? Would her daughter like her? Would she be proud of her?

The wheelchair jolted to a stop. 'Do you want to walk the rest of the way,' the woman asked, 'or do you want to ride?'

'I want to walk.' Rena looked at her foot. The scruffy blue hospital sock covered the snake bite, but she could picture it small and drying. And she knew she wouldn't be alive if not for Kendra's fast action, hers and Leighton's.

She let the woman help her from the chair, then stood firmly on her own two feet.

'There's a rail here,' the woman told her, and touched the wide piece of wood along the wall of glass.

'Thank you,' Rena said. She looked at the woman's name tag. 'Thank you, Betty.' Then, she hugged the woman who had taken her this far. She would have to go the rest of the way on her own.

With her hand on the rail, she slowly made her way down the rest of the hall. This was how she wanted to meet her daughter: walking through the front entrance, not in a wheelchair.

She looked through the glass. Someone was walking toward her on the other side of it. Her face was scraped, and her long hair frizzed all over the place, but she was beautiful standing there in her torn shirt. Rena remembered the shirt, remembered when and how it had been torn. It wasn't a dream. It was as real as anything she'd ever lived.

'Leighton's hair,' she said through the glass, but her daughter couldn't hear her. She put up both hands on the glass. Rena covered them with her own. She pressed her forehead against the glass. Rena giggled and pressed her own head against the other side.

'Oh, baby,' she whispered, 'my baby,' although she knew only she could hear the words. The sound was real, though, and she could no longer hear the nail gun.

Her daughter put her hand on the glass and began to slowly move. Rena placed her hand against it and took the last steps that led her out of the hall and into her daughter's arms.

'You're real,' she said. Then, she added, 'Kit.' She needed to remember to use her name.

'You better believe I am.' She broke away from the hug. 'Are you really here?'

'I think I am,' Rena said, and even though she felt as if she needed to sleep for a week, she knew she'd be able to walk to the car. She could walk anywhere, as long as she could hold on to her daughter's arm like this. 'I have a secretarial certificate,' she said. 'From the city college here. And I own a gas and convenience store in Buckeye.'

'That's wonderful,' Kit said, her voice hoarse. 'That's really wonderful, Mother.'

'I like to make my own way, and I want you to know I can do that.'

262

Kit threw her arms around Rena, and again, Rena was struck by her scent, the only memory linking them. She pulled her close. 'Mother,' she said, 'you have no idea.'

Thirty-Five

When we returned home and I arrived at work, still in a daze, I found Luis in the parking lot, staring up at the 'Amazing Grace' art on the building next door. That brought me back to reality. I got out of my car, and he walked over to me.

We hugged, and he said, 'I didn't want to bother you while you were gone. I heard about Tamera, of course. I'm so sorry.'

'She died trying to help me. It was senseless and terrible.'

'And you found your mother?'

'I did.' I pictured Rena, her fingers against the glass of the hospital wall, and all of the moments since then. Then I remembered that Luis must have a reason for showing up here. 'What's going on?' I asked. 'You didn't have to wait to get in touch with me.'

'Doesn't matter.' He blinked, and even through his glasses I could tell it wasn't because of the sun. 'I lost my job. They didn't renew my contract.'

'Carla?' I didn't know what else to say or how to express my disbelief.

'Under the guise of her family, no doubt. No one came out and said it, though. All of a sudden, I wasn't teacher material.'

'Can you fight it?'

'Jerry and I are talking about it with some lawyer friends of his, but I don't know. Teaching was my dream.'

'And they took that away from you. Oh, I'm sorry, Luis. I wish I could do something.'

'You've tried to help from the start,' he said. 'I've been doing volunteer work on the suicide hotline, and there's a possibility of a job there. At least they haven't come after my parents. My family's tight. We'll get through this, Kit.'

All day, I thought about our conversation and about what an outrage it was to take away a young man's future because he threatened someone's perceived public image. I talked to Farley about it and discussed it with Richard. Then I did what I should have done a long time ago. I wrote a blog that told the truth about the so-called Brantingham Crime Fund and the cause it pretended to represent.

I did it because I had learned first-hand that although answers alone don't heal, not much can happen until you have them. I did it for Alex, Jerry, Luis, and myself. Yes, I would be fired, but like Luis, I would survive. Because we – Luis and I – possessed something Carla Brantingham and her supporters would never have. A family.